A Book Of

E-COMMERCE TECHNOLOGY

For Semester - V : T.Y.B.B.M. (I.B.)

As Per Savitribai Phule Pune University's Revised Syllabus
Effective from June 2015

Gautam Bapat

M.C.A., P.G.D.B.M. (Marketing)
Asst. Professor, Computer Science & Applications
MITSOM College
Pune

N3461

| **E-COMMERCE TECHNOLOGY** | **ISBN 978-93-5164-764-5** |

First Edition : **August 2015**

© : **Author**

Published By :

NIRALI PRAKASHAN

Abhyudaya Pragati, 1312, Shivaji Nagar,
Off J.M. Road, Pune – 411005
Tel - (020) 25512336/37/39, Fax - (020) 25511379
Email : niralipune@pragationline.com

✦ DISTRIBUTION CENTRES

PUNE

Nirali Prakashan : 119, Budhwar Peth, Jogeshwari Mandir Lane, Pune 411002, Maharashtra
Tel : (020) 2445 2044, 66022708, Fax : (020) 2445 1538
Email : bookorder@pragationline.com, niralilocal@pragationline.com

Nirali Prakashan : S. No. 28/27, Dhyari, Near Pari Company, Pune 411041
Tel : (020) 24690204 Fax : (020) 24690316
Email : dhyari@pragationline.com, bookorder@pragationline.com

MUMBAI

Nirali Prakashan : 385, S.V.P. Road, Rasdhara Co-op. Hsg. Society Ltd.,
Girgaum, Mumbai 400004, Maharashtra
Tel : (022) 2385 6339 / 2386 9976, Fax : (022) 2386 9976
Email : niralimumbai@pragationline.com

✦ DISTRIBUTION BRANCHES

JALGAON

Nirali Prakashan : 34, V. V. Golani Market, Navi Peth, Jalgaon 425001,
Maharashtra, Tel : (0257) 222 0395, Mob : 94234 91860

KOLHAPUR

Nirali Prakashan : New Mahadvar Road, Kedar Plaza, 1st Floor Opp. IDBI Bank
Kolhapur 416 012, Maharashtra. Mob : 9850046155

NAGPUR

Pratibha Book Distributors : Above Maratha Mandir, Shop No. 3, First Floor,
Rani Jhanshi Square, Sitabuldi, Nagpur 440012, Maharashtra
Tel : (0712) 254 7129

DELHI

Nirali Prakashan : 4593/21, Basement, Aggarwal Lane 15, Ansari Road, Daryaganj
Near Times of India Building, New Delhi 110002
Mob : 08505972553

BENGALURU

Pragati Book House : House No. 1, Sanjeevappa Lane, Avenue Road Cross,
Opp. Rice Church, Bengaluru – 560002.
Tel : (080) 64513344, 64513355,Mob : 9880582331, 9845021552
Email:bharatsavla@yahoo.com

CHENNAI

Pragati Books : 9/1, Montieth Road, Behind Taas Mahal, Egmore,
Chennai 600008 Tamil Nadu, Tel : (044) 6518 3535,
Mob : 94440 01782 / 98450 21552 / 98805 82331,
Email : bharatsavla@yahoo.com

niralipune@pragationline.com | www.pragationline.com

Also find us on [f] www.facebook.com/niralibooks

Preface ...

I take this opportunity to present this book entitled as **"E-Commerce Technology"** to the students of Fifth Semester (T.Y.B.B.M.) (I.B.). The object of this book is to present the subject matter in a most concise and simple manner. The book is written strictly according to the Revised Syllabus of Savitribai Phule Pune University.

The book has its own unique features. It brings out the subject in a very simple and lucid manner for easy and comprehensive understanding of the basic concepts, its intricacies, procedures and practices. This book will help the readers to have a broader view on E-commerce Technology. The language used in this book is easy and will help students to improve their vocabulary of Technical terms and understand the matter in a better and happier way.

I sincerely thank Shri. Dineshbhai Furia and Shri. Jignesh Furia of Nirali Prakashan, for the confidence reposed in me and giving me this opportunity to reach out to the students of management studies.

I thank Mrs. Anita Panajkar for his important inputs time to time and Mr. Akbar Shaikh who painstakingly attended to all the details to make this book appear good.

I also thank Ms. Chaitali Takale, Mr. Ravindra Walodare, Mr. Mahesh Swami, Mr. Vijay Shete, Mr. Sachin Shinde, Nikunj Joshi, Nilesh Deshmukh, Ashok Bodke, Moshin Sayyed and Nitin Thorat.

I have given my best inputs for this book. Any suggestions towards the improvement of this book and sincere comments are most welcome on niralipune@pragationline.com.

Author

Syllabus ...

4. Electronic Data Exchange and E-Governance [10]

    4.1   Electronic Data Interchange (EDI)

         4.1.1   Introduction

         4.1.2   Concept of EDI

         4.1.3   Applications of EDI and Its Limitation

         4.1.4   EDI Model

    4.2   E-Governance

         4.2.1   Introduction

         4.2.2   E-Governance in India

         4.2.3   Import, Export

5. Electronic Payment System [10]

    5.1   Introduction to EPS

    5.2   Meaning of Traditional and Modern Payment System

    5.3   Types of Modern Payment System (GIRO Payment, Credit Card, Smart Cart, Direct Transfers, Stored Value Card, Point of Scale, Micropayment, Electronic Cash, E-cheque, RTGS, Security Measures of Online Transactions, Threats of Payment System etc.)

Contents ...

Chapter **1**...

Introduction to Electronic Commerce

Contents ...

1.1 Introduction to E-Commerce

• E-commerce or e-commerce is the art and science of selling products and/or services over the Internet.

• Electronic commerce, commonly known as e-commerce or eCommerce, or e-business consists of the buying and selling of products or services over electronic systems such as the Internet and other computer networks.

• The term Electronic commerce refers to the use of an electronic medium to carry out commercial transactions. Most of the time, it refers to the sale of products via Internet.

• E-commerce, means buying and selling of goods/products on the internet. E-commerce can best be described as buying and selling of goods/products and services over the Internet so this E-commerce includes both business-to-business (B2B) and business-to-consumer (B2C) transactions.

- The potential dimension of e-commerce today is the substantial cost savings that could occur if a company's business is done electronically.

- E-commerce, is the process used to distribute, buy, sell or market goods and services, and the transfer of funds online, through electronic communications or networks.

- Electronic commerce is commonly referred to as Online commerce, Web commerce, eBusiness, eRetail, eTailing, e-tailing, ecommerce, eCommerce, e-commerce, ecom or EC.

- Electronic commerce is generally considered to be the sales aspect of e-business. It also consists of the exchange of data to facilitate the financing and payment aspects of the business transactions.

- The amount of trade conducted electronically has grown extraordinarily with widespread Internet usage. The use of commerce is conducted in this way, spurring and drawing on innovations in electronic funds transfer, supply chain management, Internet marketing, online transaction processing, Electronic Data Interchange (EDI), Inventory Management Systems, and automated data collection systems.

- Modern electronic commerce typically uses the World Wide Web at least at some point in the transaction's lifecycle, although it can encompass a wider range of technologies such as e-mail as well.

- Electronic commerce that is conducted between businesses is referred to as business-to-business or B2B. B2B can be open to all interested parties or limited to specific, pre-qualified participants.

- Electronic commerce that is conducted between businesses and consumers, on the other hand, is referred to as business-to-consumer or B2C. This is the type of electronic commerce conducted by companies such as Amazon.com.

- Online shopping is a form of electronic commerce where the buyer is directly online to the seller's computer usually via the internet. There is no intermediary service.

- The sale and purchase transaction is completed electronically and interactively in real-time such as Amazon.com for new books. If an intermediary is present, then the sale and purchase transaction is called electronic commerce such as eBay.com.

- E-commerce is not just technology but it is a way of doing business differently. E-commerce has very high power that is much greater than the number of people in the company.

- E-commerce delivers a level of marketing capacity that was exclusively for larger corporations having the biggest brand and budget capabilities.

- E-commerce allows us to targeting of individuals and their needs in a way that has been the bailiwick of niche markets and small players.

- E-commerce is more about money-all about money-lots of money, a combination of lots of money, the internet and a strong economy.

Meaning of Electronic Commerce

- E-commerce involves in advertising, multimedia, product information, customer support on the world wide web (www), Internet security and payment mechanism are all covered under electronic commerce.

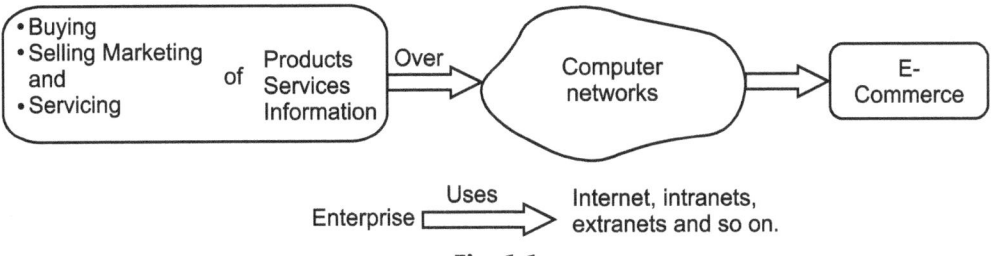

Fig. 1.1

- Electronic commerce could include following examples:
  - Use of multimedia web pages of product catalogs on the Internet.
  - Use by sales representatives to access customer records through corporate intranet.
  - Access of inventory databases by large customers through the extranet.

1. **Electronic Commerce covers following:**
   - Web retailing and wholesaling,
   - Online point-of-sale and Transaction processing,
   - Electronic Funds Transfer (EFT),
   - Electronic Data Interchange (EDI),
   - Electronic Banking,
   - Supply Chain Management, and
   - Interactive Marketing.
   - Use of multimedia web pages of product catalogs on the internet.
   - Access of inventory database by large customers through extranet.

2. **Enterprise Collaboration System (ECS) includes:**
   - Electronic Mail,
   - Voice Mail,
   - Discussion Forums,
   - Data conferencing,
   - Video conferencing, and
   - Electronic Meeting Systems (EMS)

Importance and Uses of E-Commerce

1. **Exploitation of New Business:**

   Broadly speaking, electronic commerce emphasizes the generation and exploitation of new business opportunities and to use popular phrases i.e. "generate business value" or "do more with less".

2. **Enabling the Customers:**

Electronic Commerce is enabling the customer to have an increasing say in what products are made, how products are made and how services are delivered.

3. **Improvement of Business Transaction:**

Electronic Commerce endeavors to improve the execution of business transaction over various networks.

4. **Effective Performance:**

It leads to more effective performance i.e. better quality, greater customer satisfaction and better corporate decision making.

5. **Greater Economic Efficiency:**

We may achieve greater economic efficiency (lower cost) and more rapid exchange (high speed, accelerated, or real-time interaction) with the help of electronic commerce.

6. **Execution of Information:**

It enables the execution of information transactions between two or more parties using inter connected networks. These networks can be a combination of 'Plain Old Telephone System' (POTS), Cable TV, leased lines and wireless. Information based transactions are creating new ways of doing business and even new types of business.

7. **Incorporating Transaction:**

Electronic Commerce also incorporates transaction management, which organizes, routes, processes and tracks transactions. It also includes consumers making electronic payments and funds transfers.

8. **Increasing of Revenue:**

Firm use technology to either lower operating costs or increase revenue. Electronic Commerce has the Potential to increase revenue by creating new markets for old products, creating new information-based products, and establishing new service delivery channels to better serve and interact with customers. The transaction management aspect of electronic commerce can also enable firms to reduce operating costs by enabling better coordination in the sales, production and distribution processes and to consolidate operations to reduce overhead.

9. **Reduction of Friction:**

Electronic Commerce research and its associated implementations is to reduce the "friction" in on line transactions frictions is often described in economics as transaction cost. It can arise from inefficient market structures and inefficient combinations of the technological activities required to make a transaction. Ultimately, the reduction of friction in online commerce will enable smoother transaction between buyers, intermediaries and sellers.

10. Facilitating of Network Form:

Electronic Commerce is also impacting business to business interactions. It facilitates the network form of organization where small flexible firms rely on other partner, companies for component supplies and product distribution to meet changing customer demand more effectively. Hence, an end to end relationship management solution is a desirable goal that is needed to manage the chain of networks linking customers, workers, suppliers, distributors and even competitors. The management of "online transactions" in the supply chain assumes a central roll.

11. Facilitating for Organizational Model:

It is facilitating an organizational model that is fundamentally different from the past. It is a control organization to the information based organization. The emerging forms of techno-organizational structure involve changes in managerial responsibilities, communication and information flows and work group structures.

E-Commerce Challenges

1. **Understanding customer evolution:** Invest ahead of customer needs.
2. **Charting changing technology:** Match technology choices to consumer tastes.
3. **Weathering the storm:** Reassure stakeholders with clear vision, sensible business model, and profitable venture.
4. **Integrating offline and online activities:** Align offline and online business activities, especially advertising, branding, retail and online store design, service, warranties, returns (customer-facing activities).
5. **Identifying key levers of competitive advantage:** Reallocate resources as competitive advantage levers evolve.
6. **Expanding globally:** Deal with complex internationalization issues.

E-Commerce Process

- Developing an e-commerce solution for clients can be more involved than the standard Web Development Process. Therefore, planning and developing the project scope may require more interaction whether the planner developer is starting from scratch or looking for a redesign.

   1. **Planning:** The planning process or e-commerce project looks at your complete operation. We will look at what your daily and weekly operations involve including inventory and shipping before creating a plan on presenting and selling product so that we can develop a solution that gets product shipped out the door as quick and efficiently as possible.

      Next we look at your product line and look at all the aspects of your products that your customers will need to use your website to get information. What options does the customer have when they place orders, what sort of detailed information and collateral does the client need to make a decision?

Finally, planning includes at the type of marketing and sales strategy your team has and look for ways of incorporating that into the E-Commerce solution, before, during, and after purchase. We also want to look at the data and tracking information that the team requires about customers and clients.

2. **Scope:** When we develop an e-commerce project's scope, we will provide your with a list of all the features to be included, timelines for their delivery and pre-determined goals. This way we both know what is expected before we begin.

3. **Site Mapping and Layout:** A good e-commerce site must load quickly and present consistently to all users on different browsers. We strive to make our sites XHTML and CSS compliant and optimize all images while maintaining a focus on quick load times without sacrificing style and presentation.

4. **Front and Backend development phase:** An e-commerce solution depends on a robust and efficient database solution on the back end so that the content is delivered quickly. Designing the database right the first time will allow the site and your business to grow.

5. **Design Phase:** We emphasize separating content from presentation. This means that the text and images are separated from the visual template for displaying them. This is important for two reasons. First, as your site scales up, new pages are added or existing pages are modified, there is no reason to adjust HTML code. Second, with the variety of browsers and devices such as PCs, PDAs, Phones as well as the variety of users from different countries or even physically impaired, separating content and presentation allows the information to be displayed in the best manner for the user.

6. **Development Phase:** Once, developed a goal and drawn up a project scope, the project will developed according to clearly spelled out milestones.

7. **Deliverables:** Once, a specific layout and design is agreed upon that sets the right tone and delivers a professional appearance, we will begin working on the final design. Unless otherwise specified, we will deliver a site that is good-looking, fast and standards compliant, and one that is easy to manage going forward, whether it is by developer, client or others in the future.

Features of E-Commerce

- Some features of e-commerce which makes it considerably appreciable are given below:

1. **Ubiquity:** In traditional commerce, a marketplace is a physical place we visit in order to transact. For example, television and radio are typically directed to motivate the customer to go someplace to make a purchase. E-commerce is ubiquitous, meaning that it is available just about everywhere at all times. It liberates the market from being restricted to a physical space and makes it possible to shop from your desktop. The result is called a market space. From consumer point of view, ubiquity reduces

transaction costs - the cost of participating in a market. To transact, it is no longer necessary that you spend time and money traveling to a market. At a broader level, the ubiquity of e-commerce lowers the cognitive energy required to complete a task.

2. **Global Reach:** E-commerce technology permits commercial transactions to cross cultural and national boundaries far more conveniently and effectively as compared to traditional commerce. As a result, the potential market size for e-commerce merchants is roughly equal to the size of world's online population.

3. **Universal Standards:** One strikingly unusual feature of e-commerce technologies is that the technical standards of the Internet and therefore the technical standards for conducting e-commerce are universal standards i.e. they are shared by all the nations around the world.

4. **Interactivity:** Unlike any of the commercial technologies of the twentieth century, with the possible exception of the telephone, e-commerce technologies are interactive, meaning they allow for two-way communication between merchants and consumer.

5. **Information Density and Richness:** The Internet vastly increase information density. It is the total amount and quality of information available to all market participants, consumers and merchants. E-commerce technologies reduce information collection, storage, communication and processing costs. At the same time, these technologies increase greatly the accuracy and timeliness of information, making information more useful and important than ever. As a result, information becomes plentiful, cheaper and of higher quality. Information richness refers to the complexity and content of a message.

6. **Personalization:** E-commerce technologies permit personalization. Merchants can target their marketing messages to specific individuals by adjusting the message to a person's name, interests and past purchases. The technology also permits customization. Merchants can change the product or service based on user's preferences or prior behavior.

Characteristics of E-Commerce

- The tools are electronic but the application is commerce.
  - Commerce is not accounting or decision support or any other internally focused function.
  - Commerce is externally focused on those with whom business is done.
  - Commerce is doing business, not reporting on it or sending messages about it.
- Special characteristics of electronic commerce and Web commerce are as follows:
  - Information is exchanged and processed by a communication network and computers, as well as e-commerce software.
  - Most transactions are processed automatically.

    o   Pulls together a gamut of business support services, such as:

      1.   Inter-organizational e-mail, on-line directories,

      2.   Trading support systems for commodities,

      3.   Products, and customized products,

      4.   Custom-built goods and services,

      5.   Ordering and logistic support system supports, and

      6.   Management and statistical reporting systems.

E-Commerce Framework

- This framework, first developed by **Kalakota** and **Whinston**,14 Professors of Information Systems and prolific authors on the subject, takes a holistic view and identifies the different components of business and technology that make up e-commerce.

- Using the analogy of the architecture of a building illustrated in Fig. 1.2, they explain how the different components fit and interact together, emphasising the relative importance of each component.

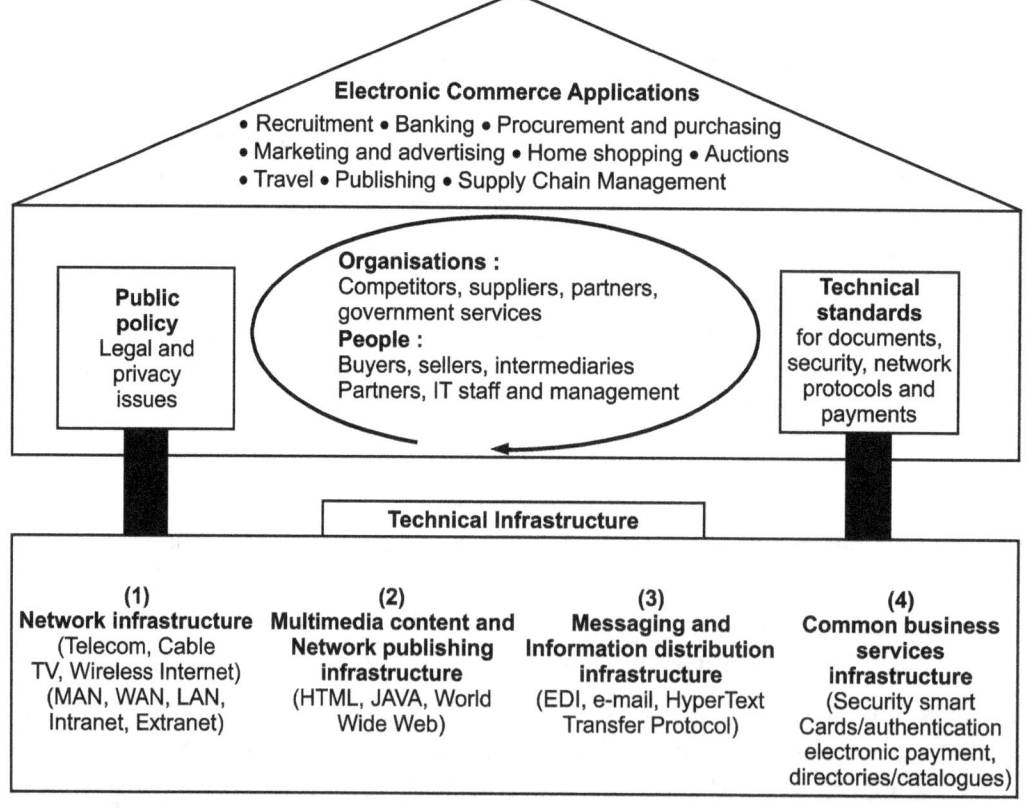

Fig. 1.2: A Framework for Electronic Commerce

- The technological foundations of e-commerce are largely hidden, but they are the base on which electronic commerce is built.
- Kalakota and Whinston use the analogy of a traditional transportation company to describe the complexity of the network and how the different components that make up the technology infrastructure are interlinked.
- The network infrastructure is like the network of roads that are interconnected and are of different widths, lengths and quality. For example, The Internet, local area networks, intranets.
- Network infrastructures also take different forms such as telephone wires, cables, wireless technology, such as satellite or cellular technology etc.
- The publishing infrastructure (including the World Wide Web, Web servers) can be seen as the infrastructure of vehicles and warehouses, which store and transport electronic data and multimedia content along the network.
- Multimedia content is created using myriad tools such as HTML and JAVA. This content can be very different with varying degrees of complexity similar to different vehicles travelling on the roads.
- For example, text only, or more complex is an application, such as a computer game, containing audio, video, graphics and a programme.
- Messaging and information distribution infrastructure are the engines and fuel, which transport the data around the network. Once, the multimedia content is created, there has to be a means of sending and retrieving this information, for example by EDI, e-mail, Hyper Text Transfer Protocol.
- Once, content and data can be created, displayed and transmitted, supporting business services are necessary for facilitating the buying, selling and other transactions safely and reliably. For example, smart cards, authentication, electronic payment, directories/ catalogues.
- The next components which facilitate and enable e-commerce and which are built on the foundations of technology are:
  - **Public policy,** regulations and laws that govern issues such as universal access, privacy, electronic contracts and the terms and conditions that govern e-commerce.
  - **Universal agreement** of technical standards dictate the format in which electronic data is transferred over networks and is received across user interfaces, and the format in which it is stored. This is necessary so that data can travel seamlessly across different networks, where information and data can be accessed by a whole range of hardware and software such as computers, palmtops, and different kinds of browsers and document readers.
- The interaction of people and organisations to manage and coordinate the applications, infrastructures and businesses are all necessary to make e-commerce work.

- All these elements interact together to produce the most visible manifestation of e-commerce. These applications include on-line banking and financial trading; recruitment; procurement and purchasing; marketing and advertising; auctions; shopping and so on.

- This is particularly useful framework for managers to understand the importance of technology and business, both within the organisation and external to it, in the planning and development of any e-commerce or e-business solution.

1.1.1 What is E-Commerce?

- Electronic commerce or ecommerce is a term for any type of business, or commercial transaction, that involves the transfer of information across the Internet.

- E-commerce covers a range of different types of businesses, from consumer based retail sites, through auction or music sites, to business exchanges trading goods and services between corporations.

- E-commerce is currently one of the most important aspects of the Internet to emerge.

- E-commerce, (electronic commerce), is online commerce verses real-world commerce.

- E-commerce includes retail shopping, banking, stocks and bonds trading, auctions, real estate transactions, airline booking, movie rentals—nearly anything one can imagine in the real world.

- Even personal services such as hair and nail salons can benefit from e-commerce by providing a website for the sale of related health and beauty products, normally available to local customers exclusively.

- E-commerce allows consumers to electronically exchange goods and services with no barriers of time or distance.

- Electronic commerce has expanded rapidly over the past five years and is predicted to continue at this rate, or even accelerate.

- In the near future the boundaries between "conventional" and "electronic" commerce will become increasingly blurred as more and more businesses move sections of their operations onto the Internet.

- Business to Business or B2B refers to electronic commerce between businesses rather than between a business and a consumer.

- B2B businesses often deal with hundreds or even thousands of other businesses, either as customers or suppliers. Carrying out these transactions electronically provide vast competitive advantages over traditional methods.

- When implemented properly, ecommerce is often faster, cheaper and more convenient than the traditional methods of bartering goods and services.

- Electronic transactions have been around for quite some time in the form of Electronic Data Interchange or EDI.

- EDI requires each supplier and customer to set up a dedicated data link (between them), where ecommerce provides a cost-effective method for companies to set up multiple, ad-hoc links.
- Electronic commerce has also led to the development of electronic marketplaces where suppliers and potential customers are brought together to conduct mutually beneficial trade.
- The road to create a successful online store can be a difficult if unaware of ecommerce principles and what ecommerce is supposed to do for your online business.
- Researching and understanding the guidelines required to properly implement an e-business plan is a crucial part for becoming successful with online store building.

1.1.2 Definition of E-Commerce

- Some of the definitions of e-commerce often heard and found in publications and the media are listed below:

Doing business online is known as e-commerce.

OR

Electronic Commerce (EC) is where business transactions take place via telecommunications networks, especially the Internet.

OR

Electronic commerce describes the buying and selling of products, services, and information via computer networks including the Internet.

OR

Electronic commerce is about doing business electronically.

OR

E-commerce, ecommerce, or electronic commerce is defined as the conduct of a financial transaction by electronic means.

OR

E-commerce is the buying and selling of goods and services on the Internet, especially the World Wide Web.

OR

E-commerce is the buying products and services through web store fronts.

OR

E-commerce is buying and selling, marketing and servicing and delivery and payment of products, service and information over the Internet, intranets, extranets and other networks, between an inter-networked enterprise and its prospects, customers, suppliers and other business partners.

OR

E-commerce is buying and selling of products, information and services over the Internet.

OR

E-commerce is also a particular type of e-business initiative that is focused around individual business transactions that use the Internet as medium of exchange, including business to business, as well as business to consumer.

OR

E-commerce is defined as a modern business methodology that addresses the desire of firms, consumers and management to cut costs while improving the quality of goods and increasing the speed of services.

1.2 Main Activities of E-commerce

- The functions included in E-commerce are:
  1. Buying and selling of products,
  2. Shipping of products, and
  3. Producing financial statements.
- All this functions are without human intervention, which is termed as real 'E' in e-commerce.
- Humans cannot vanish from the scene and humans will be moving to other tasks that generate real value like:
  - Corporate development,
  - Personalised customer service,
  - Sales, and
  - New products research etc.
- You will avoid tasks that can be handled faster and more efficiently by a computer such as sending purchase orders, creating journal entries, or confirming shipments etc.
- When a company or oganisation uses computers extensively to perform tasks within the organisations, we call it "e-commerce ready for capable".
- E-commerce is a range of online business activities that include explaining products or services are providing a mechanism for customers to buy those products and services from a website or internet and it encompasses online shopping and online purchasing.
- Four major sequential activities related to a prospective customer are as shown in Fig. 1.3.

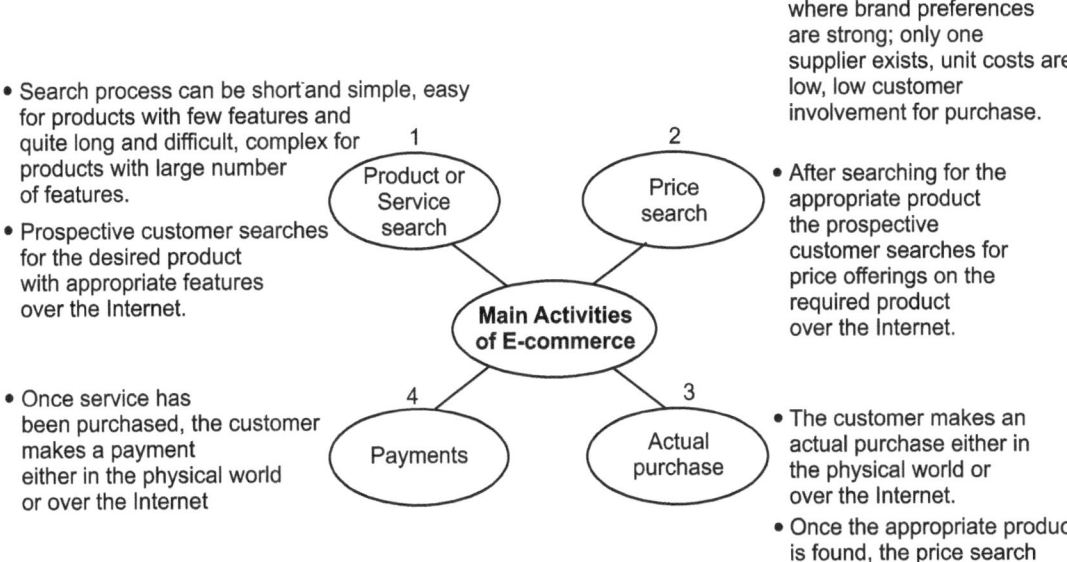

- Search process can be short and simple, easy for products with few features and quite long and difficult, complex for products with large number of features.
- Prospective customer searches for the desired product with appropriate features over the Internet.
- Once service has been purchased, the customer makes a payment either in the physical world or over the Internet
- Search process can be limited in scope in cases where brand preferences are strong; only one supplier exists, unit costs are low, low customer involvement for purchase.
- After searching for the appropriate product the prospective customer searches for price offerings on the required product over the Internet.
- The customer makes an actual purchase either in the physical world or over the Internet.
- Once the appropriate product is found, the price search ends appropriately.

Fig. 1.3: Activities related to a prospective customer in e-commerce

1. **Product or Service Search:** Internet sites offer product feature search and comparison services for relatively complex consumer products that have multiple suppliers. This facilitates the search and evaluation process.

2. **Price search:** It can be extensive in scope in cases where low or no brand preferences exist, multiple reliable suppliers exist, unit costs are high or the product requires high involvement for purchase. Products and price search can be interactive in some cases.

3. **Actual purchase:** The sequential activities are in Fig. 1.3 may end at the first or second point without any economic transaction being effected. When the actual purchaser utilises the internet, the economic transaction will be part of electronic commerce.

   o   E-commerce firms/organisations act directly/indirectly in several ways as under, to effect and influence one or more of the four major sequential activities by the prospective customer. The Table 1.1 gives E-commerce activities.

4. **Payments:** Once product has been purchased the customers makes the payment either physical or internet world.

Table 1.1: Electronic commerce activities

• Direct selling of goods and/or services over the Internet	• This activity involves providing product information, price details on the Internet to enable a customer to buy a product through off-line or on-line payment mechanisms.

contd. ...

• Provision of company information on a company homepage	• Though not E-commerce, provides important information about the company's products and provokes direct or indirect enquiries and subsequent purchase.
• Priced information	• Firms or organisations may provide priced information regarding products or provide comparative information that may be of value to niche customer. In some cases, the information may be provided free to end-customers as the featured firms/products pay for the service.
• Advertising banners on popular internet sites for publicity and marketing	• Communicates packaged information regarding the company advertised and provides links to the company's homepage. The host company also earns some revenue by providing advertising space.
• Research and Development	• Firms or organisations may gather product preference and use information through popular general sites like **double click.com** through information or through contents and use the information to provide targeted products.
• Agent services	• Firms or oragnisations may act as internet based agents and provide an internet site that helps in bringing the buyer and seller together and thereby earn commission income.

1.3 Goals of E-commerce

- E-commerce is a modern business methodology which addresses the needs of the organisations, consumers and merchants to cut costs while improving the quality of goods and services and increasing the speed of service regarding delivery.
- E-commerce is associated with the buying and selling of the information products and services via computer network today and in the future via any one of the myriad of networks that make up the information super highway.

- E-commerce is well suited to facilitate re-engineering of business processes occurring at many firms or organisations. The goals of E-commerce are:

  1. Reduced costs,
  2. Lower product cycle time,
  3. Faster customer response, and
  4. Improved service quality.

- E-commerce is a new way of managing, conducting and executing business transactions using computer and telecommunication networks.

- E-commerce is expected to improve the productivity and competitiveness of participating businesses, by providing unprecedented access to an online global market place with millions of customers and thousands of services and products.

1.4 Technical Components of E-commerce

- Various e-commerce technical components are given below and shown in Fig. 1.4.

  1. Client or PC workstation,
  2. Transaction server,
  3. Database server,
  4. Database transaction,
  5. Router, and
  6. Internet communication line.

1. **Client or PC workstation:**

   A client is an application or system that accesses a remote service on another computer system, known as a server, by way of a network. A workstation is a high-end microcomputer designed for technical or scientific applications. Intended primarily to be used by one person at a time, they are commonly connected to a local area network and run multi-user operating systems.

2. **Transaction server:**

   A transaction server is a software component that is used in implementing transactions. A transaction involves multiple steps which must be completed atomically, as though it is a single operation which can not be interrupted, even though it may require multiple steps. For example, a bank moving money from account A to account B must remove it from A and also add it to B; it would be unacceptable to do only one of these steps. If the server is unable to accomplish all of the steps it must be sure to perform none of them. This will mean ensuring that transactions are guaranteed, or that if a transaction fails the system can tell about the failure has happened. A transaction server will consist of a system providing the safety described above, and an environment where programs can be written to make use of these features. It will also have various connection protocols to allow it to connect to the databases involved, and to the front end software, (For example the computer of a telesales person or the web interface of an online bank).

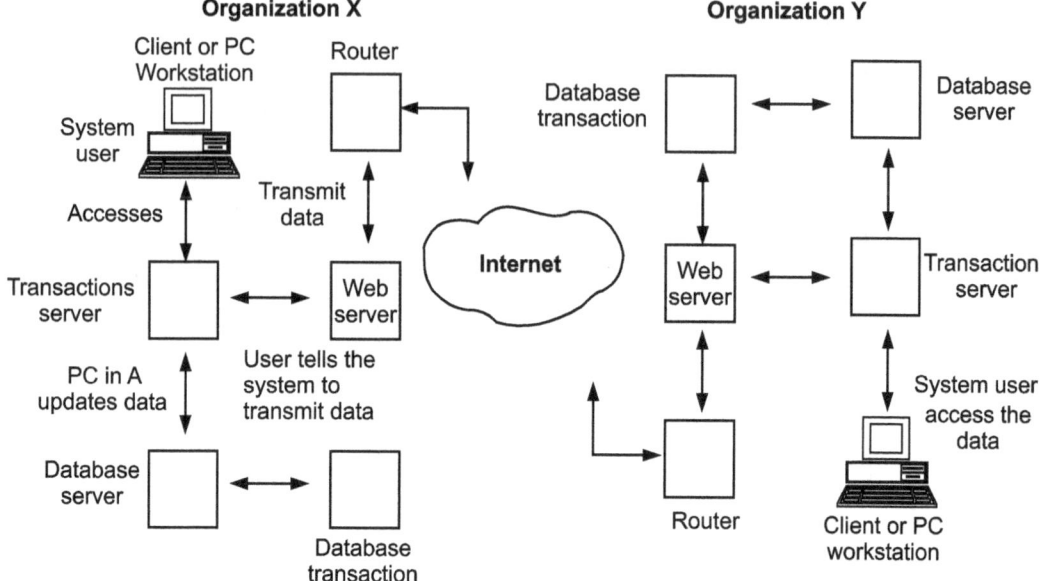

Fig. 1.4

3. **Database server:**

   A database server is a computer program that provides database services to other computer programs or computers, as defined by the client–server model. The term may also refer to a computer dedicated to running such a program. Database management systems frequently provide database server functionality, and some DBMSs (For example: MySQL) rely exclusively on the client–server model for database access.

4. **Database transaction:**

   A database transaction is a logical unit of database operations which are executed as a whole to process user requests for retrieving data or updating the database. A database transaction comprises a unit of work performed within a database management system against a database, and treated in a coherent and reliable way independent of other transactions. Transactions in a database environment have two main purposes:

   1. To provide reliable units of work that allow correct recovery from failures and keep a database consistent even in cases of system failure, when execution stops (completely or partially) and many operations upon a database remain uncompleted, with unclear status.

   2. To provide isolation between programs accessing a database concurrently. Without isolation the programs' outcomes are possibly erroneous.

5. Router:

A router is a device that interconnects two or more computer networks, and selectively interchanges packets of data between them. Each data packet contains address information that a router can use to determine if the source and destination are on the same network, or if the data packet must be transferred from one network to another. A router is a networking device whose software and hardware are customized to the tasks of routing and forwarding information. A router has two or more network interfaces, which may be to different physical types of network such as copper cables, fiber, or wireless or different network standards. Each network interface is a specialized device that converts electric signals from one form to another.

6. Internet communication line:

Communication lines makes internet connections.

1.5 Functions of E-commerce

- The four functions of E-commerce are given below:
    1. Communication
    2. Process management
    3. Service management, and
    4. Transaction capabilities.

1. **The communication function:** This function is aimed at the delivery of information and/or documents to facilitate business transactions. E-mail is an best example of this.

2. **The process management:** This function covers the automation and improvements of business processes. For example, networking two computers together so that they can share and transfer data rather than have a person to take data from one computer to another computer.

3. **Service management function:** The quality of service can be improved by the application of technology. For example, the Federal express web site. This web site permits customers to track shipments and the schedule pickups 24 hours a day with a worldwide network having to talk to a service representative. Customer service is greatly enhanced due to the web sites capabilities.

4. **Transaction capability function:** This provides the ability to buy/sell on the Internet or some, other on-line service. The retail websites of Amazon.com, REI and websites of business offers good examples of the transaction capabilities of E-commerce.

1.6 Advantages and Disadvantages of E-commerce

1.6.1 Advantages of E-Commerce

* Various advantages of e-commerce are given below:

1. **Advantages of E-commerce to Organisations:**

    (i)   **International marketplace:** What used to be a single physical marketplace located in a geographical area has now become a borderless marketplace including national and international markets. By becoming e-commerce enabled, businesses now have access to people all around the world. In effect all e-commerce businesses have become virtual multinational corporations.

    (ii) **Saves Operational cost:** The cost of creating, processing, distributing, storing and retrieving paper-based information has decreased.

    (iii) **Mass customization:** E-commerce has revolutionised the way consumers buy good and services. The pull-type processing allows for products and services to be customised to the customer's requirements. In the past when Ford first started making motor cars, customers could have any colour so long as it was black. Now customers can configure a car according to their specifications within minutes on-line via the www.ford.com website.

    (iv) **Enables reduced inventories and overheads by facilitating 'pull'-type supply chain management:** This is based on collecting the customer order and then delivering through JIT (Just-In-Time) manufacturing. This is particularly beneficial for companies in the high technology sector, where stocks of components held could quickly become obsolete within months. For example, companies like Motorola (mobile phones), and Dell (computers) gather customer orders for a product, transmit them electronically to the manufacturing plant where they are manufactured according to the customer's specifications (like colour and features) and then sent to the customer within a few days.

    (v)   **Lower telecommunications cost:** The Internet is much cheaper than Value Added Networks (VANs) which were based on leasing telephone lines for the sole use of the organisation and its authorised partners. It is also cheaper to send a fax or e-mail via the Internet than direct dialling.

    (vi) **Digitisation of products and processes:** Particularly in the case of software and music/video products, which can be downloaded or e-mailed directly to customers via the Internet in digital or electronic format.

    (vii) **No more 24-hour-time constraints:** Businesses can be contacted by or contact customers or suppliers at any time.

2. **Advantages of E-commerce to Consumers:**

(i)   **24/7 access:** Enables customers to shop or conduct other transactions 24 hours a day, all year round from almost any location. For example, checking balances, making payments, obtaining travel and other information. In one case a pop star set up web cameras in every room in his house, so that he/she could check the status of his home by logging onto the Internet when he/she was away from home on tour.

(ii) **More choices:** Customers not only have a whole range of products that they can choose from and customise, but also an international selection of suppliers.

(iii) **Price comparisons:** Customers can 'shop' around the world and conduct comparisons either directly by visiting different sites, or by visiting a single site where prices are aggregated from a number of providers and compared (For example www.moneyextra.co.uk for financial products and services).

(iv) **Improved delivery processes:** This can range from the immediate delivery of digitised or electronic goods such as software or audio-visual files by downloading via the Internet, to the on-line tracking of the progress of packages being delivered by mail or courier.

(v)   **An environment of competition:** Where substantial discounts can be found or value added, as different retailers via for customers. It also allows many individual customers to aggregate their orders together into a single order presented to wholesalers or manufacturers and obtain a more competitive price (aggregate buying). For example www.letsbuyit.com.

3. **Advantages of E-commerce to Society:**

(i)   **Enables more flexible working practices:** It enhances the quality of life for a whole host of people in society, enabling them to work from home. Not only is this more convenient and provides happier and less stressful working environments, it also potentially reduces environmental pollution as fewer people have to travel to work regularly.

(ii) **Connects people:** Enables people in developing countries and rural areas to enjoy and access products, services, information and other people which otherwise would not be so easily available to them.

(iii) **Facilitates delivery of public services:** For example, health services available over the Internet (on-line consultation with doctors or nurses), filing taxes over the Internet through the Inland Revenue website.

1.6.2 Disadvantages of E-commerce

*   Disadvantages of E-commerce are given below:

1. **Disadvantages of E-commerce to organisations:**

(i)   **Lack of sufficient system security, reliability, standards and communication protocols:** There are numerous reports of websites and databases being hacked into, and security holes in software. For example, Microsoft has over the years issued many security notices and 'patches' for their software. Several banking and other business websites, including Barclays Bank, Powergen and even the Consumers' Association in the UK, have experienced breaches in security where 'a technical oversight' or 'a fault in its systems' led to confidential client information becoming available to all.

(ii)   **Rapidly evolving and changing technology,** so there is always a feeling of trying to 'catch up' and not be left behind.

(iii)   **Under pressure to innovate and develop business models** to exploit the new opportunities which sometimes leads to strategies detrimental to the organisation. The ease with which business models can be copied and emulated over the Internet increase that pressure and curtail longer-term competitive advantage.

(iv)   **Facing increased competition:** From both national and international competitors often leads to price wars and subsequent unsustainable losses for the organisation.

(v)   **Problems with compatibility of older and 'newer' technology:** There are problems where older business systems cannot communicate with web based and Internet infrastructures, leading to some organisations running almost two independent systems where data cannot be shared. This often leads to having to invest in new systems or an infrastructure, which bridges the different systems. In both cases this is both financially costly as well as disruptive to the efficient running of organisations.

2. **Disadvantages of E-commerce to Consumers:**

(i)   **Computing equipment** is needed for individuals to participate in the new 'digital' economy, which means an initial capital cost to customers.

(ii)   **A basic technical knowledge** is required of both computing equipment and navigation of the Internet and the World Wide Web.

(iii)   **Cost of access to the Internet,** whether dial-up or broadband tariffs.

(iv)   **Cost of computing equipment,** Not just the initial cost of buying equipment but making sure that the technology is updated regularly to be compatible with the changing requirement of the Internet, websites and applications.

(v)   **Lack of security and privacy of personal data,** There is no real control of data that is collected over the Web or Internet. Data protection laws are not universal and so websites hosted in different countries may or may nothave laws which protect privacy of personal data.

(vi)   **Physical contact and relationships are replaced by electronic processes,** Customers are unable to touch and feel goods being sold on-line or gauge voices and reactions of human beings.

(vii)   A lack of trust because they are interacting with faceless computers.

3. **Disadvantages of E-commerce to Society:**

(i)   **Breakdown in human interaction:** As people become more used to interacting electronically there could be an erosion of personal and social skills which might eventually be detrimental to the world we live in where people are more comfortable interacting with a screen than face to face.

(ii) **Social division:** There is a potential danger that there will be an increase in the social division between technical haves and have-nots – so people who do not have technical skills become unable to secure better-paid jobs and could form an underclass with potentially dangerous implications for social stability.

(iii) **Reliance on telecommunications infrastructure, power and IT skills,** which in developing countries nullifies the benefits when power, advanced telecommunication infrastructures and IT skills are unavailable or scarce or underdeveloped.

(iv) **Wasted resources:** As new technology dates quickly there arises a problem of disposing all the old computers, keyboards, monitors, speakers and other hardware or software.

(v)   **Facilitates Just-In-Time manufacturing:** This could potentially cripple an economy in times of crisis as stocks are kept to a minimum and delivery patterns are based on pre-set levels of stock which last for days rather than weeks.

(vi) **Difficulty in policing the Internet,** which means that numerous crimes can be perpetrated and often go undetected. There is also an unpleasant rise in the availability and access of obscene material and ease with which pedophiles and others can entrap children by masquerading in chat rooms.

1.7 Scope of E-commerce

-   Companies involved in e-commerce as either buyers or sellers, rely on Internet based technologies, and E-commerce applications and service to accomplish marketing, discovery, transaction, processing, and product and customer service processing.

-   For example, electronic commerce can include interactive, marketing, ordering, payment, and customer support process at E-commerce catalog and auction site on the World Wide Web, extranet access of inventory databases by customers and suppliers, intranet access of customer relationship management systems by sales and customer collaboration in product development via E-mail and internet newsgroup.

-   Many companies today are participating in or sponsoring three basic categories of electronic commerce applications, business-to-consumer, business-to-business and consumer-to-consumer E-commerce. However, many E-commerce concepts apply to such applications.

    The scope of E-commerce is shown in Fig. 1.5, which is self explanatory.

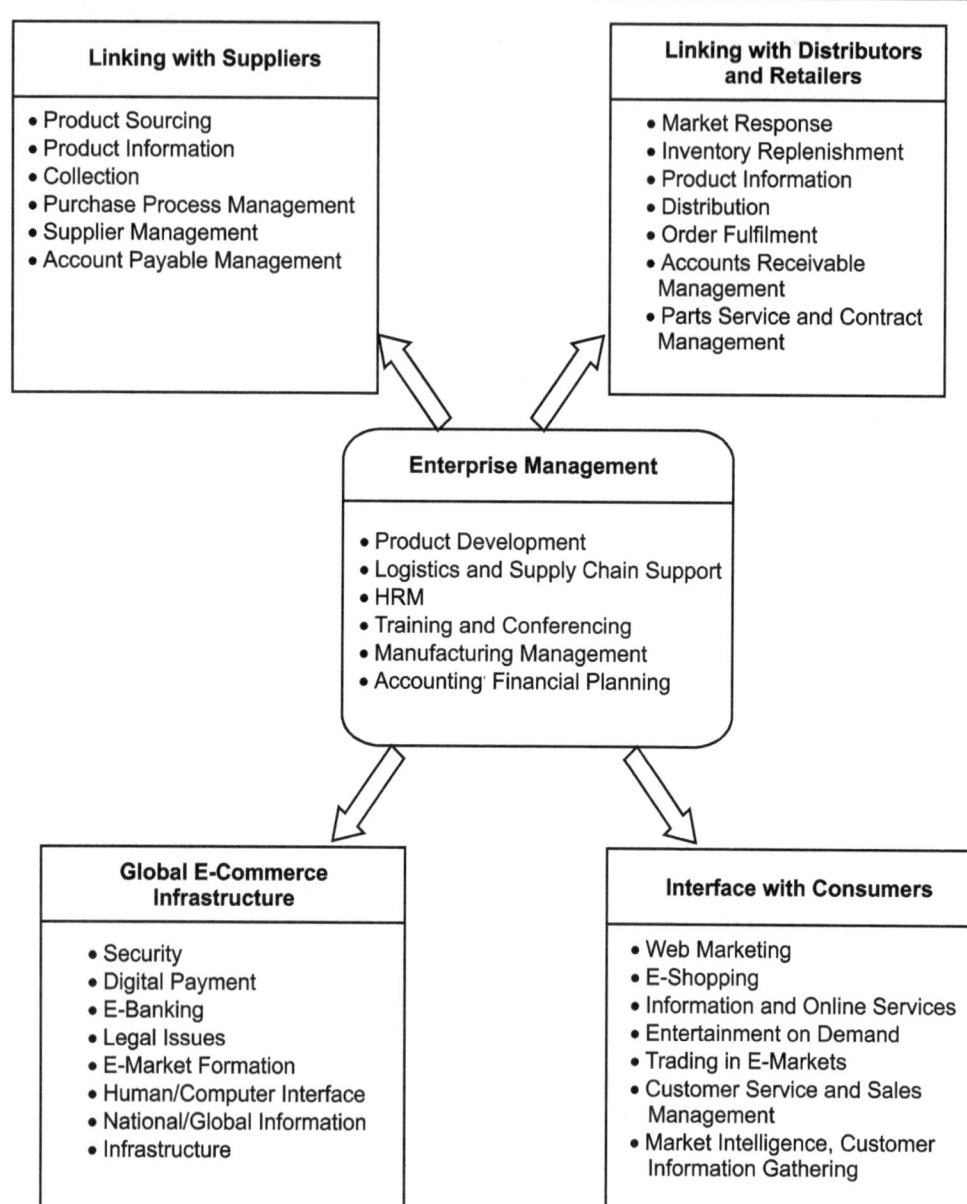

Fig. 1.5

1.8 Electronic Commerce Applications

- Various E-commerce applications are listed below:

  1. E-commerce used in retail stores such as book stores, music stores, toy stores and so on.

  2. E-commerce used in Railways, airlines, cinema theatre for booking ticket online and payment through credit cards.

3.   E-commerce used in services provided to customers from connected banks such as deposits, payments, providing information on status of an account.

4.   E-commerce used in auction sites wherein an individual buyer and seller participates in buying and selling goods.

5.   E-commerce used in filing tax returns to the government and obtain an immediate acknowledgement on the real time.

6.   E-commerce used in co-operating business connect to each other using their own private telecommunication network carrying out transactions in semi-automated way.

7.   E-commerce used in electronic publishing to promote marketing, advertising, sales and customer support.

8.   E-commerce used in online training of employees etc.

9.   The Internet looks for the following companies (as an example).

    (i)   To a big media conglomerate   :   An opportunity to create best such as television, book sellers, newspapers and dominant brands publishing etc.

    (ii)   To a software company   :   An opportunity for an early foot in the door that leads to market dominance as users standardize on a few well known packages.

    (iii) To a cable company   :   Thousands of a couch potato to surf through.

10. E-commerce is used in web-based educational material allowing the students to learn any time and at any place.

1.9 Electronic Commerce and Electronic Business

- E-commerce is the use of Internet and the web to transact business but when we focus on digitally enabled commercial transactions between and among organizations and individuals involving information systems under the control of the firm it takes the form of e-business.

- Now-a-days, 'e' is gaining momentum and most of the things if not everything is getting digitally enabled. Thus, it becomes very important to clearly draw the line between different types of commerce or business integrated with the 'e' factor.

1.9.1 E-Commerce

- There are many acronyms similar to the transactions of B2B, B2C and so on.

   1.   C2C (Customer to Customer),

   2.   B2A (Business to Administration),

   3.   C2G (Customer to Government),

4. C2A (Consumer to Administration),

5. G2G (Government to Government),

6. B2G (Business to Government),

7. B2P (Business to Peer),

8. P2P (Peer to Peer), and

9. B2B (Business to Business)

1. Business-to-Business (B2B):

B2B is an online business selling to other businesses. e.g. eSteel.com is a steel industry exchange that creates an electronic market for steel producers and users.

It is the business that dedicates the exchange of information, goods and services to two businesses. B2B is all about transaction between your organization and your partner. Any transaction or information associated with development, manufacturing, delivery, sales and support of product or services is a candidate for B2B transactions. This includes use of EDI and E-mail for purchasing goods and services, buying information and consulting services, submitting request for proposal and receiving proposals.

For example: A wholesaler places an order through the companies website for fresh stock and receives processed order in the form of shipped suppliers.

The exchange of products, services or information between business entities. According to market research studies published in early 2000, the money volume of B2B exceeds that of B2C by 10 to 1. The Gartner Group estimates B2B revenue worldwide will be $7.29 trillion by 2004, a compound annual growth of about 41 per cent.

It is the largest form of e-commerce involving business of trillions of dollars. In this form, the buyers and sellers are both business entities and do not involve an individual consumer. It is like the manufacturer supplying goods to the retailer or wholesaler. For example, Dell sells computers and other related accessories online but it is does not manufacture all those products. So, in order to sell those products, it first purchases them from different businesses i.e. the manufacturers of those products.

Web-based B2B includes:

o **Direct selling and support to business,** (as in the case of Cisco where customers can buy and also get technical support, downloads, patches online).

o **E-procurement,** (also known as industry portals) where a purchasing agent can shop for supplies from vendors, request proposals, and in some cases, bid to make a purchase at a desired price. For example the autoparts wholesaler (reliableautomotive.com); and the chemical B2B exchange (chemconnect.com).

o **Information sites** provide information about a particular industry for its companies and their employees. These include specialised search sites and trade and industry standards organisation sites. For example, newmarket makers.com is a leading portal for B2B news. Many B2B sites may also fall into one or more than one of these groups.

Advantages of B2B:

1. Direct interaction with customers.
2. Focused sales promotion.
3. Building customer loyalty.
4. Scalability.
5. Saving in distribution costs.

Type	Description	Examples
B2B storefront	Provide businesses with purchase, order fulfillment and other value added services.	Staples.com
B2B vertical markets	Provide a trading community for a specific industry.	HotelResource.com
B2B aggregators	Provide a single marketspace for business purchasing from multiple suppliers.	metalSite.com
B2B trading hubs	Provide a marketspace for multiple vertical markets.	VerticalNet.com
B2B post and browse markets	Provide a marketspace where participants post buy and sell opportunities.	CATEX.com CreditTrade.com
B2B auction markets	Provide a marketspace for buyers and sellers to enter competitive bids on contracts.	e-STEEL.com Altra.com Freemarkets.com
B2B fully automated	Provide a marketspace for the automatic matching of standardized buy and sell contracts.	PaperExchange.com

2. **Business-to-Consumer (B2C):**

    The exchange of products, information or services between business and consumers in a retailing relationship. Some of the first examples of B2C e-commerce were amazon.com and dell.com in the USA and lastminute.com in the UK.

    B2C is an online business selling to individual consumer. e.g. Amazon.com is a general merchandiser that sells consumer products to retail consumers. In B2C all transactions take place between business house and the final consumer.

For example, A consumer would log in to a website which is the virtual processing office of a business organization. After going through the product details and catalogue the customer may want to buy certain goods an order would be place and send as e-mail office of business organization. The e-mail would be dispatched the customer would be receive order goods.

For example, Etrade.com, Expedia.com, Monster.com, processors of online sales transactions, such as stock brokers and travel agents, that increase customers productivity by helping them get things done faster and more cheaply.

B2C e-business includes retail sales, often called e-retail and other online purchases such as airline tickets, entertainment venue tickets, hotel rooms, and shares of stock. B2C e-business provides high value content to consumers for a subscription fee. B2C e-business models include virtual malls, which are nothing but websites that host many online merchants. Virtual malls typically charge setup, listing, or transaction fees to online merchants and may also include transaction handling services and marketing options. E.g. of virtual malls include excite.com, choicemall.com, women.com, networkweb.com, amazon.com, Zshops.com, yahoo.com etc.

B2C e-business allowed businesses and consumers to get connected in entirely new ways and hence many people were very excited about the use of B2C on the internet. The opportunities and the challenges posed by the B2C E-business are enormous.

Some reasons of why one should opt for B2C:

1. Inexpensive costs, big opportunities.
2. Globalization.
3. Reduces operational costs.
4. Customer convenience.
5. Knowledge Management.

Working of B2C:

1. **Visiting the virtual mall:**

   The customer visits the mall by browsing the online catalogue. Finding right product becomes easy by using a search engine.

2. **Customer registration:**

   The customer has to resister to become part of the sites shopper registry. This allows the customer to get the shop's complete services.

3. **Customer buys products:**

   Through a shopping card system, order details, shipping charges, taxes, additional charges and price totals are presented in an organized manner, so customer can buy the product if he wants.

4. **Merchant process the order:**

   The merchant processes the order that is received from the previous stage and fill the necessary form.

5. **Credit card is processed:**

   The credit card of the customer is authenticated through a payment gateway or a bank.

6. **Operations management:**

   When the order is passed on to the logistics people, the traditional business operations will still be used.

7. **Shipment and delivery:**

   The product is then shipped to the customer. The customer can track the delivery.

8. **Customer receives:**

   The product is received by the customer and verified.

9. **After sales service:**

   After the sale has been made, the firm has to make sure that it maintain a good relationship with its customers, and is done through CRM.

As the name suggests, it is the model involving businesses and consumers. This is the most common e-commerce segment. In this model, online businesses sell to individual consumers. When B2C started, it had a small share in the market but after 1995 its growth was exponential. The basic concept behind this type is that the online retailers and marketers can sell their products to the online consumer by using crystal clear data which is made available via various online marketing tools. For example: An online pharmacy giving free medical consultation and selling medicines to patients is following B2C model.

3. **Business-to-Government (B2G):**

   B2G is the exchange of information, services and products between business organisations and government agencies on-line. This may include:

   o **E-procurement services**, in which businesses learn about the purchasing needs of agencies and provide services.

   o **A virtual workplace** in which a business and a government agency could co-ordinate the work on a contracted project by collaborating on-line to co-ordinate on-line meetings, review plans and manage progress.

   o **Rental of on-line applications and databases** designed especially for use by government agencies.

4. **Business-to-Peer Networks (B2P):**

   This would be the provision of hardware, software or other services to the peer networks. An example here would be Napster who provided the software and facilities to enable peer networking.

5. Consumer-to-Business (C2B):

This is the exchange of products, information or services from individuals to business. A classic example of this would be individuals selling their services to businesses.

6. Consumer-to-Consumer (C2C):

C2C helps consumers connect with other consumers who have items to sell. C2C provides a way for consumers to sell to each other, with the help of an online market maker such as an auction site eBay.com

In C2C all transaction take place between customer to customer and the website is acting as a platform that brings buyers and sellers together.

The customers located in Atlanta and Washington can register. A customer from Atlanta places an advertisement on the website. A customer from Washington while surfing the website looks at the advertisement and decide to purchase the product then the deal is finalize between two customers through the website without an actual meaning.

For example: eBay.com is a popular online Auction house which creates a marketplace where consumers can auction or sell goods directly to other consumers.

Consumers that don't like auctions but still want to find used merchandise can visit Half.com, which enables consumers to sell off unwanted books, movies, music, and games to other consumers.

In this category consumers interact directly with other consumers. It facilitates the online transaction of goods or services between two people. Though there is no visible intermediary involved but the parties cannot carry out the transactions without the platform which is provided by the online market maker such as eBay. They exchange information such as:

- o **Expert knowledge** where one person asks a question about anything and gets an e-mail reply from the community of other individuals, as in the case of the New York Times-affiliated abuzz.com website.

- o **Opinions** about companies and products, for example epinions.com. There is also an exchange of goods between people both with consumer auction sites such as e-bay and with more novel bartering sites such as swapitshop.com, where individuals swap goods with each other without the exchange of money.

7. Consumer-to-Government (C2G):

Examples where consumers provide services to government have yet to be implemented. See Government-to-Business.

8. Consumer-to-Peer Networks (C2P):

This is exactly part of what peer-to-peer networking is and so is a slightly redundant distinction since consumers offer their computing facilities once they are on the peer network.

9. **Government-to-Business (G2B):**

G2B is the exchange of information, services and products between government agencies and business organisations.

Consumer to Business is a growing arena where the consumer requests a specific service from the business.

Example: Harry is planning a holiday in Darwin. He requires a flight in the first week of December and is only willing to pay $250. Harry places a submission with in a web based C2B facility. Budget Price Airways accesses the facility and sees Harry's submission. Due to it being a slow period, the airline offers Harry a return fare for $250.

Government sites now enable the exchange between government and business of:

o **Information**, guidance and advice for business on international trading, sources of funding and support (ukishelp), facilities (For example: www.dti.org.uk).

o **A database of laws**, regulations and government policy for industry sectors.

o **On-line application** and submission of official forms, (such as company and value added tax).

o **On-line payment** facilities.

This improves accuracy, increases speed and reduces costs, so businesses are given financial incentives to use electronic-form submission and payment facilities.

10. **Government-to-Consumer (G2C) (Also known as E-government):**

Government sites offering information, forms and facilities to conduct transactions for individuals, including paying bills and submitting official forms on-line such as tax returns.

11. **Government-to-Government (G2G):**

Government-to-government transactions within countries linking local governments together and also international governments, especially within the European Union, which is in the early stages of developing coordinated strategies to link up different national systems.

12. **Government-to-Consumer (G2C):**

It is an attempt by the Government to reach out people in general. The government regularly conducts auctions and sells of vehicles, machinery and other material which are visited by customer. These websites also provides access to various official records and applications forms such as for birth, marriage and death certificate.

13. **Peer–to-Peer (P2P):**

This is the communications model in which each party has the same capabilities and either party can initiate a communication session.

Peer-to-peer technology enables Internet users to share files and computer resources directly without having to go through a central web server.

The focus in P2P companies is on helping individuals make information available for anyone's use by connecting users on the web.

For example: Napster.com, which was established to aid Internet users in finding and sharing online music files. Gnutella is a software application that permits consumers to share music with one another directly, without the intervention of a market maker. Another music sites, MP3.com, took a slightly different tack than Napster with its My.MP3.com service. It is used to share and download free MP3 songs at MyMP3.com. MP3.com makes money through advertising and charging for some downloads and has been recently acquired by Vivendi Universal, a major music industry player.

Though it is an e-commerce model but it is more than that. It is a technology in itself which helps people to directly share computer files and computer resources without having to go through a central web server. To use this, both sides need to install the required software so that they can communicate on the common platform. This type of e-commerce has quite low revenue generation as from the beginning it has been inclined to the free usage due to which it sometimes got entangled in cyber laws.

In recent usage, peer-to-peer has come to describe applications in which users can use the Internet to exchange files with each other directly or through a mediating server.

14. Peer-to-Consumer (P2C):

This is in effect peer-to-peer networking, offering services to consumers who are an integral part of the peer network.

15. Peer-to-Government (P2G):

This has not yet been used, but if it was, it would be used in a similar capacity to the P-to-B model, only with the government as the party accepting the transaction.

16. Peer-to-Business (P2B):

Peer-to-peer networking provides resources to business. For example, using peer network resources such as the spare processing capacity of individual machines on the network to solve mathematical problems or intensive and repetitive DNA analyses which requires very high capacity processing power. This framework can be used by organisations to segment their customers and distinguish the different needs, requirements, business processes, products and services that are needed for each.

17. Business-to-Consumer (B2C)

The Business-to-Consumer type of e-commerce is distinguished by the establishment of electronic business relationships between businesses and final consumers. It corresponds to the retail section of e-commerce, where traditional retail trade normally operates.

When compared to buying retail in traditional commerce, the consumer usually has more information available in terms of informative content and there is also a widespread idea that you'll be buying cheaper, without jeopardizing an equally personalized customer service, as well as ensuring quick processing and delivery of your order.

18. Business-to-Administration (B2A)

This part of e-commerce encompasses all transactions conducted online between companies and public administration. This is an area that involves a large amount and a variety of services, particularly in areas such as fiscal, social security, employment, legal documents and registers, etc. These types of services have increased considerably in recent years with investments made in e-government.

19. Consumer-to-Administration (C2A)

The Consumer-to-Administration model encompasses all electronic transactions conducted between individuals and public administration.

Examples of applications include:

- Education – disseminating information, distance learning, etc.
- Social Security – through the distribution of information, making payments, etc.
- Taxes – filing tax returns, payments, etc.
- Health – appointments, information about illnesses, payment of health services, etc.

Both models involving Public Administration (B2A and C2A) are strongly associated to the idea of efficiency and easy usability of the services provided to citizens by the government, with the support of information and communication technologies.

1.9.2 E-Business

- Electronic business (e-business) represents transformation of an organisations business and functional processes through the application of technologies, computing paradigms and philosophies of the new digital economy.
- Electronic business or E-business is any Internet initiative – tactical or strategic that transforms business relationships, whether those relationships be business-to-business, business-to-consumer, intra-business or even consumer-to-consumer.
- E-business includes:
  1. Shipping,
  2. Pricing and Promotions,
  3. Customer Relationship Management (CRM),
  4. Functional Accounting and Reporting,
  5. Merchandise Planning and Analysis,
  6. Other Logistics,
  7. Warehousing,
  8. Returns,
  9. Fulfilment,
  10. Knowledge management, and
  11. Order entry.

- E-business is really a new way to drive the following in an organisation or firm
  1. Speed,
  2. Innovation,
  3. Efficiencies, and
  4. New value creation.
- As with e-commerce, e-business (electronic business) also has a number of different definitions and is used in a number of different contexts.
- One of the first to use the term was IBM, in October 1997, when it launched a campaign built around e-business.
- Today, major corporations are rethinking their businesses in terms of the Internet and its new culture and capabilities and this is what some see as e-business.
  - E-business is the conduct of business on the Internet, not only buying and selling but also servicing customers and collaborating with business partners.
  - E-business includes customer service (e-service) and intra-business tasks.
  - E-business is the transformation of key business processes through the use of Internet technologies. An e-business is a company that can adapt to constant and continual change.
  - The development of intranet and extranet is part of e-business.
  - E-business is everything to do with back-end systems in an organisation.

Electronic Commerce Vs Electronic Business

- E-commerce is a subset of e-business.
- For the purpose of clarity, the distinction between e-commerce and ebusiness in this topic is based on the respective terms commerce and business.
- Commerce is defined as embracing the concept of trade, 'exchange of merchandise on a large scale between different countries'. By association, e-commerce can be seen to include the electronic medium for this exchange. Thus electronic commerce can be broadly defined as the exchange of merchandise (whether tangible or intangible) on a large scale between different countries using an electronic medium – namely the Internet. The implications of this are that e-commerce incorporates a whole socio-economic, telecommunications technology and commercial infrastructure at the macro-environmental level. All these elements interact together to provide the fundamentals of e-commerce.
- Business, on the other hand, is defined as 'a commercial enterprise as agoing concern'. E-business can broadly be defined as the processes or areas involved in the running and operation of an organisation that are electronic or digital in nature. These include direct business activities such as marketing, sales and human resource management but also indirect activities such as business process re-engineering and change management, which impact on the improvement in efficiency and integration of business processes and activities.

- Fig. 1.6 illustrates the major differences in e-commerce and e-business, where e-commerce has a broader definition referring more to the macro-environment, e-business relates more to the micro-level of the firm.

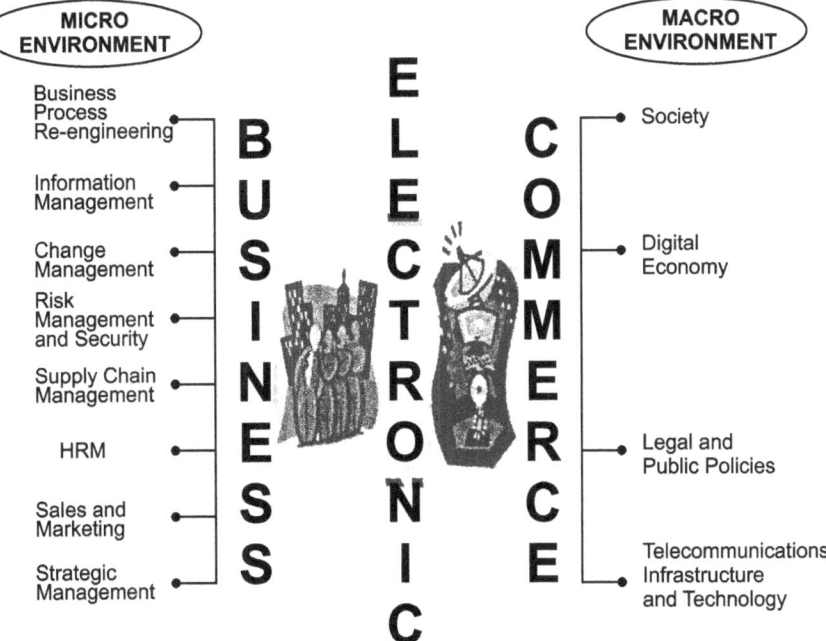

Fig. 1.6: Electronic commerce and electronic business

Objectives of E-Business

- Various objectives of E-business are:
  1. Improve service.
  2. Save time:
     (a) Time taken by customers.
     (b) Elapsed time for processes.
  3. Reduce process errors.
  4. Reduce the cost of core service provision.
  5. Free staff to provide value added services.
  6. Improve morale.
  7. Give people the tools and time they need.

Meaning of Electronic Business

- E-business is about transforming the way key business processes as done by integrating Internet technology and services into a companies essential business process.
- E-business links employees, partners, suppliers and customers and so on.
- E-business is a term now used broadly for the act of doing business using the Internet on online.
- Basically, the term E-business applies at all Net-based business applications of B2B, B2C, B2S and B2E.

- E-business is marketplace where businesses are using Internet technologies to securely transform:
  1. Their business relationship (via Extranets),
  2. Their business and selling services, goods and information (via E-commerce), and
  3. Their internal business processes (via Intranets).

Essential Elements of an E-Business

- Fig. 1.7 shows elements of e-business.
  1. **Business model:** How businesses interwork, How businesses influences the way they are established, the way in which technology is deployed.
  2. **Technical aspects:** Software, hardware, networks that are needed to connect a community of interest and allow them to share information, presentation and design of that information.
     (a) **Specialised software:** This softwares are used for payments such as billing, charging, invoicing, account management etc. and the security such as authenticity, authorization, privacy, data integrity, audit etc.
     (b) **Service supports:** Such as configuration control, problem management and order handling.

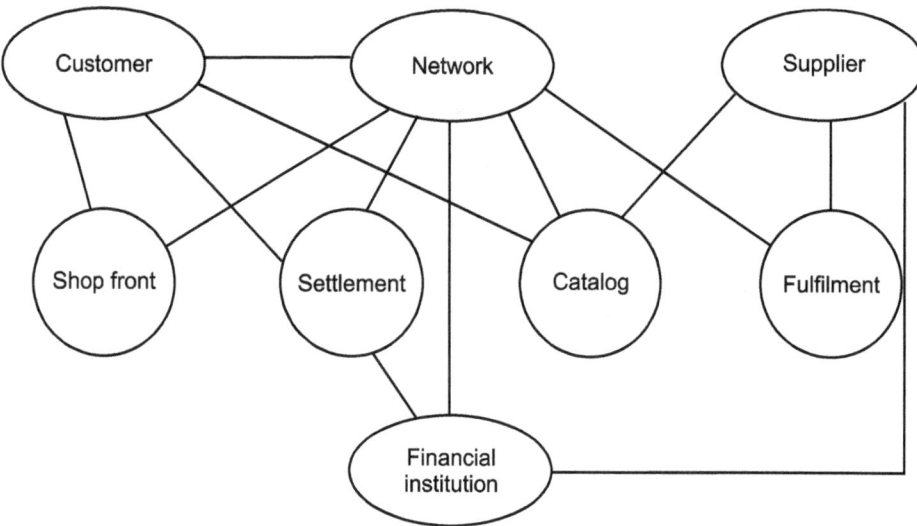

Fig. 1.7

- We can daily chain the picture and some on take the:

  role of supplier   :   to one set of customers

  role of customer   :   to different suppliers.

- All have to be on a shared network from the same catalogue, we have some means of delivering goods and be able to settle up after the transaction.

$$\text{E-business} = \frac{\text{Mass marketing}}{\text{capability}} = \frac{\text{Internet's global}}{\text{search}} + \frac{\text{Vast resources of}}{\text{traditional IT}}$$

- Constituent parts of trading over a network are:

o Conventional market difference	Including bogus traders, inferior goods, doing bargains.
o Size and scope of the market place	Different from conventional (high steel model) – size does not matter.
o The market place	Market place is a virtual trading area where the deals are struck over a network.
o Shop Front	Computer, server is the warehouse.

- One supplier might provider the online content, service support and a means of fulfillment.
- One supplier might provide the online content; another the application hosting.
- An e-business that looks like a cogent entity to the consumer may in reality be a host of co-operating suppliers.

An Architecture for E-Business

- Before considering an architecture for e-business we will analyse the e-business areas first.
- Global transaction volumes between business on the Internet is expected to reach trillions of dollars by 2008. Hence, the areas to be focused are many.
- B2B initiatives like participation in e-market places supply and distribution collaboration through the web and so on are needed.
- Further, the organisations will have to take all necessary steps to build and retain skills, capabilities across the entire employee community.
- There are four key areas as mentioned in C10 Web business magazine.
  1. Empowering employees
  2. Building customer intimacy
  3. Energising business processes (For example: extended ERP, web application etc.)
  4. Channel connections to value chain partners.

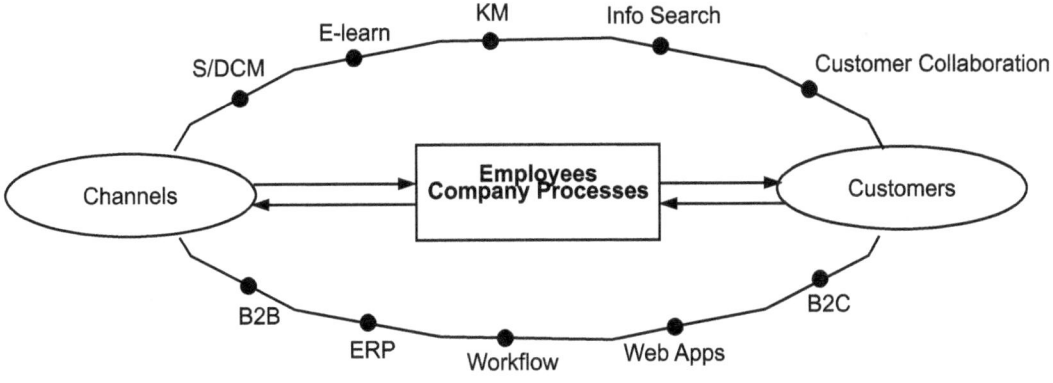

Fig. 1.8

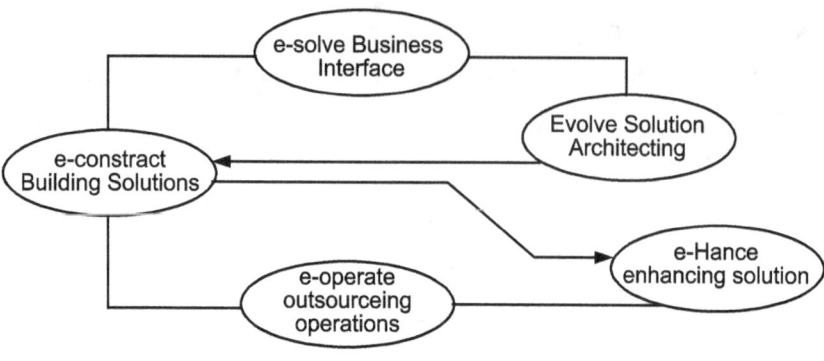

Fig. 1.9

Advantages of E-Business

* Various advantages of e-business are listed below:
  1. **Worldwide presence:** This is the biggest advantage of conducting business online. A firm engaging in e-business can have a nationwide or a worldwide presence. IBM was one of the first companies to use the term e-business to refer to servicing customers and collaborating with business partners from all over the world. Dell Inc. too had a flourishing business selling PCs throughout the US, only via telephone and the Internet till the year 2007. Amazon.com is another success story that helps people buy internationally from third parties. Hence, worldwide presence is ensured if companies rethink their business in terms of the Internet.
  2. **Cost effective marketing and promotions:** Using the web to market products guarantees worldwide reach at a nominal price. Advertising techniques like pay per click advertising ensure that the advertiser only pays for the advertisements that are actually viewed. Affiliate marketing, where customers are directed to a business portal because of the efforts of the affiliate who in turn receive a compensation for their efforts meeting with success, has emerged on account of e-business. Affiliate marketing has helped both the business and the affiliates. Firms engaging in e-business have managed to use cost effective online advertising strategies to their advantage.
  3. **Developing a competitive strategy:** Firms need to have a competitive strategy in order to ensure a competitive advantage. Without an effective strategy, they will find it impossible to maintain the advantage and earn profits. The strategy, that the firms can pursue, can be a be a cost strategy or a differentiation strategy. For instance, till the year 2007, Dell Inc. was selling computers only via the Internet and the phone. It adopted a differentiation strategy by selling its computers online and customizing its laptops to suit the requirements of the clients. Thus, e-business resulted in Dell Inc. managing to capture a vast segment of the market using the differentiation strategy.
  4. **Better customer service:** E-business has resulted in improved customer service. Many times, on visiting a website, the customer is greeted by a pop-up chat window. Readily available customer service may help in encouraging the customer to know

2. **Let the world hear what you have to say and share**: You can share your knowledge, experience and enthusiasm with people who have common interests across the globe, with whom you might never otherwise crossed paths. With your very own website, you can create a discussion board, a very popular idea-voicing tool, better known as a 'forum'. You can also have a guestbook, where people can discuss your postings.

3. **Make extra profit with minimum investment:** With the latest technology at your service, your website will make money for you while you are asleep or out having fun. Earn easy money by simply having visitors click on certain product or service promos or links that are relevant to your site content pages, (For example, Google Adsense/Adwords ad solutions) without any initial investment.

4. **Enjoy complete creative freedom**: Even though social media is constantly on a campaign to cater to the users' personalisation needs, having your own website means you can not only decide the content but also design the look and feel of it as well.

   So go crazy on colours and fonts, create logos, and enjoying the process of building through website from scratch.

5. **Specialise and expand**: Probably the greatest feature about owning a website is that you can build one domain name around a number of unique themes.

   Each web 'page' on the same domain name can be based on a certain theme. For instance you can have complete personal information on your home page while the rest of the pages can be dedicated to each of your interests or hobbies.

6. **Add a blog**: Of course, what website is complete without a blog. Blogs have shot up to immense popularity due to the creative vent it offers majority of the world- be it with words or with pictures.

   The search engines too seem to like blogs, so set one up and bring in the visitors.

7. **Affordability**: The affordability factor is the icing on the cake. Be it for business purposes or for personal use, setting up your own website does not cost much.

2.2 Benefits of Website

- Various benefits of website are given below:

1. **Increases awareness of products/services:** A website provides the opportunity to publish the who, what, where, when and why of your business in a powerful and effective manner. How many potential customers might be saved if they could learn a little more about you, your company, your products, etc., without having to phone or taking the time to meet with you in person? A website makes it easy for customers to learn more about your business at their own pace.

2. **Expands market place:** A website can expand your reach to a market that may have been difficult or expensive to reach through traditional advertising. Increasingly, people search the Web rather than the Yellow Pages when looking for a service or product. You'd be amazed how much shopping occurs on the World Wide Web overnight! With an e-commerce site you can even make sales when your offices are closed. Currently over 75% of the people in the US access the Internet, up from over 40% at the end of 1999.

3. **Increases hours of operation:** Not only will your website be there 24 hours a day, 365 days a year with the possibility of reaching millions of people every day, but now your customers are able to contact you outside of your normal business hours. Your website is still working for you while you are at leisure or asleep, and is not dependent on your having a PC or leaving your PC switched on.

4. **Marketing tool: Replace or complement existing sales and marketing channels:** It's a very low-cost method of promoting your business. By advertising your website, in addition to your product or services, you give potential customers the opportunity to learn far more about your product or services than you could ever place in an ad. Advertising experts agree the Internet will become an increasingly popular advertising medium, with anticipated spending eclipsing $15 billion and have an 8% increased share of all advertising spending by 2005.

5. **Reduce costs / Improve efficiency:**

   (i)   **Reduce publishing costs:** One of the largest expenses a business can incur is designing, printing, and delivering marketing materials. Websites are quicker, easier and more cost-effective to update than print based media. You can keep your website more current, more affordably than any other media can. With a website, you can instantly publish that same information: new product announcements, employment opportunities, contact information, coupons, almost anything, without material or delivery costs. People can learn about it instantly just by visiting your website. Imagine how much it would cost to produce a catalog for 200 different products, and keep it in consumers' hands for an entire year. You can accomplish this with a website very easily, with low development cost and almost no distribution cost.

   (ii) **Reduce marketing costs:** Buying advertising space, whether it's a newspaper ad, billboard or radio spots, can be expensive. In addition is the burden of the hours spent trying to figure out the perfect words to say in a limited space. A website is an unlimited number of full-page ads that you can change at will!

   (iii) **Reduce communication costs:** A website can do far more than sell products. You can have pictures, details and prices of your products/services, the very latest company information, hours of operation and maps indicating the location of your

more about the product or service. Moreover, payments can be made online, products can be shipped to the customer without the customer having to leave the house.

With the use of e-commerce you can promote your product globally.

5. Reduces Time and money spent.
6. Gives a competitive advantages.
7. Removes Location and availability restrictions.
8. Heightens customer service.

Disadvantages of E-Business

- Disadvantages of E-business are given below:
  1. **Sectoral limitations:** The main disadvantage of e-business is the lack of growth in some sectors on account of product or sector limitations. The food sector has not benefited in terms of growth of sales and consequent revenue generation because of a number of practical reasons like food products being perishable items. Consumers do not look for food products on the Internet since they prefer going to the supermarket to buy the necessary items as and when the need arises.
  2. **Costly E-business solutions for optimization:** Substantial resources are required for redefining product lines in order to sell online. Upgrading computer systems, training personnel, and updating websites requires substantial resources. Moreover, Electronic Data Management (EDM) and Enterprise Resource Planning (ERP) necessary for ensuring optimal internal business processes may be looked upon, by some firms, as one of the disadvantages of e-business.
  3. **Security:** There are still some people who do not think it is save to buy on-line therefore, as there is not a high-street shop will loss their custom.
  4. You may not recieve what you believe you have purchased.
  5. Things such as viruses cpould meanlosing the site or affecting your customers computers while on your website.

E-Business Applications

- Electronic business is any information system or application that empowers business processes. Today this is mostly done with web technologies.
- Applications can be divided into three categories:

1. **Internal business systems:**
   - Customer relationship management,
   - Enterprise resource planning,
   - Employee information portals,
   - Knowledge management,
   - Workflow management,
   - Document management systems,
   - Human resource management,
   - Process control, and
   - Internal transaction processing.

2. **Enterprise communication and collaboration:**
    *   E-mail,
    *   Voice mail,
    *   Discussion forum,
    *   Chat systems,
    *   Data conferencing, and
    *   Collaborative work systems.
3. **Electronic commerce:**
    *   Electronic Funds Transfer (EFT),
    *   Supply Chain Management,
    *   E-marketing, and
    *   Online transaction process.

Questions

1. List four uses of E-commerce.
2. Define the term E-commerce.
3. Enlist various goals of E-commerce.
4. Describe various technical components of E-commerce.
5. What are the main activities of E-commerce?
6. With suitable diagram describe meaning of E-commerce.
7. What is meant by E-business?
8. State advantages and disadvantages of E-commerce to organisation.
9. What are the functions of E-commerce?
10. Compare E-commerce and E-business.
11. Enlist various application of E-commerce.
12. Explain the following terms with suitable example.
    *   (i)   B2B
    *   (ii)   B2C
    *   (iii)   C2C
    *   (iv)   B2G
    *   (v)   P2P
    *   (vi)   B2A
13. With suitable example describe G2G.
14. Describe the importance of E-commerce.
15. Enlist the various challenges of E-commerce.
16. List the characteristics of E-commerce.
17. List four advantages of E-commerce to consumers.
18. Describe the term scope of E-commerce.
19. List the objectives of E-business.
20. What are the essential elements of E-business.
21. List four advantages and disadvantages of E-business.
22. Enlist various application of E-business.

■■■

Chapter 2...

Building Own Website

Contents ...

2.1 Reasons for Building Own Website

- Before we study reasons for creating own website it is essential first to understand what is website?

- A website is a collection of related web pages, images, videos or other digital assets that are addressed relative to a common Uniform Resource Locator (URL), often consisting of only the domain name, or the IP address, and the root path ('/') in an Internet Protocol-based network.

- A web site is hosted on at least one web server, accessible via a network such as the Internet or a private local area network.

- A web page is a document, typically written in plain text interspersed with formatting instructions of Hypertext Markup Language (HTML, XHTML).
- A web page may incorporate elements from other websites with suitable markup anchors.

Definition of Website

- A website is a collection of documents known as webpages (or pages for short) that contain information: images, words, digital media, and the like. The main page in a website is called a homepage, and other pages in a website are called subpages. These are connected by hyperlinks, which are spots on a page (usually text or images) that, when clicked, take the user to different location. This can be another subpage, another location on the same page, or another website altogether.

OR

- A website, Web site or WWW site is a collection of Web pages, that is, HTML/XHTML documents accessible generally via HTTP on the Internet; all publicly accessible websites in existence comprise the World Wide Web.
- The pages of a website will be accessed from a common root URL, the homepage, and usually reside on the same physical server.

OR

- A website is just a bunch of web pages connected together through something called links.

OR

- A collection of interlinked web pages with a related topic, usually under a single domain name, which includes an intended starting file called a "home page".
- A website of your own with information about your name, family, or business and so on. It is the quickest and fastest way to let people all over the world know that you have arrived.
- For example, Number of actors, actresses and players have their own websites with information about themselves and their movies their sport carrier. This only goes to prove how vast the audience for the is medium is.
- Any information or data that you would like to spread over a wide area economically could be done through the website, just put all the information or data in place, decide how you want the world to see it... and presto, you are on !
- Here, are some reasons why you should create your very own website:
  1. **Showcase your virtual portrait**: You need not rely on Facebook and Twitter any more to showcase your virtual portrait. With your very own website, you can indulge in some popular ways of presenting yourself online such as maintaining a webblog, (online diary) or a photo gallery.

company's outlets on your website. It can supply your staff, suppliers and business partners with important and timely information. Just about any printed matter can be converted to a web page and distributed by email at far less cost and time than by fax, mail or courier.

2.3 Cost, Time and Reach

2.3.1 Cost

- It is of prime importance in any business or organisation.
- Setting up a website is one of the cheapest and easiest forms of promotion.
- For example, newspapers charge a sizeable amount of limited space where you can just say that you want to Television and Radio are good media, but their rates are likely to be out of your budget.
- On the other hand, a website can be designed at a negligible cost and yet give you ample space to show case your company or organisation and its services.

2.3.2 Time

- Imagine paying through your nose for newspaper space or a radio/TV slot-the ad runs for a day or a few seconds.
- Now compare these with your website which is on the Internet for a period of one whole year.

2.3.3 Reach

- It is another important factor for any sort of promotion.
- The advertiser is always concerned about the size of the audience he/she will cover by this promotion.
- Radio and print ads are effective only on a regional level and the television has a wider reach but even this is not a good indicator.
- How can you be sure that you have the full attention of the person who is browsing your website?
  1. First of all, he/she is paying for every minute that he/she spends online.
  2. Secondly, he/she probably goes to your site because he/she queried for it in a search engine.
  3. Thirdly, there is nothing on your web-page to distract him from your sales-pitch! Yes, with a website, you can have the whole world as your audience.
- You have to note the following points:
1. **Registering a Domain Name:** To register a domain name with Network Solutions i.e. InterNIC, you need to send an e-mail to hostmaster@internic.net with a precise format including registrant name, technical, administrative and billing contract information and nameserver information. Today, however, the procedure has been greatly simplified

through an online form at networksolutions.com. This procedure is interesting to note that this form, once filled out correctly, is actually e-mailed to you and you have to reply to it to complete the registration. Somethings never change.

To save us the burden of remembering long numeric addresses, experts devised a mechanism to represent computers through levels constructed using alphanumeric characters and these codes are called "domain name" and it is unique and nobody can use this without permission. Domain names have so far been assigned on a First Come-First Served basis (i.e. FCFS).

2. **Type of Domains:** There are four types of domains available for registration, they are:
    1. .com
    2. .net
    3. .org
    4. .int

    When you have probably come across the first three domains sometime during your sufing sessions. The fourth and last is harder to come by. According to definition, Int is meant for Internet infrastructure providers, possibly large ISPs, bandwidth backbones and so on. One site that uses this extension is The Phone Company i.e. www.tpc.int which provides free e-mail to fax services. You probably do not want to register a name ending with .int domain.

3. **Costs:** Domains such as .com, .net and .org domains cost $80 for the first 2 years and $40 for every subsequent year. There was a time when .org domains were free, but that has changed. Competition in the name registration of domain name, game is likely to push down prices quite a bit. Some registration authorities have expressed that they intended to push the price down to $45-$50 half the present rates charged.

    This is just the cost of keeping your domain alive. Even if you do not have a website, yet feel that your domain name is important, register it before someone else does. Your payment option include following things:
    1. Your friendly neighbourhood Internet-wallah,
    2. The dollar draft, the most annoying of them all, and
    3. An International Credit Card.

    All in all, it is usually best to let someone else handle the money as long as you are paying the correct amount and own rights to the domain.

4. **Feedback:** In any business or organisation quick feedback or response time from both parties is of utmost importance. The dynamic nature of websites makes this easy and simple.

    Number of websites feedback and query forms that make customer support and query handling much more efficient. All this activities is done from your website itself without having the user have to make any extra effort or telephone calls.

Ideal Website

- First analyse the objectives you want to achieve through your website. Number of websites have been total failures due to the lack of planning and proper objectives.

- For example, an educational site which people access for purely academic reasons does not need a heavy complement of graphics, especially when the graphics serve no purpose besides making the site look attractive and on the other hand, if you are a music/movie organisation, it is required of your site to be flashy and graphical so as to create an atmosphere.

- A website can be an interactive advertisement or a comprehensive brochure, or even take on the role of a spokesperson-all this to an international audience not limited by factors such as time and distance.

- Someone should always plan what sort of website he/she would like to have. Very often, corporate organisations that spend huge amounts of money on advertising and other forms of promotion have very poorly designed websites.

Build Own Website

- For building own website first, consider the Internet as an extension of our corporate identity and also as the look you would like it to have just as you would plan the other aspects of our business.

- For example: Each and every corporate house has a style in which they print their letterheads, visiting cards, brochures etc., to maintain a sense of corporate and uniformity identity. This style could be extended to the look of the website as well, so that a person who has seen the advertisements and promotions of the company or organisation would already be familiar with the look of the website even when he/she visits it for the first time. This look would also help the surfer to associate the website with your company/organisation without your having to explicitly emphasise it.

- Secondly, when deciding on the look and feel of the website, always consider the image you want to project. Make sure the information you put on your website is useful and relevant.

- If yours is a serious type of an organisation, avoid heavy graphics and animations, on the other hand, if your site is more of a fun-and-frolic type, go ahead and use pastel animation and shades. The look of the site helps greatly in creating the right ambience; so it should in no way contradict the actual content of the site.

- Another point to be noted is that overdoing the graphics makes a site load much less quickly; so it is better to show some restraint.

2.4 Domain Names - Meaning And Types Of Internet Organisations (.edu, .com, .mil, .gov, .net)

- Before we study domain name registration we discuss what is mean by domain name?

What is a Domain Name?

- A domain name is an identification label that defines a realm of administrative autonomy, authority or control on the Internet, based on the Domain Name System (DNS).
- Domain names are used in various networking contexts and application-specific naming and addressing purposes.
- Domain names are organized in subordinate levels (subdomains) of the DNS root domain, which is nameless.
- The first-level set of domain names are the Top-Level Domains (TLDs), including the generic Top-Level Domains (gTLDs), such as the prominent domains.com.net and .org, and the country code Top-Level Domains (ccTLDs).
- Below these top-level domains in the DNS hierarchy are the second-level and third-level domain names that are typically open for reservation by end-users that wish to connect local area networks to the Internet, run web sites or create other publicly accessible Internet resources.
- The registration of these domain names is usually administered by domain name registrars who sell their services to the public.
- This is the name that identifies an Web site. For example, "microsoft.com" is the domain name of Microsoft's Web site.
- A single Web server can serve Web sites for multiple domain names, but a single domain name can point to only one machine.
- For example, Apple Computer has Web sites at www.apple.com, www.info.apple.com, and store.apple.com. Each of these sites could be served on different machines.
- Then there are domain names that have been registered, but are not connected to a Web server.
- The most common reason for this is to have e-mail addresses at a certain domain name without having to maintain a Web site. In these cases, the domain name must be connected to a machine that is running a mail server.

Definition of Domain Name:

- A domain name is a name that uniquely identifies a site (For example, web site or ftp site) on the Internet or other TCP/IP network.

OR

- The domain name is the piece of a URL that is the property of the website owner. Domain names are typically preceded by 'www.', which identifies the server the site is stored on and end with '.com' or '.edu' or another extension that represents the type of website (commercial, educational, nonprofit, etc.) although with the explosion of domain name demand, extensions have lost some of their relevancy.

OR

- A domain name, simply put, is a name with a common domain name extension on the end. It is typically put in the form of domain.com, domain.net, domain.org or domain.info. There are other extensions available as well, but these four are the most common and most people that are on the Internet recognize them. A domain name is simply a placeholder for an IP address. Whenever you type a domain name into the browser something interesting happens. The browser will send that name to a server which will translate the domain name into an IP address. That server will then forward the request to the server that contains that IP address. What comes back to you are the contents of that final server.

Basic Term of Domain Name:

1. **A domain name** is textual representation of a numeric number i.e. IP address used to locate specific areas of the Internet. It is simpler, easier to remember a name than a series of numbers.

2. **A Top Level Domain** (TLD) is the extension that is attached at the end of your domain name. Example, in myname.com, .com is the top level domain. The two types of top level domains available right now are global (GTLD) and country code (CCTLD).

3. **A URL** (Uniform Resource Locator) is your full address on the Internet. For example, http//www.myname.com includes the prefix http://www, and the TLD extension.com as well as the actual domain name.

4. **IP i.e. Internet Protocol** address is the numerical equivalent to your domain name. IP is easier to remember a name than the string of numbers that make up the IP address. Without a number assigned, a domain name is not accessible on the Internet.

5. **DNS i.e. Domain Name Server** is the server connected to the Internet that translates the URL/domain name into the IP address to direct you to the correct location on the Internet.

- Every domain name has to be directed to a computer server somewhere. When someone types in your- new domain name, they need to be directed to some location on the Internet.

Importance of a Domain Name:

- There are a number of good reasons for having a domain name. They are:

1. If you ever change your web host, your domain name goes with you. Your regular visitors or customers who knew your site name as www.thesitewizard.com (for example) would not have to be informed about a change of URL. They would simply type your domain name and they'd be brought to your new site.

2. If you are a business, a domain name gives you credibility. Few people would be willing to do business with a company with a dubious URL like http://www.geocities.com/whatever/12345.

3. If you get a domain name that describes your company's business or name, people can remember the name easily and can return to your site without having to consult their documents. In fact, if you get a good name that describes your product or service, you might even get people who were trying their luck by typing "www.yourproductname.com" in their browser.

4. If you want good sponsors (advertisers) for your website, a domain name is usually helpful. It tends to give your website an aura of respectability.

2.5 Internet Service Providers

- An **Internet Service Provider** (ISP, also called **Internet Access Provider** or **IAP)** is a business or organization that provides consumers or businesses access to the Internet and related services. In the past, most ISPs were run by the phone companies. Now, ISPs can be started by just about any individual or group with sufficient money and expertise. In addition to Internet access via various technologies such as dial-up and DSL, they may provide a combination of services including Internet transit, domain name registration and hosting, web hosting, and colocation.

2.5.1 What is an ISP?

- An Internet Service Provider (ISP) is an organisation through which you can arrange Internet access. ISPs are typically commercial or community organisation offering broadband or dial-up access, usually alongwith other services such as, Web hosting and, e-mail etc.

2.5.2 History of ISP

- The internet started off as a closed network between government research laboratories and relevant parts of universities. It became popular and then universities and colleges started giving more of their members access to it.

- As a result, commercial Internet Service Providers occurred to provide access for mainly those who missed their university accounts.

2.5.3 ISP Connection Options

- ISPs employ a range of technologies to enable consumers to connect to their network. For "home users", the most popular options include dial-up, DSL (typically ADSL), Broadband wireless access, Cable modem, FTTH, and ISDN (typically BRI). For customers who have more demanding requirements, such as medium-to-large businesses, or other ISPs, DSL (often SHDSL or ADSL), Ethernet, Metro Ethernet, Gigabit Ethernet, Frame Relay, ISDN (BRI or PRI), ATM, satellite Internet access and SONET are more likely. With the increasing popularity of downloading music and online video and the general demand for faster page loads, higher bandwidth connections are becoming more popular.

2.5.4 How ISPs Connect to the Internet?

*   Just as their customers pay them for Internet access, ISPs themselves pay upstream ISPs for Internet access. In the simplest case, a single connection is established to an upstream ISP using one of the technologies described above, and the ISP uses this connection to send or receive any data to or from parts of the Internet beyond its own network; in turn, the upstream ISP uses its own upstream connection, or connections to its other customers to allow the data to travel from source to destination.

*   In reality, the situation is often more complicated. For example, ISPs with more than one Point of Presence (PoP) may have separate connections to an upstream ISP at multiple PoPs, or they may be customers of multiple upstream ISPs and have connections to each one at one or more of their PoPs. ISPs may engage in peering, where multiple ISPs interconnect with one another at a peering point or Internet exchange point (IX), allowing the routing of data between their networks, without charging one another for that data - data that would otherwise have passed through their upstream ISPs, incurring charges from the upstream ISP.

*   ISPs that require no upstream and have only customers and/or peers are called Tier 1 ISPs, indicating their status as ISPs at the top of the Internet hierarchy. Routers, switches, Internet routing protocols, and the expertise of network administrators all have a role to play in ensuring that data follows the best available route and that ISPs can "see" one another on the Internet.

2.5.5 Virtual ISP

*   A Virtual ISP (vISP) purchases services from another ISP (sometimes called a **wholesale ISP** or similar within this context) that allow the vISP's customers to access the Internet via one or more point of presence (PoPs) that are owned and operated by the wholesale ISP. There are various models for the delivery of this type of service; for example, the wholesale ISP could provide network access to end users via its dial-up modem PoPs or DSLAMs installed in telephone exchanges, and route, switch, and/or tunnel the end user traffic to the vISP's network, whereupon they may route the traffic toward its destination.

*   In another model, the vISP does not route any end user traffic, and needs only provide **AAA** (**A**uthentication, **A**uthorization and **A**ccounting) functions, as well as any "value-add" services like email or web hosting. Any given ISP may use their own PoPs to deliver one service, and use a vISP model to deliver another service or use a combination to deliver a service in different areas. The service provided by a wholesale ISP in a vISP model is distinct from that of an upstream ISP, even though in some cases, they may both be one and the same company. The former provides connectivity from the end user's premises to the Internet or to the end user's ISP, the latter provides connectivity from the end user's ISP to all or parts of the rest of the Internet.

- A vISP can also refer to a completely automated white label service offered to anyone at no cost or for a minimal set-up fee. The actual ISP providing the service generates revenue from the calls and may also share a percentage of that revenue with the owner of the vISP. All technical aspects are dealt with leaving the owner of vISP with the task of promoting the service. This sort of service is however declining due to the popularity of unmetered internet access also known as **flatrate**.

2.5.6 ISP Services

1. Digital Subscriber Line (DSL):

- To understand DSL, you first need to know a couple of things about a normal telephone line the kind that telephone professionals call **POTS** (Plain Old Telephone Service). One of the ways that POTS makes the most of the telephone company's wires and equipment is by limiting the frequencies that the switches, telephones and other equipment will carry. Human voices, speaking in normal conversational tones, can be carried in a frequency range of 0 to 3,400 Hertz. This range of frequencies is tiny. For example, compare this to the range of most stereo speakers, which cover from roughly 20 Hertz to 20,000 Hertz. And the wires themselves have the potential to handle frequencies up to several million Hertz in most cases.

- The use of such a small portion of the wire's total bandwidth is historical remember that the telephone system has been in place, using a pair of copper wires to each home, for about a century. By limiting the frequencies carried over the lines, the telephone system can pack lots of wires into a very small space without worrying about interference between lines. Modern equipment that sends digital rather than analog data can safely use much more of the telephone line's capacity. DSL does just that.

- **Types of DSL:**

  CDSL: CDSL (Consumer DSL) is a version of DSL, trademarked by Rockwell Corp., that is somewhat slower than ADSL (1 Mbps downstream, probably less upstream) and has the advantage that a "splitter" does not need to be installed at the user's end.

  G.Lite or DSL Lite: G.lite (also known as DSL Lite, splitterless ADSL, and Universal ADSL) is essentially a slower ADSL that does not require splitting of the line at the user end but manages to split it for the user remotely at the telephone company. This saves the cost of what the phone companies call "the truck roll." G.Lite, officially ITU-T standard G-992.2, provides a data rate from 1.544 Mbps to 6 Mpbs downstream and from 128 Kbps to 384 Kbps upstream. G.Lite is expected to become the most widely installed form of DSL.

  HDSL: HDSL (High bit-rate Digital Subscriber Line), one of the earliest forms of DSL, is used for wideband digital transmission within a corporate site and between the telephone company and a customer. The main characteristic of HDSL is that it is symmetrical: an equal amount of bandwidth is available in both directions. HDSL can carry as much on a single wire of twisted-pair cable as can be carried on a T1 line (up to 1.544 Mbps) in North America or an E1 line (up to 2.048 Mbps) in Europe over a somewhat longer range and is considered an alternative to a T1 or E1 connection.

IDSL: IDSL (ISDN DSL) is somewhat, of a misnomer since it's really closer to ISDN data rates and service at 128 Kbps than to the much higher rates of ADSL.

RADSL: RADSL (Rate-Adaptive DSL) is an ADSL technology from Westell in which software is able to determine the rate at which signals can be transmitted on a given customer phone line and adjust the delivery rate accordingly. Westell's FlexCap2 system uses RADSL to deliver from 640 Kbps to 2.2 Mbps downstream and from 272 Kbps to 1.088 Mbps upstream over an existing line.

SDSL: SDSL (Symmetric DSL) is similar to HDSL with a single twisted-pair line, carrying 1.544 Mbps (U.S. and Canada) or 2.048 Mbps (Europe) each direction on a duplex line. It's symmetric because the data rate is the same in both directions.

UDSL: UDSL (Unidirectional DSL) is a proposal from a European company. It's a unidirectional version of HDSL.

VDSL: VDSL (Very high data rate DSL) is a developing technology that promises much higher data rates over relatively short distances (between 51 and 55 Mbps over lines up to 1,000 feet or 300 meters in length). It's envisioned that VDSL may emerge somewhat after ADSL is widely deployed and co-exist with it. The transmission technology (CAP, DMT, or other) and its effectiveness in some environments is not yet determined. A number of standards organizations are working on it.

x2/DSL: x2/DSL is a modem from 3 Com that supports 56 Kbps modem communication, but is upgradeable through new software installation to ADSL when it becomes available in the user's area. 3 Com calls it "the last modem you will ever need".

2. Asymmetric Digital Subscriber Line (ADSL):

- ADSL technology is asymmetric. It allows more bandwidth downstream-from an NSP's central office to the customer site-than upstream from the subscriber to the central office. This asymmetry, combined with always-on access (which eliminates call setup), makes ADSL ideal for Internet/intranet surfing, video-on-demand, and remote LAN access. Users of these applications typically download much more information than they send.

- ADSL transmits more than 6 Mbps to a subscriber, and as much as 640 Kbps more in both directions (shown in Fig. 3.11). Such rates expand existing access capacity by a factor of 50 or more without new cabling. ADSL can literally transform the existing public information network from one limited to voice, text, and low-resolution graphics to a powerful, ubiquitous system capable of bringing multimedia, including full motion video, to every home this century.

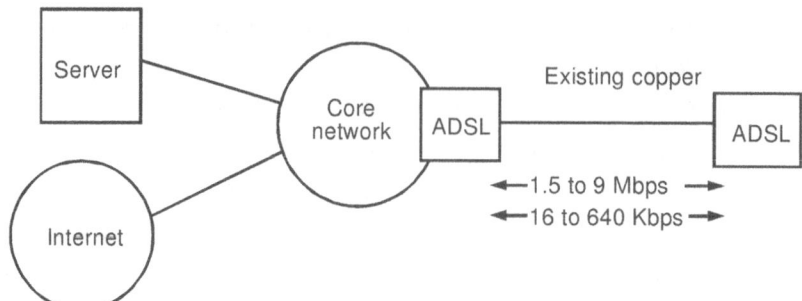

Fig. 2.1: The components of a ADSL network include a telco and a CPE

- ADSL will play a crucial role over the next decade or more as telephone companies enter new markets for delivering information in video and multimedia formats. New broadband cabling will take decades to reach all prospective subscribers. Success of these new services will depend on reaching as many subscribers as possible during the first few years. By bringing movies, television, video catalogs, remote CD-ROMs, corporate LANs, and the Internet into homes and small businesses, ADSL will make these markets viable and profitable for telephone companies and application suppliers alike.

2.6 Registering Domain Name

Domain Name Registration Overview

- Getting a domain name involves registering the name you want with an organisation called ICANN through a domain name registrar. For example, if you choose a name like "example.com", you will have to go to a registrar, pay a registration fee that costs around US$10 to US$35 for that name. That will give you the right to the name for a year, and you will have to renew it annually for the same amount per annum.
- Some web hosts will register it and pay for the name for free, while others will do it for you but you will have to foot the ICANN fees.

Step By Step Instructions

- If you want to register a domain name, here's what you need to do. Please read it all before acting.
  - Think of a few good domain names that you'd like to use. It won't do to think of only one — it might already be taken (it probably is!). You can find some tips on choosing a good domain name from my article, Tips on Choosing a Domain Name, at http://www.thesitewizard.com/ archive/domainname.shtml.
- There's more to it than meets the eye.
  - o You will need either a credit card or a PayPal account to pay for the domain. This is a requirement of most if not all registrars. It will allow you to claim and get the domain name immediately on application. This is not an option, (unfortunately).

o If you already have a web host, obtain from your web host the names of their primary and secondary nameservers. Don't worry if you do not understand what these things mean. Just save the information somewhere. The information can usually be obtained from their FAQs or other documentation on their site, usually under a category like "domain name" or "DNS" or "domain name transfer" and the like. If you cannot find it, email them. You'll need the information to point your domain name to your website after you buy your domain. Don't worry if you do not have a web host yet. Just read on.

o If you do not have a web host, you can always allow the registrar to you to park your domain name at a temporary website specially set up for you. This way you can quickly secure your domain name before it's too late and still take your time to set up the other aspects of your site. As far as I can tell, many registrars automatically park your domain by default whether you ask them to or not, so if this is your situation, you probably do not have to do anything special to get it done. Some of those registrars also provide you with a free email address at your own domain name while it is parked at their site, like sales@example.com (where "example.com" is your domain).

Rules for Domain Name Registgration

- Web hosting is renting space on a server connected 'to the Internet so that you can have an active website. There are a few guidelines to follow the rules for domain name registration:

  1. Your domain name cannot exceed 63 characters.
  2. Domain name is not case sensitive, it can be both lower case and upper case.
  3. Domain name must begin and end with a number/letter.
  4. Domain name can only use the hyphen; no other character/symbols are permitted.

- Someone, who wants to establish a presence on the Internet or wants to secure for future use, the first step is to check if the domain name is available. After which, follow the following steps: Select the name(s) you would like to register.

  1. Log in as internet user by entering a user name and password.
  2. Complete the Registration Information Page and confirm the information.
  3. Complete the Payment Information Page, click Register.

- A Thank you page will appear letting you know your domain name has been registered and you will also receive an e-mail confirmation.

- After doing all these procedure you are the user of the domain. You have the right to use the name as long as youpa yearly fees required.

Procedure for Registration of Domain Name

- The procedure for the registration of a domain name could not be simpler it is complex and critical

    1. First Check whether the domain name you desire is available. It is not just enough to try and type www.mycoolco.com to see if the page loads. Some domain hoarder may have registered it just to blackmail a future prospective customer. What you need to do is go to www.internic.net and type in your desired domain name in their form. This will tell you if it has been registered already.

    2. Next, to actually register, there are two options; do it yourself, or have a local Internet company do it for you. People offering domain registration services locally charge anywhere from Rs. 3500 upwards, which makes it better to get your facts straight before you approach any of them. However, that being said, it is usually far easier to let someone else bother with the details of registration as it would involve trips to the bank, couriers and so on. which can be an headache to you.

    3. There are essentially two different ways of registering a domain, provided by Network Solutions. The simpler of the two, just reserves the name and even gives you a free **"Under Construction"** page at your domain. However, this costs $119 and not really worth it if you are armed with a bit of technical know-how. Instead, we concentrate on the more technical approach.

    4. Go to www.networksolutions.com and find your way into the registration area. Usually, it's an icon that says **"Confused? Click here!"** It's nice to see someone taking the casual surfer's point of view.

    5. A simple single-line input field lets you check if your requested domain name is available. If it is, you can add it to your **"order"**. The next step takes you to the actual form.

    6. At this stage, you will see your **"order"** or your requested domain name listed, along with the price in dollars. A few fields for your name, address, e-mail address etc. are included which you need to fill out.

- Every registered domain name has a total of four people involved in it's maintenance:

    1. **Registrant:** Who ultimately has authority over the domain. This is the most important person and you should make sure you specify yourself as the registrant.

    2. **Billing contact:** Who gets the bill.

    3. **Technical contact:** Usually the person responsible for hosting your website or the service provider.

    4. **Administrative contact:** Who is a decision-maker in cases such as transfer of domain.

- Since, you are registering a domain name independently, you can use the registrant's info as Administration, Billing and Technical contacts. You register yourself and then next for the billing and technical contact, you may specify "same as administrative contact".

- Technically, all domains need to be **"parked"** once they are registered. It is something like buying a bike. If you buy it, you can not expect the manufacturer to keep it for you in the event that you do not have a garage! So, you need to specify a name server that will handle your domain. This will be the nameserver of the Web host or service provider who will host your domain.

- If you have not decided to host your domain just yet, or are in the process of deciding, it can be done in a simple way. Almost all web service providers will provide what is called **"free domain parking"** that you can provide their nameservers for your domain without paying them a rupee. Usually, this is tied into your buying an account from them or something similar, so it's never totally "free".

- Thereafter, you can specify just about any nameserver you fancy, and it does not make a difference. When you decide on a good domain host, you can always change this information. Suppose you know of a domain hosting service, say, xyz.com. While registering your domain, you can specify your primary nameserver to be xyz"ns.xyz.com". You will also need to find the IP address of xyz.com and specify that as well. Similarly, you need to fill in a secondary nameserver and IP address. Note that the owner of the host will be informed of this. If he/she objects, you have a problem. Anyway, you should ask first.

- After this procedure, submit the form by pressing the large button on the form and you will be taken to a confirmation page. An agreement will be e-mailed to you which you have to reply to, in order to complete the transaction.

- When you are paying via dollar, take a copy of the invoice that Network Solutions sends you and take it to your bank. They will tell you how to go about it.

- Your domain name will be registered as soon as you submit the application. You have a 3-month grace period in which your payment must reach them.

- When you want to use a service provider to register your domain, you can just pay him in rupees and let him handle the dollar payments in this condition, he/she will have to be the billing contact, and he/she will receive the invoices. All the same, it's a good idea to keep track of when your domain was registered and when payments are-due.

- You do not want your domain going out of service, just because someone else forgot to pay. One of the three things has happened to you:

  - You are sufficiently armed with knowledge to go ahead and register your domain all by yourself.

  - You are totally confused and think that you should not be doing this yourself. You have a friend that does this stuff anyway.

  - You are reasonably well informed to know that the pain of registering yourself may not be worth it.

List of Domain Name Registrars

- There are numerous domain name registrars. Listed below are just a few, along with my comments, if I know anything about them.
- Note that the domain name industry is highly competitive, with prices wildly fluctuating throughout the year, every year, so it's impossible to really mention accurate prices below unless I spend all my time updating this page.

    1. **GoDaddy.com :** This extremely popular registrar (possibly the biggest today) offers .com domain names for $9.99 (plus 20 cents) per year ($6.99 plus 20 cents if you transfer from another registrar). They have a web interface to manage your domains, free web redirection, free starter web page, free parked page or free "for sale" page, and an optional private domain registration where your domain is registered in the name of a proxy company. They offer .com, .us, .biz, .info, .net, .org, .ws, .name, .tv, .co.uk, .me.uk and .org.uk. Note that the exact price varies depending on which domain you are registering. Both credit card and PayPal payments are accepted.

    2. **Dotster.com :** This fairly popular registrar provides fairly cheap domain prices ($15.75 plus 20 cents per domain), a convenient web interface to manage your domains, an optional privacy facility where your domain name is registered in the name of a proxy company, etc. They offer .com, .net, .org, .biz, .info, .us, .ca, .tv, .name, .cc, .de, .sr, .md, .co.uk, .us.com domains, etc. If you are transferring a domain here from other registrars, the price is even cheaper ($6.99 plus 20 cents). Both credit card and PayPal payments are accepted here.

    3. **Register.com :** This domain name registrar has been in business for a very long time: they were one of the biggest around when I started my first websites. They are currently running an offer where they charge $9.99 for the first year for a domain name with a free business email account. Domains qualifying for this offer include .com, .net, .org, .biz, .us and .info. Country-specific domains have different prices.

    4. **Moniker:** This domain name registrar allows domain name registrations for a plethora of Top Level Domains (TLD), including .com, .org, .net, .info, .mobi, .biz, .us, .co.uk, and so on. Prices for domain names differ, depending on the extension. Their normal prices are about $10.49 for .com, $6.04 for .net, $10.95 for .org, $5.49 for .info, etc., although at the time I write this entry, it seems like they are having a sale, with $7.59 for .com, $5.59 for .net, $7.97 for .org, and so on. Their web interface allows you to manage matters pertaining to your domain, such as DNS, web forwarding etc. You also have the option to add "Whois privacy", where your domain is registered in the name of a proxy company. Both credit card and PayPal payments are accepted by this registrar, although PayPal payments have a surcharge.

    5. **1&1 Internet :** This is primarily a large web host that is also a domain name registrar. You are charged $6.99 for .com, .org, .net, .us domains. They also offer .info domains for $0.99 and .biz at $8.99. The fee includes private domain registration, which means that your particulars are hidden from public view. You also get a free email account, DNS management, domain forwarding and masking, and a starter website with each domain. Both credit card and PayPal payments are accepted by this registrar.

2.7 Web Promotion - Meaning and Concept

- Web site promotion is a collection of techniques that serve to boost the popularity of, or to promote, a website.

- Definition of website promotion is the continuous process of promoting a website on the Web in order to maintain its Web visibility and attract more visitors to increase the sale of website's products and services.

- Web promotion is the means of promoting your site to your prospective clients on the internet. This is done in various ways such as getting your site listed in various directories, linking your site from other sites, getting you in the top pages of search engines and much more.

- After establishing the project a business must define how it is going to market its web site. One of the biggest fallacies in establishing a web site is the notion that, "if you build it, they will come." It takes continued promotions, both off and on-line, to build any meaningful traffic to a site.

- Without effective promotion, your website would be lost in the maze of the Internet, this does not mean that people around the world would really care to come to check it out instead of the 34000 new Web sites that flood the Internet daily.

- Most Indian companies and organisations stop after getting themselves a Web site and then after a few months down the line complain that their Internet project did not work and they now regret all those investments they made.

- This is the usual outcome or output of those who do not know about the principles of the World Wide Web (WWW) and the basics of selling products on the internet. Once, your Web site is complete, it needs promotion.

- Any Web site such as shopping mall in the middle of the jungle with no roads leading unless one paves the roads to it by proper promotion.

- For successful promotion, a complete and highly effective package starts with planning the routes to your site, which includes:
  1. Identifying those search terms by which viewers will search for your material.
  2. Identifying search engines and directory listings which will be important to you due to specialisation or location.
  3. Recognising pages which are most search–engine critical.

- Second, comes the actual constructions of the paths the more paths that lead to your Web site the easier it is to access the site and the greater is the chance of the user visiting your Web site.

- To increase your chances of achieving the optimum search engine performance it is required that you make certain changes to your Web page such as adding Meta Tags etc.

- Then comes the actual submission of your site to as many search engines and directories can bring about a massive boost in the number of people visiting your Web site.

- Some of the more popular search engines, such as google.com, yahoo.com, are actually 'directories' i.e. vast resources of information fed in by real people and categorised and sub-categorised according to specific content.

- These search engines, have a fairly simple method of submitting your URL. Simply go to the category and sub-category of your choice, depending on how well that fits your Web site's content and click 'Add URL' or something similar.

- The second type of search engine, someone that can truly be called a 'search' is a Web Spider. Spider are programs designed to browse the Internet and look for information to add to a search tool's database. Altvisata.com is a commonly used search that relies on spidering techniques to add your Web site into it's database.

Other Ways of Promotion

- Free For All (FFA) pages is yet another method of online marketing and works on the concept of Multi Level Marketing.

- Here, anybody is allowed to place a link on your FFA page.

- You in turn can send all those people whose link you add an e-mail. The user who posts his/her link on your page has agreed to receiving an e-mail from you.

- You in turn can submit a link to your website on thousands of FFA pages automatically by using software like FFA Blaster available at www.ffbiaster.com website.

- Another small but crucial dimension for web promotion is including your URL in all your documents, letterheads, advertisements and in any other material you use to interact with your customers, peers and friends.

Web Phases

- Promoting your site takes a lot of time and may involve waiting several weeks or even months to get into certain directories and search engines.

- **Phase 1 – Directories:**

  You should start your website promotion efforts by listing your site at the most popular Internet directories. Because they can send you substantial amounts of traffic and affect your ranking in various search engines, it is wise to make sure that your site is present in all of the major directories before doing anything else.

  Step 1: General information: Submitting to directories is easy and doesn't require much effort. It's ensuring that your submission will be accepted that makes this task a hard one.

  1. First, read "Boost your traffic with website directories" to get a basic idea on what directories are and how to submit to them.

  2. Examine the article about web page design to get some tips on how to improve your site and reduce the chances of it being rejected.

  Step 2: The Open Directory Project: Start with the Open Directory Project. While your site has to offer good, unique content to be accepted to the ODP, its editors usually review sites quickly and won't reject them without a good reason for doing so. This, along with the fact that submitting to the ODP is free of charge, makes it a perfect starting point. Completing this step successfully will also provide you with experience that will prove to be very valuable later on.

1. Read my thoughts on how Google's ranking algorithm works and notice how an ODP listing seems to affect your ranking at Google. Keep this information in mind when you submit.

2. Take a look at the advice on submitting your website to the ODP.

3. Finally, submit your site to the ODP.

4. If your submission is not successful, consider becoming an editor at the Open Directory and listing your own site.

Step 3: Yahoo: After securing a listing at ODP, your next task is to get the folks at Yahoo to notice that your site exists and is worth a place in their directory. This might cost you a fair amount of money if you are running a commercial site, but is usually worth it. Non-commercial sites can get in for free, but might require several submissions and a lot of patience before they are accepted.

1. Check out the Yahoo-specific guidelines and hints and the article about how Yahoo's search feature ranks sites.

2. Bite the bullet and submit your site to Yahoo.

- **Phase 2 - Search Engines:**

Now that your site has been included in ODP and Yahoo, you should already be receiving clearly more traffic than before. The next task is to get to know search engines and use them to bring even more people to your pages. Because you have completed phase one, you have established a good foundation for making your site perform well in the search engines.

Step 1 - Search Engine Optimization, Basics: In order to gain good rankings, you will need to learn the basics of search engine algorithms (ranking systems) and adjust your pages to meet their criteria as well as possible. This will take some time and effort, but doing some work now will save you from a lot of trouble in the future.

1. First, try to make the design of your site as search engine friendly as possible.

2. Next, you will need to do some keyword optimization. Sounds frightening, but in plain English it simply means choosing the correct keywords for your pages. Using the wrong words is perhaps the most common reason why people do not get satisfying results from their search engine optimization work.

3. Continue by reading these search engine optimization tips.

4. Read the article about META tags and add them to all of your pages. The META keywords tag is not absolutely necessary, but the META description tag is very important.

5. Learn what link popularity is and how search engines use it to rank your pages.

6. Unless you have already done so, read about Google's algorithm. Google is among the most popular search services of today, so it is wise to take its requirements into account.

7. Use all of this information to optimize your pages for the search engines.

Step 2 - Search engine optimization, advanced: Your site is now adequately prepared to really start bringing in traffic from search engines. But if you want to widen your knowledge about them and increase your chances of success, you still have some work to do. On the other hand, if you are totally exhausted and just want to get this thing over with, you will be delighted to know that this step is not absolutely necessary.

1. Study some of the more advanced things related to search engine optimization. Among them are cloaking, css tricks, doorway pages, themes and how to improve your search engine ranking with click popularity.

2. Read about the things you should avoid doing from this topic that outlines common web site promotion mistakes.

Step 3 - Submitting to search engines?: Now is the time to make sure that your site has a presence in the indexes of major search engines. Fortunately, they are quite good at finding your site on their own. There are things you can do to help them, though:

1. Get to know how search engine submission works and how the search engines determine which sites to list.

2. Read the article "Targeting your search engine marketing" to see which engines are the most popular ones.

3. If you are running a commercial site, you might also want to consider paying for search engine placement. Take a look at how you can use PPC search engine advertising to buy your way to the top.

- **Phase 3 - More Techniques:**

After being accepted into the largest directories and having pages of your site come up in answer to searches done at the major search engines, the long hours that you have spent on website promotion have begun to pay off and your daily visitor count is starting to look good. But there is still plenty you can do to help your site attract even more traffic.

In phase three, we will examine different promotion methods that you might want to try. However, in order to prevent you from wasting your time on things that do not work, we will also go over a few techniques that have proven to be less than spectacular when I experimented with them.

Step 1 - Keep these in mind: First, let's take a look at the good stuff. The topic introduced in this step are about the website promotion methods that are at least partially effective. Some of them work better than others, but if used correctly, all of them can produce results that will be worth your while. Of course, most of the topics include advice on what you need to do to obtain the best possible results with the method discussed.

1. If you sell something on your site, you might want to try banner ads. Usually banner campaigns are seen as expensive and ineffective, but it is partially because advertisers do not know how to design good banners.

2. Read the article on how to increase traffic with return visitors. Getting people to come back is the secret to why some sites get amazingly many hits per day.

3. Learn what reciprocal links are and how to get them, then put that knowledge into use. In addition to sending you visitors, reciprocal links will also increase your link popularity and help your site rank higher in the search engines.

4. Start using E-mail signatures. They might not produce thousands of visitors, but are a great way to promote your site a bit without having to actually do anything.

5. Evaluate whether your site could benefit from joining a topsite list. These lists have their good and bad sides, but might be at least worth a try.

6. Consider trying to build traffic with Usenet advertising. It can give you a nice traffic boost and help spread the word about your site, but only if done properly. Read the article to learn why Usenet promotion should only be done with great care.

7. Writing newsletter articles often works well and can send you large amounts of targeted traffic in a short period of time, for free.

Step 2 - Forget these: As said, everything just does not always work the way it should in the world of promotion. In step two, our attention is focused on website promotion methods that are more trouble than they are worth. They might not be entirely useless, but your time would be better spent on improving your site or spreading the word about your site in other ways.

1. Click exchange programs are easy, fast, free and will get you a lot of visitors. That is why it might be a surprise to hear that they really are not good website promotion tools.

2. A lot has been written about FFA (Free For All) pages and for the past few years, most of it has been negative. The only thing they are good for is increasing the flow of spam to your E-mail address.

3. Winning website awards can occasionally be useful, especially if the awards are well-known. However, sometimes the winner of the award is not the real winner.

2.8 Types of Website Promotion

2.8.1 Target E-Mail

• It is another very productive method of getting online results or feedback.

• Targeting e-mail gets hold of as many e-mail addresses as possible of your targeted audience only. When a person who is a website designer receives an e-mail about a good deal in spices, he/she is sure to get aggravated by it, though another exporter or importer of spices might find it very useful for this reason it is very important that you do not use spamming as a marketing tool and rather e-mail only to a list of targeted people who have agreed to receive mails on topics related to your site.

- Such lists of addresses can be purchased from places like www.yesmail.com or other similar sites.

2.8.2 Banner Exchange

- It is a method in which advertisers work together and allow each other to place their banner ads at the other's website.
- A banner exchange program is a program designed to allow marketers to exchange banners (a form of bartering) to enable marketers to promote their sites without the outlay of cash. A program typically allows a marketer to display one advertisement, across the network, for every two advertisements it hosts on its site.
- Unlike a straight exchange with one entity, exchange programs allow for the possibility for the banner to be displayed on many web sites (those sites that participate in that particular network). The Free Banner Exchange Megalist is a good resource for identifying these exchanges.
- These programs help in the growth of your online revenue and traffic.
- The mechanics are easy and simple, by joining, you agree to display advertising banners for other members, and they agree to display banners for you for this reason the more hits that you get, the more banner views you earn on other sites and hence you further increase your hits.
- There is a general click-through rate of 2% which means that 2 out of every 100 people who see your banner will visit your site.
- A good banner exchange program is Microsoft's www.linkexchange.com.
- Another technique that works out amazingly and which is totally unexploited is the use of ICQ groups and IRC channels.
- Chatting online with people in channels and groups, related with what you can sell can be one of the easiest ways to click your online deal.
- For example, A person selling computer hardware can go to channels and groups where he/she would find other people who are using computers daily such as software developers/engineers and web designers who would definitely be interested in good deals for their next purchase.
- Online chatting gives a personal touch to your online marketing and improves the chances of sales by 72%.
- So going in for a chat room on your website is also something which you should be really looking into; this however could be an option only if you are a really big business outfit as maintaining a chat site would not be a feasible idea for everyone.
- The downside to this technique is that you need to manually do the promotion, i.e., sit in chat channels and throw your sales pitch around.

2.8.3 Shopping Bots

• They are like Shopping bots little search engines and type in the name of a product and these binary buyers scour the Web, looking for bargains.

• Shopping bots are price comparison sites on the World Wide Web that automatically search the inventory of several different online merchants to find the lowest prices for consumers. We can define shopping bot as "A program that searches the Web for the best price for a particular item you wish to purchase".

• In theory, shopping bots are wonderful tools, finding the cheapest books, computer games, videos, sound cards and home fitness equipment in cyberspace.

• However, not all bots are so hot, the best deals often go unfound, and searches lack the sort of precision savvy surfers now demand.

• Like most of the web's new and advanced technologies, shopping agents are works in progress, destined to be better tomorrow than they are today.

1. **Bottom Dollar.com (www.bottomdollar.com):**

   Bottomdollar.com lets you pick a category and search from there. The bot searches all the major merchants for each category and lets you sort results by price. We can limit book searches to hard cover, paperback, or audio titles music searches to cassettes or CDs and video searches to VHS, DVD is a nice touch. Links to products often took up to merchants', home pages and not to the products themselves. And prices were sometimes inaccurate. Bottomdollar.com's queries were frequently unsuccessful, returning empty handed from merchants. The results is the best deals often went undiscovered.

2. **Excite Shopping (www.excite.com/shopping):**

   www.excite.com does not look for books and music. For other categories such as computer hardware are brokendown into useful sub categories such as monitors, laptops, desktops, and PDAs. You can search for products or reviews a convenient feature. Advertisers do get preferential treatment. For books and music, excite has entered into exclusive partnerships Amazon.com, CD now respectively.

3. **Yahoo! Shopping (www.shopping.yahoo.com):**

   www.shopping.yahoo.com bot searches Yahoo!, initially. Only when this search has been completed, we can choose to search other merchants-an annoying extra step. When we enter key words, yahoo! scans its database and lists all items that fit the description. We click on the best match and the bot searches only that product, eliminating all irrelevant hits. Yahoo! also searches auctions but only its own.

4. **Web Market (www.webmarket.com):**

   www.webmarket.com covers specifications of products such as books, consumer electronics and office supplies but within these categories, you are limited to specific types of goods like modems, printers-but not PDAs in consumer electronics.

5. **My Simon (www.mysimon.com):**

www.mysimon.com queried so many sites more than over 1000. www.mysimon.com did a better job of finding the best deals than the other shopping agents. www.mysimon.com offers dozens of categories, which cover just about any item we are likely to buy on the Web. We can also search auction sites such as EBay and classified ads.

Questions

1. Enlist various reasons for building your own website.
2. Describe various benefits of website.
3. State following advantage of website:
   (i)   Time
   (ii) Cost
   (iii) Reach
4. What is meant by ideal website?
5. Define the following terms:
   (i) Domain name
   (ii) Website
6. How to register a domain name? Explain in detail.
7. What is meant by web promotion?
8. Describe the following terms:
   (i) Target email
   (ii) Banner exchange.
9. Explain the term shopping Bots.

■■■

Chapter **3**...

Internet, Extranet and Intranet

Contents ...

3.1 Introduction

- The Internet began as a project of the US Defense Department in the late 1960's.

- It was intended to link scientists working on defense and research projects around the country.

- During the 1980's, the National Science Foundation took over responsibility for the project and expanded the network to include the major universities and research sites in the United States. Links were then established to similar emerging networks in other countries.

- During the mid 1990's, the commercialization of the Internet began with the creations of dial-up services and was fueled by the creation of the World Wide Web.

- The Internet derived from the Advanced Research Projects Agency network (ARPANET), which was created by packet switching researchers in the early 1970s.

- It is important to understand that the Internet is not a single entity:
  - The Internet is made up of many separate networks, which are able to communicate with each other using standard languages or protocols.

- o   Each separate network is managed by its own network administration staff.
- o   The Internet works because all connected networks comply with a set of standards or protocols.
- o   There is no single governing body in charge of all the networks connected to the Internet.
- Internet is a computer network made up of thousands of network made up of thousands of network worldwide. The pre cursor of the Internet is 'ARPANET' was originally designed by department of the defense in consumption with universities and research facilities.
- In beginning ARPANET was used mainly for communication technology research and development with scientist at various sites around the world connected to each other so that they could share information.
- In 1989 and important evolutionary state occurred, those networks created for military were disseminated and replace by National Science Foundations NET (NSF). This makes a significant shift as the Internet began to survive not for the military but also civilian community.
- The Internet is the largest computer network in the world. Internet is actually network of network. Internet is also called Public Network.
- The National Science Foundations network originated in 1986 and linked researches across the country with five super computer centers. The seamless internetworking's of all these network give to Internet.
- Basically Intranet is a closed, business wide network, but uses open standards such as TCP/IP, instead of proprietary protocols traditionally used for LAN's (Local Area Networks) and WANs (Wide Area Networks).
- An Intranet is an internet network that is located inside the organisation and not generally accessible by the general public.
- Intranet is based on the same technology components as the Internet.
- To create our own internal Internet, we need following:
  1. FTP
  2. A browser or Client software application,
  3. A TCP/IP network,
  4. E-mail server,
  5. Chat,
  6. Web server, and
  7. E-mail client software.

- All the advantages of the Internet could be obtained using the above list but to suit the internal requirements, the technology is to be customized.
- Intranets are accessible only to their employees and their known users.
- Intranet is built on internet technology developed by the corporations.
- Intranets are used not only for posting documents but also for linking software, database and hardware into a universal network and so on.
- Number of companies uses intranet to link design centres for e-mail purposes, benefit sharing, travel authorizations and project reports, as an information resource for marketing, product and corporate information. Intranets are very useful because of:
  1. Learning is easy and simple,
  2. They can take with ease complex data and applications,
  3. Low costs, and
  4. The resources are accessible to everyone who have a computer, modem and a password.

3.2 Definition of Internet

- The Internet, sometimes called simply "the Net," is a worldwide system of computer networks - a network of networks in which users at any one computer can, if they have permission, get information from any other computer.

OR

- An internet is a vast computer network linking smaller computer networks worldwide. The Internet includes commercial, educational, governmental, and other networks, all of which use the same set of communications protocols.

OR

- The Internet is millions of computers around the world connected to each other.

OR

- The Internet is a global system of interconnected computer networks that use the standard Internet Protocol Suite (TCP/IP) to serve billions of users worldwide. Internet is a network of networks that consists of millions of private, public, academic, business, and government networks of local to global scope that are linked by a broad array of electronic and optical networking technologies. The Internet carries a vast array of information resources and services, most notably the inter-linked hypertext documents of the World Wide Web (WWW) and the infrastructure to support electronic mail.

Uses of Internet

- In each and every field there is use of Internet for accessing worldwide information. Here some uses of Internet are as follows:

  1. Scientist use Internet for their research and development works to save the problems.

  2. The education use Internet to educate people in their expertise area.

  3. Professionals use it to complete with others.

  4. Businessmen's use Internet to complete with others.

  5. Government use Internet to distribute information, knowledge etc.

  6. Physician use Internet to health.

  7. Journalist use Internet to report.

  8. Doctors can help the doctors from around the world in remote and can save lives.

  9. College students can send E-mail to his/her parents asking for required things and information for work on a project, collecting data from questionary send out via E-mail.

  10. A person can search jobs with the help of Internet and also apply for the same.

Internet Service

- There are different services provided by Internet such as

  1. Communication,

  2. Information Retrieval, and

  3. World Wide Web.

(a) Communication:

Both personal and business communication is available using the communication services. Communication service include E-mail, chatting, Newsgroups, Usenet, TELNET, LIST SERVERS, Internet Telephony and Internet Fax.

(i) **E-Mail:** Electronic mail is one of the most popular tools made available through the Internet. It is an efficient and effective means of network communication. One of the most valuable features of communicating via E-mail is that it is asynchronous, meaning the recipient need not be at a computer to receive the message you send. The message will be stored and available to be read when the recipient is ready to read it.

In order to send and receive E-mail, you must have access to an E-mail account. Preferably this account will be at your academic institution. If you have any problems or questions about using E-mail you can ask your instructor for assistance.

E-mail connects so many people and organization. E-mail is an application that allows an electronic message to be send between individuals through telephone wires or over wireless networks. Users can embed sound and images in their messages and attach files that contain text documents, spreadsheets, graphs etc. E-mail allows persons separated by long distances to Internet with and informality and speed. It is low cost, quick and convenient way to transmit messages across the world E-mail increases the efficiency as it enables to people to communicate quickly providing a close two way information exchange.

Features of E-mail:

(a) It is widely used network service.

(b) It is a system for sending messages or files to other competitors. Users based on E-mail book address.

(c) You can attach the various files.

(d) Support mail exchange.

(e) The message which are not deliver within specific time are returned to the sender.

(f) Every user on the network uses a private mailbox.

(g) Spooling mechanism is used.

(h) Messages are delivered within a few minutes or even seconds.

(i) Delivery of letter, anywhere in the world.

(ii) Chatting: It allows two or more people who are simultaneously connected to the Internet to hold live, interactive, return conversation, Internet Relay Chat (IRC) is a general chat program for the Internet. Chat Groups are divided into channels.

(iii) USENET: Users network is a collection of thousands of ongoing topic discussion called newsgroups. It is a system of carrying on discussions that can be delivered in a number of ways.

(iv) TELNET: It allows users to be on one computer while doing work on another. TELNET is the protocol that establishes an error free link between two computers.

(v) Internet Telephony: Users talk across the Internet to any p.c. equipped to receive call around the world for the price of only the Internet connection.

(b) Information Retrieval Services:

It allows users to access to the Internet thousands of library catalogues that are online as well as thousands of database that have been open to the public by corporations, government agencies and Non-profit organizations. The information retrieval services include Gopher, Archie, WAIS, FTP, and Veronica.

(i) **File Transfer Protocol (FTP):** It enables user to access a remote computer and retrieve files for it. After users have log on to the remote computers they can search the directories that are accessible to FTP. Looking for the files they want to retrieve.

(ii) **Archie:** It is a tool that allows user to search the files at FTP site. It regularly monitors hundreds of FTP sites and update a database on software documents and data files available for download. Archive database searches subject keywords.

(iii) **GOPHER:** A Gopher is a computer client tool that enables user to locate information stored on Internet GOPHER servers, through a series of hierarchical menus. Each Gopher server contains it's own system of menus listing subject matter topics, local files and other relevant Gopher sites.

(iv) **VERONICA** (Very Easy Rodent Oriented Net wide Index To Computer Archives).

It provides the capabilities of search for text that appears in Gopher menu. It is an automated title-search application program like Archie using a world wide index to computerised Archives.

(v) **WAIS (Wide Area Information Server):** It allows users to locate files around the Internet for this name of databases is required. After users specify database names and key identifying words. WAIS searches for the key words in all the files in those databases.

(c) WWW (World Wide Web)

WWW is an application that uses these transport functions. The web is a system with universally accepted standards for storing, retrieving formatting and displaying information via client server architecture. The web handles all types of digital information including text, hypermedia, graphics and sound. It uses GUI so it is very easy to use.

The web is based on a standard hypertext markup language called HTML, which formats, document stored on the same or different computer.

(i) **Domains:** A domain name is the computers name that is registers on the Internet. It is unique name that identifies a device on the Internet. There is a program called as Domain Name Server (DNS) that runs on your ISP's computer. Each IP address on the network should have DNS entry. This is basically a database that associated a name to an IP address.

Domain names always have two or more parts separated by dots. The first part is the specific machine and sub networks and the part on the right is the server and type of server. The new approach two letters abbreviation are added for the country to the end of URL.

Common top-level domains are

.com - for commercial Enterprises,   .org - for non profit organizations

.net - for networks,   .edu - for educational Institutes.

.govt - for government organizations,   .mil - for militery services.

.int - for international organizations,   .ac - for academics.

Domains along with country names are as follows:

.in - for India,	.uk - for united kingdom,	.sg - for singapure
.fr - for france,	.us - for united states of America,	.pk - for pakistan
.ca - for canada,	.ja - for Japan,	.ch - for china

Establishing Connectivity on Internet

- It involve providing and synchronizing setting for various software and hardware components. Unless all these works go in completely, your Internet connection may not work at all or may work irreticaly and may cause lot of problems.

- There are many ways in which you can connect the Internet two main ways to connect to the Internet are.

  1. Dial Up Access
  2. Direct or Dedicated Access

1. Dial Up Access:

This type of connection is most commonly used by many indivisuals, You can connecct to the Internet via modem. The major advantages of dail up connection is; it is less expensive as compared to the dedicated or direct connection an inivisual use can easily afford this type of connection. Another advantage of dial up connection is that it requires very simple and cheap hardware and software.

Disadvantages:

1. They have a very slow speed and low reliability as compared to direct access.
2. Little disturbance may break the connection to the Internet.

Hardware Requirement:

1. A computer with minimum 16 MB RAM and 70 MB hard disk space.
2. Choose the right ISP (Internet Service Provider) e.g BSNL, VSNL, MTNL in your city.
3. A modem speed – 50 kbps.
4. A telephone connection.

Software Requirement:

1. Communication Software.
2. Browser.
3. E-mail Software.

2. Direct or Dedicated Access:

In this type of connection access dedicated lease phone lines is used between the PC or network and ISP therefore it is mostly suitable for organization.

Advantages:

1. Fast speed and reliability.
2. Many users of LAN can be connected to the Internet to a single leased line.
3. No modem is require by each indivisual.
4. There is no need to dial-up to connecting computer system.

Types of Internet Provider

The most general way to use/access the Internet is through a provider or host computer. The providers are connected to the Internet and provide a path or connection for individuals to use/access the Internet. Commercial Internet Service Providers (ISP) include National, Regional and wireless service providers.

1. **National Service Providers:**

   AOL are the most widely used ISP. They provide access through standard telephone connection. Users can access the Internet from anywhere within the country for a standard fee without incurring the long distance telephone charges.

   e.g. www.AOL.com, www.att.com.

2. **Regional Service Providers:**

   It also use telephone lines, their service area is smaller typically consists of several states. If users access the Internet from outside the regional area, they incur long distance connection charge in addition to the services standard fee.

   e.g. www.bellsouth.net, www.quest.net.

3. **Wireless Service Providers:**

   This do not used telephone lines. They provide Internet connections from computer without wire. i.e. wireless modem and a wide array of wireless devices.

   e.g. www.sprintpcs.com, www.omnisky.com.

3.3 Evolution of Internet

- The internet is a worldwide system of interconnected computer networks that use the TCP/IP set of network protocols to reach billions of users.
- The internet began as a U.S Department of Defense network to link scientists and university professors around the world.
- A network of networks, today, the internet serves as a global data communications system that links millions of private, public, academic and business networks via an international telecommunications backbone that consists of various electronic and optical networking technologies.

- Follow the internet Timeline below to see how the internet has evolved over the years and take a glance at what lies ahead in the future as the internet continues to change the world we live in.

  o 1957 - USSR launches Sputnik into space. In response, the USA creates the Advanced Research Projects Agency (ARPA) with the mission of becoming the leading force in science and new technologies.

  o 1962 - J.C.R. Licklider of MIT proposes the concept of a "Galactic Network." For the first time ideas about a global network of computers are introduced. J.C.R. Licklider is later chosen to head ARPA's research efforts.

  o 1962 - Paul Baran, a member of the RAND Corporation, determines a way for the Air Force to control bombers and missiles in case of a nuclear event. His results call for a decentralized network comprised of packet switches.

  o 1968 - ARPA contracts out work to BBN. BBN is called upon to build the first switch.

  o 1969 - ARPANET created - BBN creates the first switched network by linking four different nodes in California and Utah; one at the University of Utah, one at the University of California at Santa Barbara, one at Stanford and one at the University of California at Los Angeles.

  o 1972 - Ray Tomlinson working for BBN creates the first program devoted to email.

  o 1972 - ARPA officially changes its name to DARPA Defense Advanced Research Projects Agency.

  o 1972 - Network Control Protocol is introduced to allow computers running on the same network to communicate with each other.

  o 1973 - Vinton Cerf working from Stanford and Bob Kahn from DARPA begin work developing TCP/IP to allow computers on different networks to communicate with each other.

  o 1974 - Kahn and Cerf refer to the system as the Internet for the first time.

  o 1976 - Ethernet is developed by Dr. Robert M. Metcalfe.

  o 1976 - SATNET, a satellite program is developed to link the United States and Europe. Satellites are owned by a consortium of nations, thereby expanding the reach of the Internet beyond the USA.

  o 1976 - Elizabeth II, Queen of the United Kingdom, sends out an email on 26 March from the Royal Signals and Radar Establishment (RSRE) in Malvern.

  o 1976 - AT&T Bell Labs develops UUCP and UNIX.

  o 1979 - USENET, the first news group network is developed by Tom Truscott, Jim Ellis and Steve Bellovin.

  o 1979 - IBM introduces BITNET to work on emails and listserv systems.

o 1981 - The National Science Foundation releases CSNET 56 to allow computers to network without being connected to the government networks.

o 1983 - Internet Activities Board released.

o 1983 - TCP/IP becomes the standard for internet protocol.

o 1983 - Domain Name System introduced to allow domain names to automatically be assigned an IP number.

o 1984 - MCI creates T1 lines to allow for faster transportation of information over the internet.

o 1984 - The number of Hosts breaks 1,000.

o 1985 - 100 years to the day of the last spike being driven on the Canadina Pacific Railway, the last Canadian university was connected to NetNorth in a one year effort to have coast-to-coast connectivity.

o 1987 - The new network CREN forms.

o 1987 - The number of hosts breaks 10,000.

o 1988 - Traffic rises and plans are to find a new replacement for the T1 lines.

o 1989 - The Number of hosts breaks 100 000.

o 1989 - Arpanet ceases to exist.

o 1990 - Advanced Network and Services (ANS) forms to research new ways to make internet speeds even faster. The group develops the T3 line and installs in on a number of networks.

o 1990 - A hypertext system is created and implemented by Tim Berners-Lee while working for CERN.

o 1990 - The first search engine is created by Mcgill University, called the Archie Search Engine.

o 1991 - U.S green light for commercial enterprise to take place on the Internet.

o 1991 - The National Science Foundation (NSF) creates the National Research and Education Network (NREN).

o 1991 - CERN releases the World Wide Web publicly on August 6th, 1991

o 1992 - The Internet Society (ISOC) is chartered.

o 1992 - Number of hosts breaks 1,000,000.

o 1993 - InterNIC released to provide general services, a database and internet directory.

o 1993 - The first web browser, Mosaic (created by NCSA), is released. Mosaic later becomes the Netscape browser which was the most popular browser in the mid 1990's.

o 1994 - New networks added frequently.

- o 1994 - First internet ordering system created by Pizza Hut.
- o 1994 - First internet bank opened: First Virtual.
- o 1995 - NSF contracts out their access to four internet providers.
- o 1995 - NSF sells domains for a $50 annual fee.
- o 1995 - Netscape goes public with 3rd largest ever Nasdaq ipo share value.
- o 1995 - Registration of domains is no longer free.
- o 1996 - The WWW browser wars are waged mainly between Microsoft and Netscape. New versions are released quarterly with the aid of internet users eager to test new (beta) versions.
- o 1996 - Internet2 project is initiated by 34 universities.
- o 1996 - Internet Service Providers (ISPs) begin appearing such as Sprint and MCI.
- o 1996 - Nokia releases first cell phone with internet access.
- o 1997 - (Arin) is established to handle administration and registration of IP numbers, now handled by Network Solutions (IinterNic).
- o 1998 - Netscape releases source code for Navigator.
- o 1998 - Internet Corporation for Assigned Names and Numbers (ICANN) created to be able to oversee a number of Internet-related tasks.
- o 1999 - A wireless technology called 802.11b, more commonly referred to as Wi-Fi, is standardized.
- o 2000 - The dot com bubble bursts, numerically, on March 10, 2000, when the technology heavy NASDAQ composite index peaked at 5,048.62.
- o 2001 - Blackberry releases first internet cell phone in the United States.
- o 2001 - The spread of P2P file sharing across the Internet.
- o 2002 - Internet2 now has 200 university, 60 corporate and 40 affiliate members.
- o 2003 - The French Ministry of Culture bans the use of the word "e-mail" by government ministries, and adopts the use of the more French sounding "courriel".
- o 2004 - The Term Web 2.0 rises in popularity when O'Reilly and MediaLive host the first Web 2.0 conference.
- o 2004 - Mydoom, the fastest ever spreading email computer worm is released. Estimated 1 in 12 emails are infected.
- o 2005 - Estonia offers Internet Voting nationally for local elections.
- o 2005 - Youtube launches.
- o 2006 - There are an estimated 92 million websites online.
- o 2006 - Zimbabwe's internet access is almost completely cut off after international satellite communications provider Intelsat cuts service for non-payment.

o 2006 - Internet2 announced a partnership with Level 3 Communications to launch a brand new nationwide network, boosting its capacity from 10Gbps to 100Gbps.

o 2007 - Internet2 officially retires Abilene and now refers to its new, higher capacity network as the Internet2 Network.

o 2008 - Google index reaches 1 Trillion URLs.

o 2008 - NASA successfully tests the first deep space communications network modeled on the Internet. Using software called Disruption-Tolerant Networking (DTN) dozens of space images are transmitted to and from a NASA science spacecraft located about more than 32 million kilometers from Earth.

o 2009 - ICANN gains autonomy from the U.S government.

o 2010 - Facebook announces in February that it has 400 million active users.

o 2010 - The U.S House of Representatives passes the Cybersecurity Enhancement Act (H.R. 4061).

- **More people will use the Internet**

  Today's Internet has 1.7 billion users, according to Internet World Stats. This compares with a world population of 6.7 billion people. There's no doubt more people will have Internet access by 2020. Indeed, the National Science Foundation predicts that the Internet will have nearly 5 billion users by then. So scaling continues to be an issue for any future Internet architecture.

- **The Internet will be more geographically dispersed**

  Most of the Internet's growth over the next 10 years will come from developing countries. The regions with the lowest penetration rates are Africa (6.8%), Asia (19.4%) and the Middle East (28.3%), according to Internet World Stats. In contrast, North America has a penetration rate of 74.2%. This trend means the Internet in 2020 will not only reach more remote locations around the globe but also will support more languages and non-ASCII scripts.

- **The Internet will be a network of things, not computers**

  As more critical infrastructure gets hooked up to the Internet, the Internet is expected to become a network of devices rather than a network of computers. Today, the Internet has around 575 million host computers, according to the CIA World Factbook 2009. But the NSF is expecting billions of sensors on buildings and bridges to be connected to the Internet for such uses as electricity and security monitoring. By 2020, it's expected that the number of Internet-connected sensors will be orders of magnitude larger than the number of users.

- **The Internet will be wireless**

  The number of mobile broadband subscribers is exploding, hitting 257 million in the second quarter of 2009, according to Informa. This represents an 85% increase year-over-year for 3G, WiMAX and other higher speed data networking technologies. Currently, Asia has the most wireless broadband subscribers, but the growth is strongest in Latin America. By 2014, Informa predicts that 2.5 billion people worldwide will subscribe to mobile broadband.

- **More services will be in the cloud**

  Experts agree that more computing services will be available in the cloud. A recent study from Telecom Trends International estimates that cloud computing will generate more than $45.5 billion in revenue by 2015. That's why the National Science Foundation is encouraging researchers to come up with better ways to map users and applications to a cloud computing infrastructure. They're also encouraging researchers to think about latency and other performance metrics for cloud-based services.

- **The Internet will be greener**

  Internet operations consume too much energy today, and experts agree that a future Internet architecture needs to be more energy efficient. But the Internet's so-called Energy Intensity is growing at a slower rate than data traffic volumes as networking technologies become more energy efficient. The trend towards greening the Internet will accelerate as energy prices rise, according to experts pushing energy-aware Internet routing.

- **Network management will be more automated**

  Besides weak security, the biggest weakness in today's Internet is the lack of built-in network management techniques. That's why the National Science Foundation is seeking ambitious research into new network management tools. Among the ideas under consideration are automated ways to reboot systems, self-diagnosing protocols, finer grained data collection and better event tracking. All of these tools will provide better information about the health and status of networks.

- **The Internet won't rely on always-on connectivity**

  With more users in remote locations and more users depending on wireless communications, the Internet's underlying architecture can no longer presume that users have always-on connections. Instead, researchers are looking into communications techniques that can tolerate delays or can forward communications from one user to another in an opportunistic fashion, particularly for mobile applications. There's even research going on related to an inter-planetary Internet protocol, which would bring a whole new meaning to the idea of delay-tolerant networking.

- **The Internet will attract more hackers**

  In 2020, more hackers will be attacking the Internet because more critical infrastructure like the electric grid will be online. The Internet is already under siege, as criminals launch a rising number of Web-based attacks against end users visiting reputable sites.

  More than anything else, computer scientists who are working on redesigning the Internet are trying to improve its security. Experts agree that security cannot be an add-on in a redesign of the Internet. Instead, the new Internet must be built from the ground up to be a secure communications platform. Specifically, researchers are exploring new ways to ensure that the Internet of 2020 has confidentiality, integrity, privacy and strong authentication.

3.4 Advantages and Disadvantages of Internet

- Today internet has become the most ever powerful tool for man throughout the world. The internet is a collection of various services and resources.
- Although, many people still think e-mail and World Wide Web as the principle constituents of the internet, there is lot more in store than e-mail, chat rooms, celebrity web sites and search engines. It also became the best business tool of modern scenario.
- Today internet has brought a globe in a single room. Right from news across the corner of the world, wealth of knowledge to shopping, purchasing the tickets of your favorite movie-everything is at your finger tips.
- Advantages of Internet are listed below:

  1. **Sharing Information**: You can share information with other people around the world. The scientist or researchers can interact with each other to share knowledge and to get guidance etc. Sharing information through Internet is very easy, cheap and fast method.

  2. **Collection of Information**: A lot of information of different types is stored on the web server on the Internet. It means that billions websites contain different information in the form of text and pictures. You can easily collect information on every topic of the world. For this purpose, special websites, called search engines are available on the Internet to search information of every topic of the world. The most popular search engines are altavista.com, search.com, yahoo.com, ask.com etc. The scientists, writers, engineers and many other people use these search engines to collect latest information for different purposes. Usually, the information on the Internet is free of cost. The information on the Internet is available 24 hours a day.

  3. **Advertisement**: Today, most of the commercial organizations advertise their product through Internet. It is very cheap and efficient way for the advertising of products. The products can be presented with attractive and beautiful way to the people around the world.

4. **Communication:** You can communicate with other through Internet around the world. You can talk by watching to one another; just you are talking with your friends in your drawing room. For this purpose, different services are provided on the Internet such as;

   - Chatting,
   - Video conferencing,
   - E-mail, and
   - Internet telephony etc.

5. **Entertainment:** Internet also provides different type of entertainments to the people. You can play games with other people in any part of the world. Similarly, you can see movies, listen music etc. You can also make new friends on the Internet for enjoyment.

6. **Online Education:** Internet provides the facility to get online education. Many websites of different universities provide lectures and tutorials on different subjects or topics. You can also download these lectures or tutorials into your own computer. You can listen these lectures repeatedly and get a lot of knowledge. It is very cheap and easy way to get education.

7. **Online Results:** Today, most of the universities and education boards provide results on the Internet. The students can watch their results from any part of country or world.

8. **Online Airlines and Railway Schedules:** Many Airline companies and Pakistan Railway provide their schedules of flights and trains respectively on the Internet.

9. **Online Medical Advice:** Many websites are also available on the Internet to get information about different diseases. You can consult a panel of online doctors to get advice about any medical problem. In addition, a lot of material is also available on the Internet for research in medical field.

- **Disadvantages** of Internet are given below:

1. **Theft of Personal information:** If you use the Internet, you may be facing grave danger as your personal information such as name, address, credit card number etc. can be accessed by other culprits to make your problems worse.

2. **Spamming:** Spamming refers to sending unwanted e-mails in bulk, which provide no purpose and needlessly obstruct the entire system. Such illegal activities can be very frustrating for you, and so instead of just ignoring it, you should make an effort to try and stop these activities so that using the Internet can become that much safer.

3. **Virus threat:** Virus is nothing but a program which disrupts the normal functioning of your computer systems. Computers attached to internet are more prone to virus attacks and they can end up into crashing your whole hard disk, causing you considerable headache.

4. **Pornography:** This is perhaps the biggest threat related to your children's healthy mental life. A very serious issue concerning the Internet. There are thousands of pornographic sites on the Internet that can be easily found and can be a detrimental factor to letting children use the Internet.

5. **Security problems:** The valuable websites can be damaged by hackers and your valuable data may be deleted. Similarly, confidential data may be accessed by unauthorized persons.

6. **English language problems:** Most of the information on the Internet is available in English language. So, some people cannot avail the facility of Internet.

3.5 Intranet and Extranet

*   An intranet is a private computer network that uses Internet Protocol technologies to securely share any part of an organization's information or network operating system within that organization.

*   The term intranet is used in contrast to internet, a network between organizations, and instead refers to a network within an organization.

*   Sometimes the term refers only to the organization's internal website, but may be a more extensive part of the organization's information technology infrastructure.

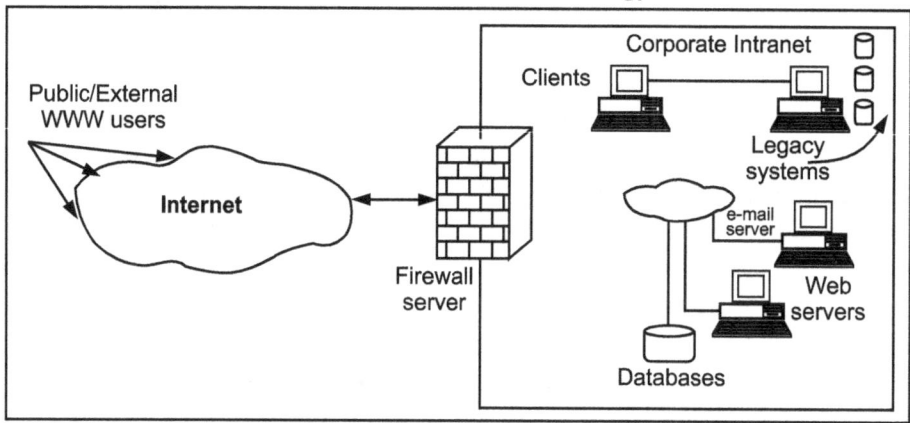

Fig. 3.1: Architecture of Intranet

*   It may host multiple private websites and constitute an important component and focal point of internal communication and collaboration. ntranets are being used to deliver tools and applications, e.g., collaboration (to facilitate working in groups and teleconferencing) or sophisticated corporate directories, sales and customer relationship management tools, project management etc., to advance productivity.

*   Intranets are also being used as corporate culture-change platforms. For example, large numbers of employees discussing key issues in an intranet forum application could lead to new ideas in management, productivity, quality, and other corporate issues.

- In large intranets, website traffic is often similar to public website traffic and can be better understood by using web metrics software to track overall activity. User surveys also improve intranet website effectiveness.

- Larger businesses allow users within their intranet to access public internet through firewall servers. They have the ability to screen messages coming and going keeping security intact.

- The intranet in the number of the organisations or companies provides the main source of working material, the vehicle for co-operating projects and the preferred reporting, accounting and supply route.

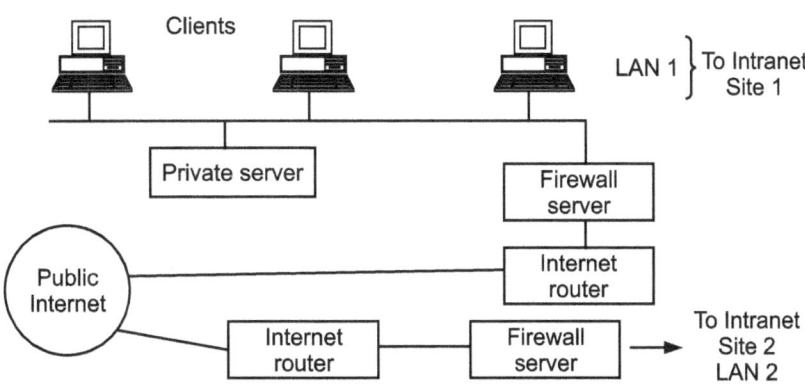

Fig. 3.2: An overview of Intranet

Definition of Intranet

- Intranet is the generic term for a collection of private computer networks within an organization. An intranet uses network technologies as a tool to facilitate communication between people or workgroups to improve the data sharing capability and overall knowledge base of an organization's employees.

OR

- An intranet is a private network that is contained within an enterprise. It may consist of many interlinked local area networks and also use leased lines in the wide area network. Typically, an intranet includes connections through one or more gateway computers to the outside Internet. The main purpose of an intranet is to share company information and computing resources among employees. An intranet can also be used to facilitate working in groups and for teleconferences.

OR

- Internet based computing networks that are private and secure are known as intranet. Intranets are typically used by corporations, government and other organisations. Intranets are based upon Internet standards and provide the means for an organisation to make resources more readily available to its employees online.

Advantages

* Advantages of intranets are listed below:

    1. **Workforce productivity:** Intranets can also help users to locate and view information faster and use applications relevant to their roles and responsibilities. With the help of a web browser interface, users can access data held in any database the organization wants to make available, anytime and - subject to security provisions - from anywhere within the company workstations, increasing employees' ability to perform their jobs faster, more accurately, and with confidence that they have the right information. It also helps to improve the services provided to the users.

    2. **Time:** Intranets allow organizations to distribute information to employees on an as-needed basis; Employees may link to relevant information at their convenience, rather than being distracted indiscriminately by electronic mail.

    3. **Communication:** Intranets can serve as powerful tools for communication within an organization, vertically and horizontally. From a communications standpoint, intranets are useful to communicate strategic initiatives that have a global reach throughout the organization. The type of information that can easily be conveyed is the purpose of the initiative and what the initiative is aiming to achieve, who is driving the initiative, results achieved to date, and who to speak to for more information. By providing this information on the intranet, staff have the opportunity to keep up-to-date with the strategic focus of the organization. Some examples of communication would be chat, email, and or blogs.

    4. **Business operations and management:** Intranets are also being used as a platform for developing and deploying applications to support business operations and decisions across the internetworked enterprise.

    5. **Cost-effective:** Users can view information and data via web-browser rather than maintaining physical documents such as procedure manuals, internal phone list and requisition forms. This can potentially save the business money on printing, duplicating documents, and the environment as well as document maintenance overhead.

    6. **Ease of publishing:** Intranets are easy and simple to publishing.

    7. **Ease of use and People friendly:** Intranets are user friendly and easy and simple to used and understand.

    8. **Low maintenance:** Intranet requires less maintenance than other.

    9. **Easy to change and Easily customized:** Some modification is intranet are done easily. Intranet customized easily.

    10. **Good performance and Well suited for most applications:** Intranet having good performance than other technologies.

11. **Promote common corporate culture:** Every user is viewing the same information within the Intranet.

12. **Enhance collaboration:** With information easily accessible by all authorised users, teamwork is enabled.

13. **Cross-platform capability:** Standards-compliant web browsers are available for Windows, Mac, and UNIX.

14. **Built for one audience:** Many companies dictate computer specifications. Which, in turn, may allow Intranet developers to write applications that only have to work on one browser.

Disadvantages

- Disadvantages of intranets are:
  1. Intranets can be expensive to maintain within an organisation.
  2. Collaborative applications for Intranets are not as powerful compared to the ones offered by traditional groupware.
  3. Intranets can reduce face to face meetings with clients or business partners.
  4. There are limited tools for linking an intranet service to databases or other back-end mainframe-based applications.
  5. With intranets, companies have to set up and maintain separate applications such as e-mail and web servers, instead of using one unified system as with groupware.

3.6 Components of Intranet

- The development of an intranet has become a major components of many electronic, business strategies organisations.

- These business strategies have established themselves at the core of many IT strategies.

- Further, the organisations or companies which have resisted the gravitational pull of the technology are adopting internet strategies.

- Earlier, intranet location was at data centres or out in the departments but recently, as the number of intranets within organisations have grown up, a necessity has arisen for the following:
  1. Creation of a need to integrate content,
  2. Sharing information,
  3. Controlling access and to deal with other intranets located at different places, and
  4. Maintaining performance.

- Multiple intranet servers, connected by LAN and WAN which provide the foundation for distributed intranets.

- Internet provides the network infrastructure upon which e-business is developed. Intranet is not an exclusive option and there are many other network that can be used such as:
  1. Closed community extranets,
  2. Community Internet Network (COINS), and
  3. Private Intranets.
- Intranet is the deployment of Internet technology to meet the needs of particular group, firm or organization and it satisfies the same need as a virtual private network or enterprise network in operation.
- Number of firms or organisations develop intranets to improve productivity and increase the speed with which information is developed inside their organisations.
- The evolution of intranet is not only for pure intranet solutions but also includes groupware as office and work group applications are becoming internet enabled. These solutions are becoming more intranet based, with browser-based interfaces, compatible with web server and supportive of web standards.
- However, the underlying databases and data structures vary according to application and platform focus.

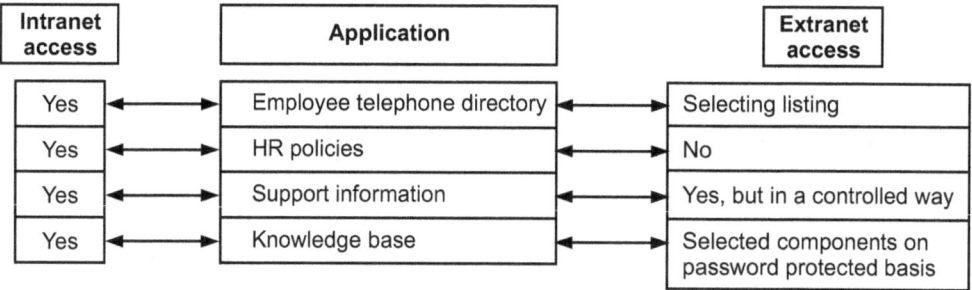

Intranet access	Application	Extranet access
Yes	Employee telephone directory	Selecting listing
Yes	HR policies	No
Yes	Support information	Yes, but in a controlled way
Yes	Knowledge base	Selected components on password protected basis

Fig. 3.3: Variations in Database and Data Structures Based on Application

- Fig. 3.4 shows various components of an intranets information technology structure.

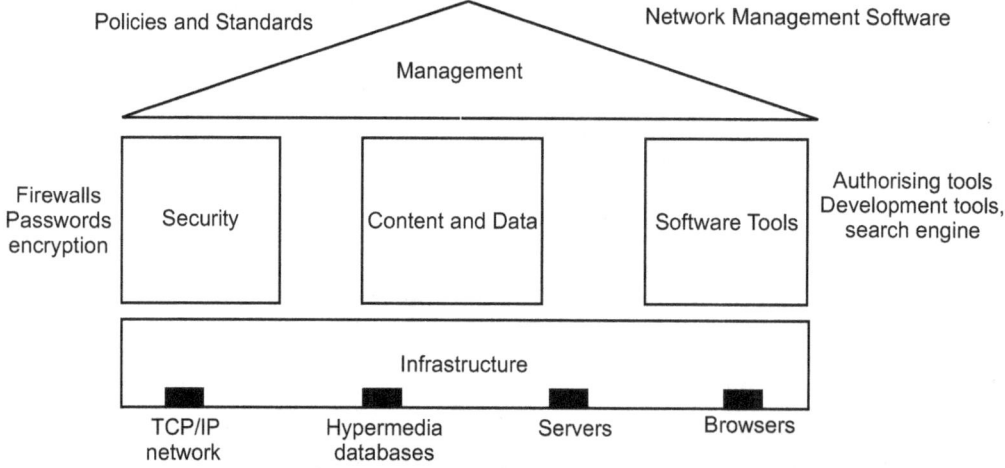

Fig. 3.4: Components of Intranet

3.7 Extranet

- An extranet is a private network that uses Internet technology and the public telecommunication system to securely share part of a business's information or operations with suppliers, vendors, partners, customers, or other businesses.
- An extranet can be viewed as part of a company's intranet that is extended to users outside the company.
- Extranets has also been described as a "state of mind" in which the Internet is perceived as a way to do business with other companies as well as to sell products to customers.
- Extranet is an Intranet for outside authorized users using same internet technology.
- An extranet is a private network that uses Internet protocols, network connectivity.
- An extranet can be viewed as part of a company's intranet that is extended to users outside the company, usually via the Internet.
- Extranet has also been described as a "state of mind" in which the Internet is perceived as a way to do business with a selected set of other companies Business-to-Business, (B2B), in isolation from all other Internet users.
- In contrast, Business-to-Consumer (B2C) models involve known servers of one or more companies, communicating with previously unknown consumer users.
- Extranet gives the channel to secure communications between intranet and shared portions of the system that are externalized to your business partners. Hence, the term as 'extranet'.
- Extranets will provide a secure gateway for visitors coming in from the outside and gives them controlled access to the portions of data that they have permission to see, modify or publish.
- In some situations, the extranet can also be used to provide access to legacy systems via a web interface or by other means.
- This approach allows business partners to gain access not just to data that is located on the extranet web, but other internal systems that are important to your business relationships.
- Companies can use an extranet to:
  - o Exchange large volumes of data using Electronic Data Interchange (EDI).
  - o Share product catalogs exclusively with wholesalers or those "in the trade".
  - o Collaborate with other companies on joint development efforts.
  - o Jointly develop and use training programs with other companies.
  - o Provide or access services provided by one company to a group of other companies, such as an online banking application managed by one company on behalf of affiliated banks.
  - o Share news of common interest exclusively with partner companies.

- Fig. 3.5 shows an example of Intranets and Extranets.

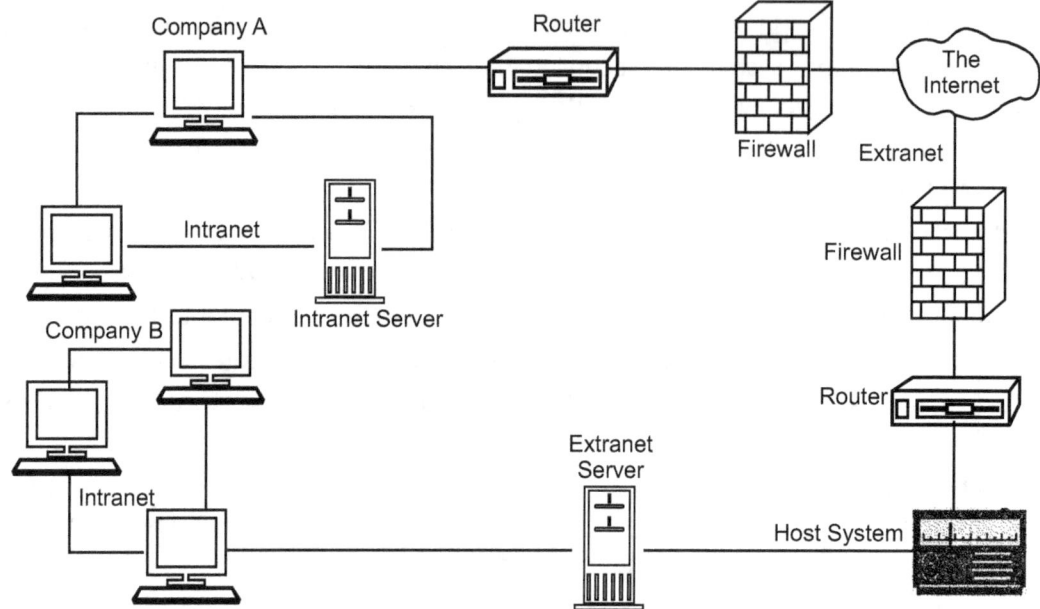

Fig. 3.5: An example of Intranets and Extranets

- Extranets are networks that links some of the intranet resources of a company with other organisations and individuals and they enable customers, suppliers, sub-contractors consultants and others to access intranet websites and other company databases.
- Organisations or companies can establish private extranets among themselves or use the Internet as part of the network connections between them.

3.7.1 Definition

- An extranet is a private network that uses the Internet protocol and the public telecommunication system to securely share part of a business's information or operations with suppliers, vendors, partners, customers, or other businesses.

OR

- Extranet refers to a group of websites, belonging to independent entities that are combined together in order to share information.

OR

- An extranet is a computer network that allows controlled access from the outside for specific business or educational purposes. Extranets are extensions to, or segments of, private intranet networks that have been built in many corporations for information sharing and ecommerce.

OR

- Extranets are private wide area networks that run on public protocols with the goal of fostering collaboration and information sharing between organisations.

3.7.2 Advantages

- Various advantages of extranets are given below:

   1. **Improved productivity:** Extranets can improve organization productivity by automating processes that were previously done manually. For example: reordering of inventory from suppliers). Automation can also reduce the margin of error of these processes.

   2. **Saving time:** Extranets allow organization or project information to be viewed at times convenient for business partners, customers, employees, suppliers and other stake-holders. This cuts down on meeting times and is an advantage when doing business with partners in different time zones.

   3. **Easy to updation:** Information on an extranet can be updated, edited and changed instantly. All authorised users therefore have immediate access to the most up-to-date information.

   4. **Improved relationship:** Extranets can improve relationships with key customers, providing them with accurate and updated information.

3.7.3 Disadvantages

- Various disadvantages of extranets are listed below:

   1. **Expensive:** Extranets can be expensive to implement and maintain within an organization (For example: hardware, software, employee training costs), if hosted internally rather than by an application service provider.

   2. **Security problem:** Security of extranets can be a concern when hosting valuable or proprietary information.

   3. **High cost:** Extranets can be costly to apply and maintain within an organization.

   4. **Protection problem:** One of big problem is the protection of extranets when dealing with precious information. System access should be controlled and checked properly to protect the system and information going into the incorrect hands.

   5. **Lack of communication:** Extranets can decrease personal face-to-face contact with clients and business partners. This can cause a lack of communication between employees, clients and organization.

3.7.4 Applications of Extranet

- Number of applications can be delivered via an extranet and are secure at the application level. i.e. the business partner submits a password to gain access to the system.

- Table 3.1 shows starter applications for a B2B application.

Table 3.1

Technology	Applications
1. Secure Electronic Mail	B2B Communications.
2. Bulletin Board	Subject review and response vehicle, FAQ (Frequently Asked Questions).
3. Instant Messaging	Sales and Customer support.
4. Document Repository	Knowledge management and customer support.
5. FTP (File Transfer protocol)	Sales support, Customer support, Software development.
6. Mail list server	Broad cash of changes and notification.
7. Calender	Scheduling.
8. Data conferencing and chat	Electronic Meetings.

3.8 Extranet and Intranet Difference

- Following table shows difference between intranet and extranet.

Intranet	Extranet
1. Intranets facilitate sharing of information by people in a single organisation.	1. Extranets facilitate sharing of information by individuals in multiple organisations.
2. Intranets are Internet based computing networks that are private and secure, typically used by corporations, government and other organisations are used to make resources more readily available to its employees online.	2. Extranets provide wide area networks that run on public protocols with the goal of fostering collaboration and information sharing between organisations or firms.
3. Intranet is an internet like network within an organisation.	3. A network that links selected resources of the intranet of an organisation with its customers, suppliers and other business partners, using the Internet or private networks to link the organisation's intranets.
4. An intranet is the generic term for a collection of private computer networks within an organization.	4. An extranet is a computer network that allows controlled access from the outside for specific business or educational purposes.

contd. ...

5. Intranet is totally internal to an organisation.	5. The Extranet is a way to connect businesses and suppliers to each other securely.
6. The internet is open to the public.	6. An Extranet is private and not open to the public.
7. An intranet is a private network that is contained within an enterprise. It may consist of many interlinked local area networks and also use leased lines in the wide area network.	7. An extranet is a private network that uses Internet technology and the public telecommunication system to securely share part of a business's information or operations with suppliers, vendors, partners, customers, or other businesses.
8. Typically, an intranet includes connections through one or more gateway computers to the outside Internet.	8. An extranet can be viewed as part of a company's intranet that is extended to users outside the company.
9. An intranet uses TCP/IP, HTTP, and other Internet protocols and in general looks like a private version of the Internet. With tunneling, companies can send private messages through the public network, using the public network with special encryption/ decryption and other security safeguards to connect one part of their intranet to another.	9. These can include firewall server management, the issuance and use of digital certificates or similar means of user authentication, encryption of messages, and the use of Virtual Private Networks (VPNs) that tunnel through the public network.
10. The main purpose of an intranet is to share company information and computing resources among employees. An intranet can also be used to facilitate working in groups and for telecom-ferences.	10. It has also been described as a "state of mind" in which the Internet is perceived as a way to do business with other companies as well as to sell products to customers. An extranet requires security and privacy.
11. Diagram for Intranet **Fig. 3.6: Intranet**	11. Diagram for Extranet **Fig. 3.7: Extranet**

3.9 Internet Marketing

- Internet marketing, or online marketing, refers to advertising and marketing efforts that use the Web and email to drive direct sales via electronic commerce, in addition to sales leads from Web sitesor emails. Internet marketing and online advertising efforts are typically used in conjunction with traditional types of advertising like radio, television, newspapers and magazines

- Internet marketing refers to the strategies that are used to market a product or service online, marketing strategies that include search engine optimization and search engine submission, copywriting that encourages site visitors to take action, web site design strategies, online promotions, reciprocal linking, and email marketing – and that's just hitting the highlights.

- Online marketers are constantly devising new Internet marketing strategies in the hopes of driving more traffic to their Web sites and making more sales; witness the increasing use of blogs as marketing tools for business, for instance.

- Online marketing refers to a set of powerful tools and methodologies used for promoting products and services through the Internet.Online marketing includes a wider range of marketing elements than traditional business marketing due to the extra channels and marketing mechanisms available on the Internet.

- Online marketing can deliver benefits such as:
  - Growth in potential
  - Reduced expenses
  - Elegant communications
  - Better control
  - Improved customer service
  - Competitive advantage

- Online marketing is also known as Internet marketing, Web marketing, digital marketing and search engine marketing (SEM).

Pros and Cons of Online Shipping

- Pros:Many companies online provide excellent values because they do not have to pay the overhead of owning a physical business that will cost them insurance, employee pay, taxes and more. Consumers can benefit from the savings of online shopping, especially when they combine it with special promotional coupons, and other consumer incentives.

- Cons: Companies offering free items online sometimes hike up the cost of shipping so high that they profit from the purchase. One example of this is the free software products that are advertised. You may get three free software CDs but the $14.95 shipping cost exceeds the real value of the products.

- The trick to getting a good value on products you purchase online is to look at the entire purchase amount and not just the amount that you will be paying for a specific product. Reading the customer service sections on e-commerce sites should provide you with clear answers on return policies, restocking fees and what guarantee is offered on the products. If you have any remaining questions call the company and get them answered before you submit your credit card to any site.

Different Techniques of Internet Marketing

- **Personal Marketing:** This is marketing at personal level and includes telling your network and friends, making a business card etc

- Article Marketing: Article marketing implies writing articles and submitting them to web article directories. When you write article, you are allowed to put a back link to your website in author's bio box. People looking for information will come and read your article. if it interests them, they would visit your web site for more information. Article marketing is a very good method to build links for your site, enhance your website's search engine ranking and getting traffic. What is more, it is absolutely free until you wish to use paid services.

- **Forum Marketing:** Forum is a place where people gather and discuss their problems, strategies etc. There are many forums on the web that you can join and participate in discussion. Most of the forums allow a link back to your website in your signature text which would appear below the post you make. Again a good traffic builder.

- **Search Engine Marketing:** This involves search engine optimization of your website design and content. Search engine use their algorithm to rank websites and when people search for something, these websites are displayed as the search engines would rank them. Search engine optimization or SEO are the methods by which you try to build your site and content so that it may please the search engines. You either learn SEO or use the paid services.

- **Pay Per Click Advertising: This** is a paid service where you pay the service provider every time your link is clicked. This kind of marketing is quite poular with internet marketers. Apart from Google and Yahoo there are many other pay per click services available

- **Link Exchange:** In this a website places a link for other website in exchange for its link on that site. Earlier it was also used for SEO purpose but a change in search engine algorithm has stripped that advantage. But it is still it is a powerful method for traffic generation.

- **Link Purchase:** You can purchase placement of your website link on other website. This is very commonly done for SEO as one way incoming backlinks are used to rank your website by search engines. This method also brings in traffic if the site that you purchased link placement from is heavily visited website.

- **Classified Advertising:** You can advertise your website on Classifieds websites on the web like Craigslist.com and USfreeads.com. Both paid and free services are available.

- **Ezine Marketing:** This refers to email marketing. You can start your own newsletter or ezine or electronic magazine which your subscribers can choose to receive. Creating an ezine is an integral part of your internet business. You can also choose to purchase an advertising space in the ezines that are already running successfully. your website gets exposed to targeted readers who may like to become your customers.

- **List Building:** This refers to building a subscribers database ,who are entered into the list of that database when they opt in for your ezine or agree to a free download against providing you their email address. You can contact these subscribers with your offers and promos.

- **Lead Purchase:** There are some paid services which will provide you with the names and email addresses of the people or leads against a payment. This method is called lead generation. This is done by them by placing your opt-in form (Form which a visitor fills in order to subscribe) on heavily visited websites, a process that you can do on your site also. Normally you are charged per lead.

- **Viral Marketing:** Here, you make a useful product like ebook or software and allow people to pass it on freely. This helps in spreading your website links and branding your site. Apart from ebook or software, you can also build some humorous video or funny email. Build anything that people would like to pass on and share.

- **Press Releases:** Here, you build a press release for your website and submit it to one or more press release sites like prweb.com. Press releases are done to create awareness among the web visitors and are displayed on various news channels or sites on the net. Also builds increased back links. Both free and paid submissions are available.

- **Joint Ventures:** Here two or more marketers come together and promote a product or service in a way that it will benefit them all. Joint ventures are a great way to build your business because the marketing efforts are combined and results are always more than individual efforts.

- **Affiliate Program:** You can launch your own affiliate program where people can join. Then they would advertise your product with their affiliate link. When a sale is made, they get a preset commission. You will need an affiliate program manager to do this. Clickbank.com offers an easy alternative.

- **Resell Rights Marketing:** You can offer resell rights to your product where people would be able to sell it and keep all the money. It increases your product value and helps in building in name because more sales are made than when you sell it just on your own. Helps in branding too.

- **RSS Marketing:** RSS stands for Really simple Syndication and it may be difficult to conceptualize in the beginning. RSS works by RSS feeds which needs to be generated by website. People can subscribe to these RSS feeds and can view the content of the website via their RSS reader. By this people are enabled to rceive the content directly on their desktop. This method is quite new as compared to others and has become really popular following spam issues in email marketing.

- **Blog Marketing:** Blog is an online journal which you can update on regular basis. You need a blogging platform like Wordpress or Blogger etc and you can publish at their site or host on your own. Blogs are immensely popular with marketers and are very much loved by search engines. A must for your business.

- **Social Bookmarking:** This is latest marketing buzz. There are online bookmarking sites available which peple can use to bookmark the places on the web they like. You can display these bookmarking buttons on your site or blog and people may submit the link for bookmarking if they like your site. Generates good traffic.

- **Video Marketing:** This is even newer. You can upload a video on the sites that allow. People would watch and then visit your site. Theory is similar to article marketing but media used is different. A popular website that allows video upload is Youtube.com.

Questions

1. Define the term Internet.
2. What is meant by Extranet.
3. What is Intranet? State its advantages.

4. What are the advantages and disadvantages of internet?

5. With suitable diagram describe syndication.

6. Enlist various components of Intranet's Information Technology Structure.

7. Describe the term development of Intranet.

8. Compare Intranet and Extranet.

9. State various advantages of Extranet.

10. Compare intranet and Internet.

■■■

Chapter 4...

Electronic Data Exchange and E-Governance

Contents ...

4.1 Introduction to Electronic Data Exchange (EDI)

- Electronic Data Interchange (EDI) is the direct computer to computer exchange between two organisations or companies of standard business transaction documents, such as invoices, bill of lading, purchase orders etc.

- EDI saves money and time because transactions can be transmitted from one information system to another through at telecommunications network, eliminating the printing and handling of paper at one end and the inputting of data at the other.

- The formats of EDI look like standard forms and highly structured.

- One widely used format of EDI is for purchase orders and consists of an outer digital 'envelope' with the address of both the sender and the receiver.

- Any organisation can establish new relationship with its suppliers. It provide strategic benefits by helping a firm 'lockin' customers, making it easier and simplier for customers or distributors.

- Electronic data interchange (EDI) is the structured transmission of data between organizations by electronic means.

- EDI is used to transfer electronic documents or business data from one computer system to another computer system, i.e. from one trading partner to another trading partner without human intervention.

- Electronic Data Interchange is a system which allows document information to be communicated between businesses, government's structures and other entities.

- EDI is a set of standards which creates a cohesive system within which all parties are able to electronically exchange data information within a set of protocols.

- In EDI information is passed electronically from one computer to another over a network without having to the read, retyped or printed.

- The information transferred must have a standard define structure agreed between every company and the company use send and receive data from that company.

- For example, EDI is used in Automatic tailor Machines (ATM) in banks, Airline reservation systems, Stock exchange transactions and car reservation systems

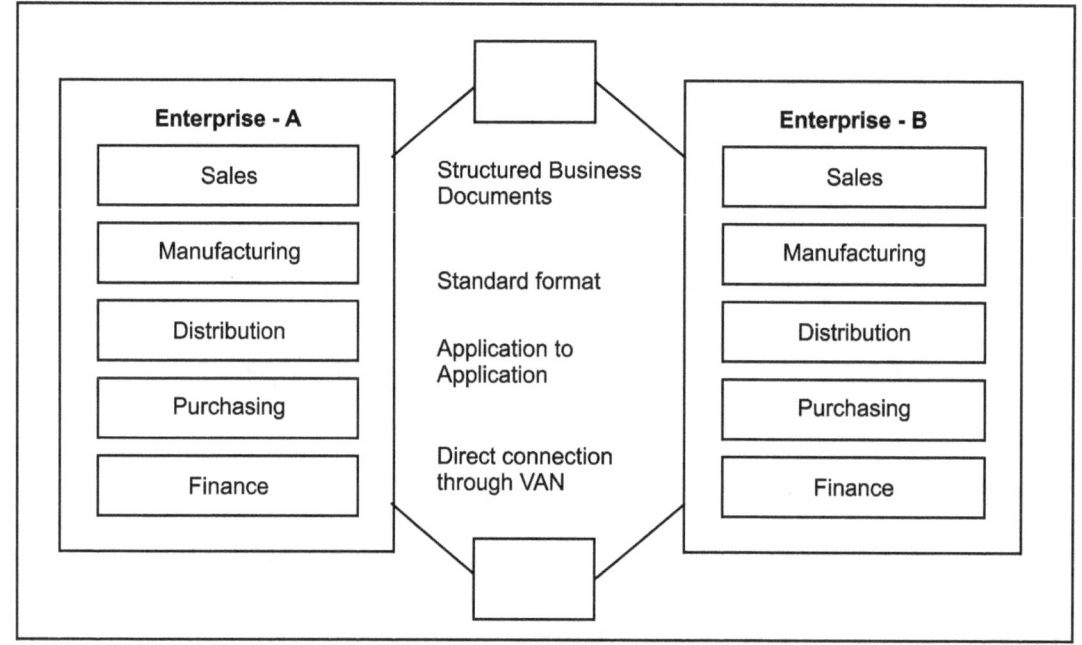

Fig. 4.1: Electronic Data Interchange

- EDI is simply a set of data definitions that permit business forms, that would have been exchanged using paper in the past, to be exchanged electronically.

- This simple set of definitions has spurred a number of organizations to put in place an operational environment in which the exchange of electronic business forms substitutes for the exchange of paper forms.

- This has resulted, in some cases, in the establishment of an EDI environment, which arguably represents the most advanced state of electronic commerce today, causing some to view EDI and electronic commerce as one and the same.

- We view EDI only as a subset of electronic commerce, albeit a very important one. As such, EDI provides an excellent example of a working electronic commerce environment and is a good starting point for examining electronic commerce.

- Electronic data interchange aims at single point collection of data for use by various agencies participating in a common activity.

- The exchange of information from one company to another using a computer network, such as the Internet. Electronic data interchange involves computer-to-computer exchanges of invoices, orders, and other business documents and therefore effects cost savings and improves efficiency because it minimizes the errors that can occur if the same information has to be typed into computers more than once.

- At the same time, EDI provides an easily accessible mechanism for companies to buy, sell, and trade information.

- In the business-to-business market, major corporations have embraced EDI systems, and in order to reduce costs and improve efficiency and competitiveness, many corporate giants are now demanding that their suppliers convert their sales and purchasing operations into EDI systems as well.

- In the retail market, the use of EDI systems allows the retailer to implement quick response strategies that can reduce the time they must hold merchandise in inventory, which can result in substantial cost savings for the retailer.

E-Commerce and EDI

- Although it appears these two systems may not be able to play together, the opposite is true. In this current climate of utilizing all the technologies available to make businesses more accessible and more user friendly, EDI can combine with e-commerce to do just that.

- While EDI is well entrenched as a major framework in many larger businesses, it is also being adopted by smaller businesses to increase their ability to make trading partners.

- EDI provides a fast and efficient way to exchange information.

- Currently, there are standards known as AS2 which govern Internet EDI transactions.

- The use of EDI through Internet modes is becoming more popular, as it does not require the same amount of set-up, costs or applications as for bigger corporate enterprises.

- The advantages of implementing EDI within the Internet environment, is that trading partners can be more efficiently and effectively communicated with, it reduces the amount of errors, and therefore improves cost effectiveness.

- It allows businesses to trade with larger enterprises that require EDI as a communication medium.
- Plus Internet EDI is relatively inexpensive, and does not carry with it the ongoing costs of other forms of EDI transmission. This can enable big and small companies to save potentially millions of dollars.
- Instead of mailing out catalogues and brochures, companies can send emails, and advise clients of discounts, and allow them to download information from the Internet.

EDI Standards and Initiatives

- There are several EDI standards that have been around for many years. But as the Internet took hold, new techniques for implementing EDI developed in groups and consortiums such as the W3C (World Wide Web Consortium), Commerce-Net, Rosetta Net, and Open Buying on the Internet (OBI).
- The Web sites for these organizations are listed on the related entries page.
- New EDI standards are currently under development. Some examples are described here.
  1. **ANSI ASC X12 (American National Standards-X12):** X12 is a standard that defines many different types of documents, including air shipments, student loan applications, injury and illness reports, and shipment and billing notices. The ANSI (American National Standards Institute) assigned responsibility for development of EDI standards to the ASC (Accredited Standards Committee) X12 organization in 1979. X12 has roots in work done in the shipping industry by the TDCC (Transportation Data Coordinating Committee) and work done in the food distribution industry by the UCC (Uniform Code Council).
  2. **UN/EDIFACT:** UN/EDIFACT (United Nations/Electronic Data Interchange for Administration Commerce and Transport) is an international set of EDI standards that are published by the United Nations Trade Data Interchange Directory (UNTDID). The standards include syntax rules and implementation guidelines; message design guidelines, directory sets defining messages, data elements, and code sets, among other definitions. It is built upon X12 and TDI (Trade Data Interchange), the latter being a generic EDI standard used in Europe.
  3. **Open-EDI:** The ISO (International Standards Organization) and IEC (International Electrical Committee) are developing an EDI reference model under a joint committee called Open-EDI. The goal of Open-EDI is to allow electronic transactions among "multiple autonomous organizations" that may or may not have any prior business relationships. In other words, businesses should be able to establish trading partners over networks like the Internet upon first contact and without any pre-agreement, assuming trust systems are in place.

EDI Software

- EDI software consists of computer instructions that translate the information from company-specific format to the structred EDI format, and then communicates the EDI message.

- EDI software also recieves the message and translates from standard format to company specific format. Thus, the major functions of the EDI software are data conversion, data formatting and message communication.
- EDI software is available for mainframes, mini comuters, and micro computers.
- The requirements for implementing EDI include a computer of any type, a communication modem and appropriate software.
- In addition a major requirement is that software should be capable of handling and controlling any incoming or outgoing EDI message to any number or combination of trading partners.
- Such software is generally called EDI converter or translater and is totally independent of the computer applications that pass data to it or recieve data from it.
- EDI solutions can be broadly configured into four categories:
   1. **Stand-alone EDI converter** software on PC which generate data with the help of data entry forms or screens.
   2. **Front-end of EDI gateway:** Connects EDI PC to the existing in-house computer and helps import/export flat-files into/from the application software.
   3. **EDI software co-hosting on in-house mainframe -** Application program interface with EDI using API or FPI (File Programme Interface or File Bridge).
   4. **Using the EDI conversion and communication** facility provided by third party Value Added Networks (VANs).

4.1.1 What is EDI?

- Electronic Data Interchange (EDI) is the inter-organisational exchange of business documents in structured, machine processable form.
- Electronic data Interchange can be used to electronically transmit documents such as purchase orders, invoices, shipping bills, receiving advices and other standard business correspondence between trading partners.
- EDI can also be used to transmit financial information and payments in electronic form. Payments carried out over EDI are usually referred to as Electronic Funds Transfer (EFT).
- EDI should not be viewed as simply a way of replacing paper documents and traditional methods of transmission such as mail, phone or in-person delivery with electronic transmission. But it should be seen not as an "end" but as a means to streamline procedures and improving efficiency and productivity.
- The electronic data interchange process is the computer-to-computer exchange of business documents between companies. EDI replaces the faxing and mailing of paper documents.
- EDI documents use specific computer record formats that are based on widely accepted standards. However, each company will use the flexibility allowed by the standards in a unique way that fits their business needs.
- EDI is used in a variety of industries. Over 160,000 companies have made the switch to EDI to improve their efficiencies. Many of these companies require all of their partners to also use EDI.

4.1.2 Definition of EDI

- We can define Electronic Data Interchange (EDI) as "the exchange of business data from one organisation's computer application to the computer application of a trading partner".

OR

- EDI (Electronic Data Interchange) is a standard format for exchanging business data.

OR

- EDI is a standardized method for transferring data between different computer systems or computer networks. EDI is commonly used for e-commerce purposes, such as sending orders to warehouses, tracking shipments, and creating invoices.

OR

- EDI is a set of protocols for conducting electronic business over computer networks.

OR

- EDI (Electronic Data Interchange) is the controlled transfer of data between business and organisations via established security standards. EDI consists of standardized electronic message formats, for business documents such as purchase change orders, requests for quotations, invoices, purchase orders, bills of lading, receiving advices and so on.

4.1.3 Components of EDI

- The following components and tools are necessary for performing EDI.

  1. **Trade Agreement:** A legally binding trade agreement between you and your trading partner.

  2. **Standard Document Format:** The standard agreed upon format for the document to be electronically transmitted.

  3. **EDI Translation Management Software:** Software used to convert the document your application's format into the agreed upon standard format. For optimum performance the translation software should be on the same platform as your business application.

  4. **Communications Software:** A programming tool that enables you to write communications protocols, or a separate application. It can be a module to the translator or a separate software application.

  5. **Modem:** A hardware device used to transmit electronic information between computer systems. The higher the baud rate, the faster the communications will be.

  6. **VAN:** Stands for Value Added Network. A network to which you can connect to transmit data from one computer systems to another. One network can act as a gateway to another.

  7. **Point-to-Point:** A direct communication link from one computer to another. Some trading partners offer a direct connection to their EDI computer. Trading partners may opt for this method of communication instead of using a VAN.

Operation of EDI

- EDI starts with a trading agreement between you and your trading partner. You make joint decisions about the standard to be used, the information to be exchanged, how the information is to be sent, and when information will be sent.
- The information can be sent through a direct connection (Point-to-Point), or through a VAN.
- To send a document, you use your EDI translation software to convert the document format into the agreed upon standard.
- The translator creates and wraps the document in an electronic envelope and puts the ID for your trading partner on it.
- If the information is to be sent Point-to-Point, the communications software sends the document directly from your computer system to your partners computer system.
- If a VAN is used, the communications software dials the phone number for the network and transmits the envelope containing the document.
- The VAN reads the ID on the envelope and places it in the correct mailbox.
- Your trading partner's modem calls the network and retrieves everything in the mailbox. The EDI translator opens the envelope and translates the data from the standard form to their application's format.
- If you attempt to do EDI without translation, you run a great risk of transmitting data that your trading partner will not be able to read.
- Your trading partners may use business applications on computers that are different than yours.
- The translator ensures that the data you send is converted into a format that your trading partner can use.
- **For example:** Consider the relationship between purchaser and vendor.

1. **Purchaser:**

   Suppose a department orders for an item to the purchasing department. Purchasing department first prepares the Purchase Orders (POs) and sends it to the vendor via its mail office under copies to accounts and shipping departments.

2. **Vendor:**

   Vendor receives or gets the Purchase Order (PO) from its mail office, route it to its sales. Sale department will take action through shipping and deliver the goods to the receiving department of the purchaser. The copies of order confirmation, bill will be delivered to the mail office of the purchases.

- EDI differs from electronic mail in that it transmits an actual structured transaction in contrast to an unstructured text message like a letter. It can also curb inventory costs by minimizing the amount of time, components are in inventory.
- Organisation can most benefits from EDI when they integrate the data supplied by EDI with applications such as inventory control, accounts payable, shipping and production planning.

- For proper EDI working four key requirements exist they are:
    1. **Appropriate 'mail box' facilities:** Companies using EDI must select a third party, value-added network with mail box facilities that allow messages to be sent, sorted and held until they are needed by the receiving computer.
    2. **Transaction software:** Special software to be developed to convert incoming and outgoing messages into a form suitable to other companies.
    3. **Transaction standardization:** Transaction formats and data must be standardized.
    4. **Legal restrictions:** To comply with legal requirements, certain transactions require "writing" or the "original document" in hard copy form.

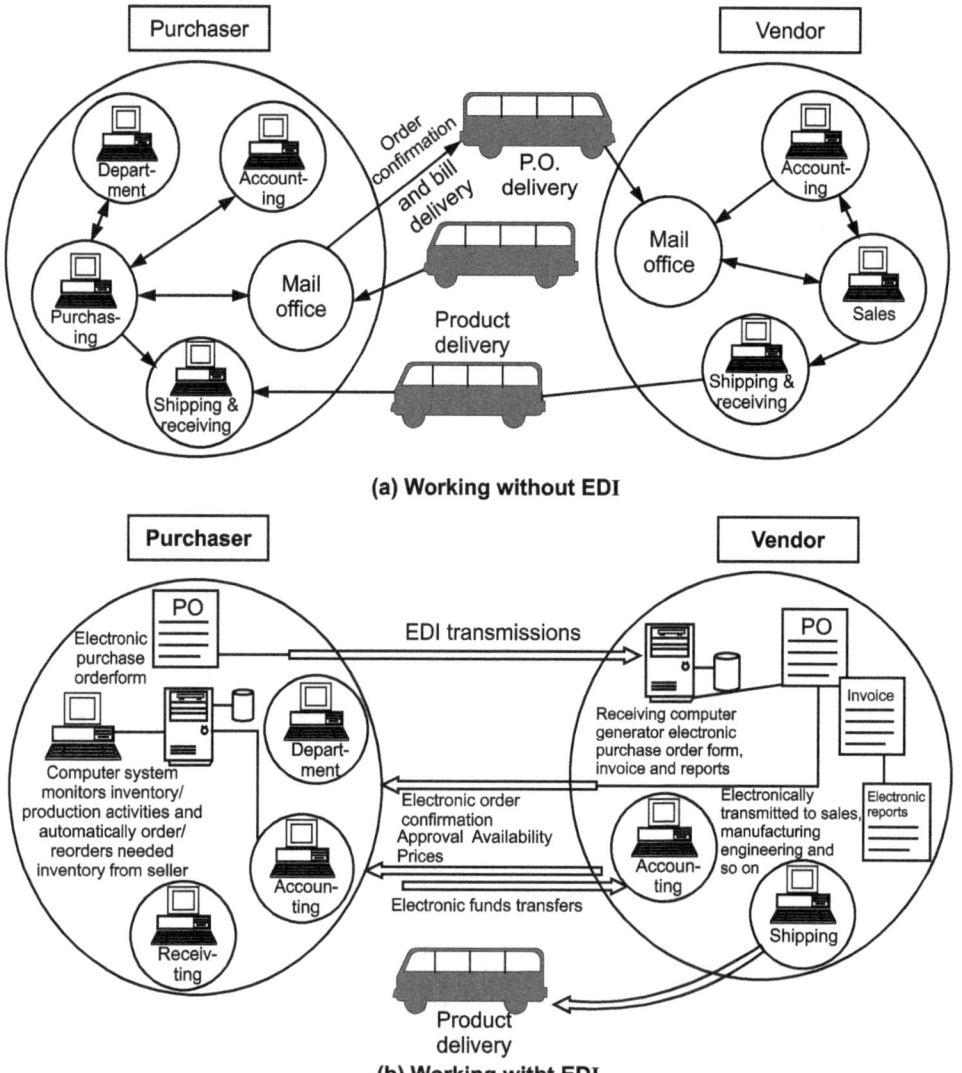

(a) Working without EDI

(b) Working witht EDI

Fig. 4.2: An illustration of how EDI would improv: and benefit business relationships among organisations or companies

- Organisations uses EDI to automate price, receiving, shipping and payment transactions with its customers as an example.
- Price updates and shipping notices are entered by the appropriate departments directly into organisations computer system, which then transmits to the customer's computer system.
- Similarly, customers material releases, payment data and receiving reports are also transmitted directly through the computer system back to the organisation.
- **EDI lowers or reduces:**
  1. Turn around time,
  2. Routine transaction processing cost,
  3. Inventory costs,
  4. Transcription errors, and
  5. Associated costs occurring during entry of data and printed out many times.

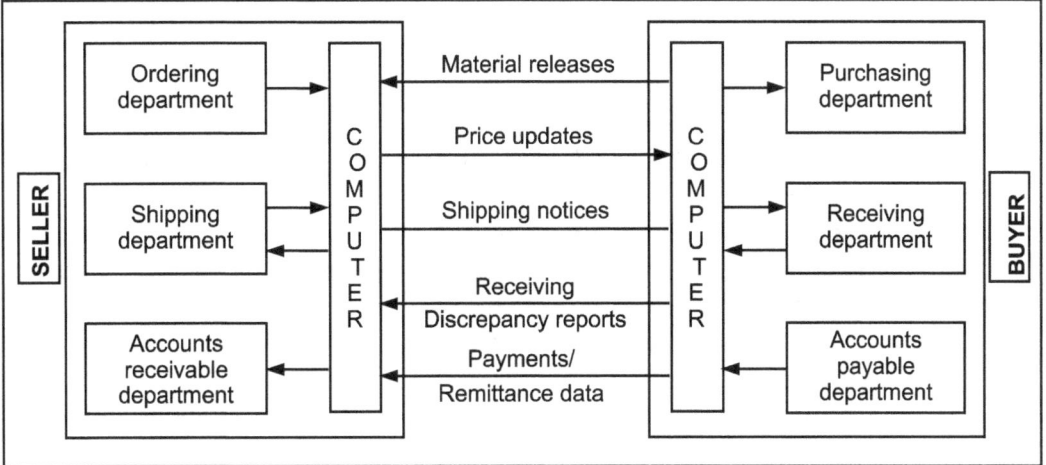

Fig. 4.3: EDI as an example

4.1.4 Advantages of EDI

- Various advantages of EDI are listed below:
  1. **Save money:** The cost of paper and paper processing is incredibly high compared to a properly implemented EDI program. RJR Nabisco estimates that processing a paper purchase order costs the company $70. Processing an EDI purchase order reduces the cost to a mere 93%.
  2. **End Repetition:** If your trading partner wants a copy of a document, instead of calling you they simply check their mailbox. This results in a great time saving from not having to copy and fax/mail copies of business documents.
  3. **Save Time:** EDI also saves time over paper processing since the transfer of information from computer to computer is automatic. There is no need to rekey information with EDI. And the chance for error drops to near zero, with no data entry.

4. **Improve Customer Service:** The quick transfer of business documents and marked decrease in errors allow you to do business faster and more efficient. KMart is an example of a retailer that implements a Vendor Stock Replenishment (VSR) program. With VSR, the KMart warehouse sends stock as their EDI system reports it and automatically bills the client. It can cut weeks from the order fulfillment cycle and ensures that product is always on the shelf.

5. **Expand your Customer Base:** Thus, with improved customer service, you can ultimately expand your customer base. Many large manufacturers and retailers are ordering their suppliers to institute an EDI program. So, when evaluating a new product to carry or a new supplier to use, the ability to do EDI is a big plus.

6. **Inventory reduction:** EDI permits faster and more accurate filling of orders, helps reduce inventory, assists in JIT (Just in Time) inventory management.

7. **Better Decision-Making:** It provides better information for management decision making. EDI provides accurate information and audit trails for transactions, enabling business to identify areas offering the greatest potential for efficiency improvement or cost reduction.

8. **Saves manpower:** By using EDI we avoid the need to rekey data.

9. **Fast Method:** It is used for sending invoices, Purchase Orders (POs), custom documents, shipping notices and other types of business documents in a fast and expensive method.

10. **Improvements in overall quality:** Using EDI we keep better record keeping, fewer errors in data, reduction in processing time, less reliance on human interpretation of data, minimized unproductive time and so on.

11. Data arrives in EDI much faster than it could be by mail and there is an automatic acknowledgement.

12. EDI eliminates the errors introduced by rekeying.

13. Reduces time of processing cycle.

14. **Reduces paperwork:** The EDI process can be handled without using a single piece of paper.

15. **Availability of data in electronic form:** Data from EDI is in electronic form, which makes it easy to share across the organisation.

16. **Reduces data entry errors:** With EDI data goes directly from one computer to another computer without involving a human being.

4.1.5 Disadvantages of EDI

- Disadvantages of EDI are given below:
    1. **Too Many Standards**: There are too many standards bodies developing standard documents formats for EDI. For example your company may be following the X12 standard format, while your trading partner follows the EDIFACT standard format.
    2. **Changing Standards**: Each year, most standards bodies publish revisions to the standards. This poses a problem to EDI users. You may be using one version of the standard while your trading partners are still using older versions.

3. **EDI is Too Expensive**: Some companies are only doing business with others who use EDI. If a company wants to do business with these organizations, they have to implement an EDI program. This expense may be very costly for small companies.

4. **Limit Your Trading Partners**: Some large companies tend to stop doing business with companies who don't comply with EDI. For example Wal Mart is only doing business with other companies that use EDI. The result of this is a limited group of people you can do business with.

5. **Less transparent:** EDI is less transparent than paper-based systems.

6. **Structured Method:** EDI is a structured way of working, companies usually change operating procedures.

7. **High flexibility:** Certain EDI system are highly flexible, other are very simple to implement.

4.2 Concept of EDI

- EDI i.e. Electronic Data Interchange which is a very simple concept.
- EDI uses direct links between computers, even between computers on different sites, to transmit data to eliminate data sent in printed form.
- It is generally thought of as replacing standardized documents such as orders forms, delivery notes and invoices, the techniques is highly flexible. It's application is vast and used in wide range of industries.
- EDI is Electronic Data Interchange. It uses direct link between computers and also computers in different sites to transmit data to eliminate data sent in printed form.
- EDI is direct computer-to-computer exchange between two organizations of standard business transaction documents in such as invoices, billing, and purchase order.
- EDI is the control transfer of data between business and organization via security standards. EDI consists of standardized electronic message format for business documents.
- Paper based Business versus EDI based Business:

	Paper based Business		EDI based Business
1.	A software application generates a paper document on a form.	1.	A application programme generates a file which contains a processed document.
2.	Copies of the documents are made, some are passed to internal departments to be filled, and other copies are sent to the trading partners through the postal service.	2.	The document is converted to an agreed standard format.

contd. ...

3.	The trading partners receive the documents and retype the information on the form, which often introduces an error.	3.	The file containing the document is send electronically over the network. This network links the originating company and his trading partners.
4.	The trading partner generates paper acknowledgement and this is send to the originating company.	4.	The files containing the document arise at the trading partner. It is translated in to a correct format and transfer to the resequence applications.
5.	The transfer of document in a paper-based system could take a considerable length of time.	5.	A report is automatically generated and sends over the network to the originating company. It transmits documents in a very short period of time without errors and with no human interaction.

4.3 Limitations of EDI

- Though there are accepted benefits, EDI technique do not find wide spread acceptance because of the following:
    1. **Limited accessibility:** EDI does not allow consumers to communicate or transact with vendors in an easy way. A subscriber must subscribe to an online service called VAN.
    2. **High costs:** Applications are costing to develop and operate in EDI. Specially, new entrants find this more difficult and complex to have EDI.
- The cost of EDI shown in Fig. 4.4.

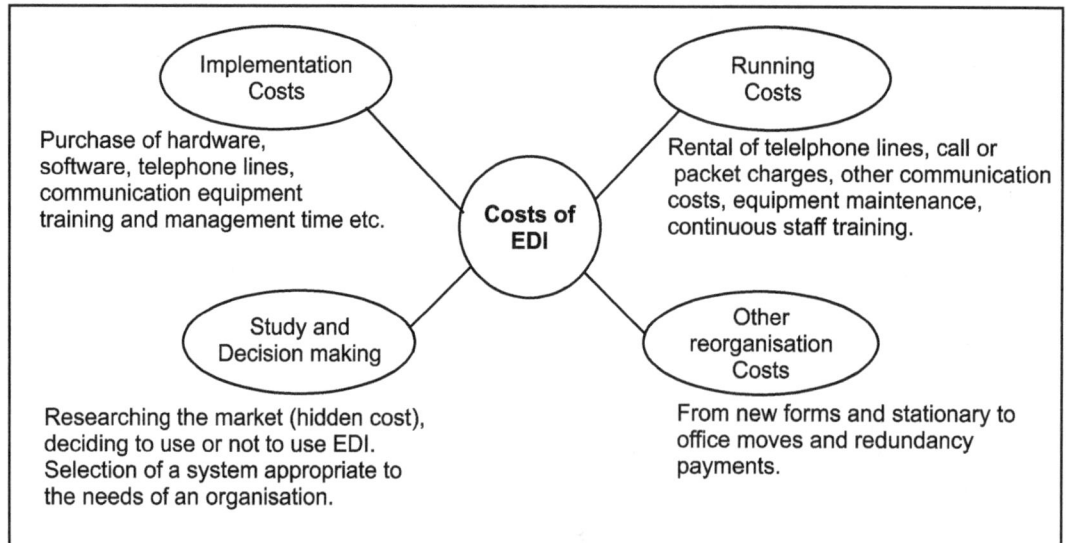

Fig. 4.4

3. **Rigid requirements:** Needs highly structured protocols, previously established arrangement, unique proprietary bilateral information exchanges.
4. Applications are narrow in scope in EDI.
5. EDI applications automate any certain portion of the transactions.

4.4 Applications of EDI

EDI is used in following:
1. Manufacturing,
2. Shipping,
3. Warehousing,
4. Utilities,
5. Pharmaceuticals,
6. Construction,
7. Petroleum,
8. Metals,
9. Banking,
10. Insurance,
11. Retailing,
12. Government,
13. Healthcare, and
14. Textiles among others.

4.5 EDI Model

- EDI Model involves trading partners who wants to exchange data from the organisations or companies.
- There may be two companies or firms with a common customer or two banks whose customers wants to deal with one another or between two divisions of the same company or firm, although if they have an integrated computer system, normally this would not be treated as EDI.
- Trading partners will have the flow of data between them through exchanges.
- The simplest and the most common form of exchange is where one partner wants to send a single message to the other and to know whether or not the message received by the other.
- Further, exchanges may be sequential messages following the first one, in some way linked to the first which would be part of the same exchange, which is similar to the telephone conversation carried on by telephone answering machine between two people who are not present when the other calls.
- The exchange is divided into messages on which most EDI standards concentrate.

- The messages is passed successfully and reliably from one partner to the other, it is said EDI is operated.

- An message has an originator who is the creator of the message and a destination which is the other trading partner.

- There may be one message to reach several destinations, though the procotol of the EDI system usually not permit this.

- Fig. 4.5 shows EDI model.

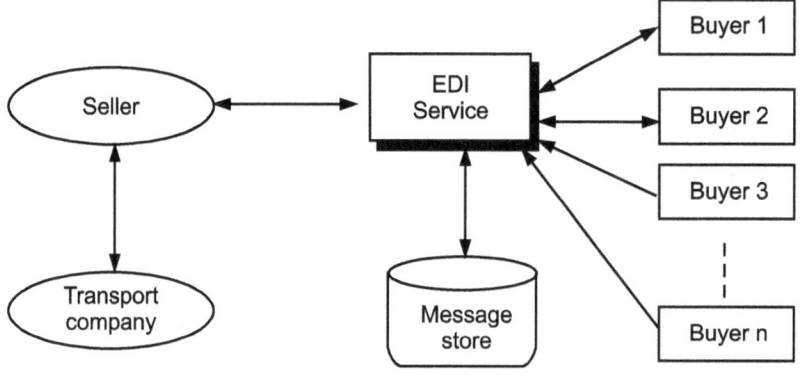

Fig. 4.5

Data Standards used in EDI

- The two data standards commonly used in EDI systems are Data Encryption Standard (DES) and Rivert-Shamier-Adelmann (RSA).

- DES standard was developed by IBM for the U.S. department of defence and RSA standard was developed by a group of mathematicians who believed that it would not be possible to devise a code that could be deciphered using a public key without giving away the encryption key.

4.6 E-governance

- Electronic Governance refers to the online delivery of information and services related to the activities and processes involved in governing a country or state through internet or other digital means.

- Electronic Governance is the application of information technology to government functioning in order to bring about Simple, Moral, Accountable, Responsive and Transparent (SMART) Governance. E-Governance involves processes like online delivery of information and services related activities governing a country or state through the internet or other digital means. In short, e-Governance refers to the use of information technologies like local area network, wide area network, the internet and mobile computing etc. by the government agencies. Such use of information technologies will be beneficial to give better delivery of government services to citizens, improved interactions with business and industry, citizen empowerment through access to information, or more efficient government management. Increased transparency, less corruption, greater convenience, cost reduction, revenue growth etc. are the resulting benefits of e-governance. E-commerce helps businesses to transact with each other more efficiently (B2B) and brings the customers closer to business (B2Q. On the similar lines, e-governance aims to make interaction between government and citizens (G2Q, government and business enterprise (G2B) and inter-agencies relationships (G2G) more friendly, convenient, transparent and inexpensive. Information Technology should be used strategically to radically improve organizational effectiveness.

- Traditionally, the interaction between citizens or business and government agencies use to take place in a government office. Now, it has been observed that e-governance enhances the citizens and business access to government information and services and provides new ways to increase citizen participation in democratic functioning of the Government. Effective change management is necessary for the success of e-governance. Along with proper telecom infrastructure, technology and software, a successful transition from a manual to electronic process requires change in various established procedures.

4.6.1 E-governance in India

- India has to respond to the emerging needs of the digital economy, and for integration into the networked world.

- The Government of India has recently approved the National E-Governance Action Plan for implementation during the years 2003-2007. The E-Governance seeks to lay the foundation and provide an impetus for long-term growth of e-governance within the country. Action plans seeks to create the right governance and institutional mechanisms, set up the core infrastructure and policies, and implement a number of mission mode projects at the Centre, state and integrated service levels, to create a citizen-centric and business-centric environment for governance. Overall the programme content, implementation approach and governance structures are in the process of being established.

- In 1998, the National IT Task Force had set up a Citizen-IT Interface Working Group with the mandate of formulating projects as well as policy guidelines for promoting the beneficial impact of IT to deliver government services to citizens electronically.

- The Working Group recognized that IT is an agent of change, an agent which can transform every facet of human life, and that it is possible to bring about revolutionary changes in the lives of citizens through the deeper penetration of IT in society. The working group examined the use of IT both at the Central Government and the State Government level.

- The Working Group under the National IT Task Force had made 25 recommendations under the following categories:
  1. Government-wide information infrastructure
  2. Re-engineering of government processes
  3. Service delivery to citizens
  4. Service delivery on commercial basis
  5. Best practices
  6. HRD requirements
- The Government of India needs and requires to create websites for the effective dissemination of information, i.e. the publish mode, or the first generation of electronic delivery of information.
- This websites have to be designed with a view to move from the publish mode of information dissemination to the interact mode and then to the transact mode.
- The necessary infrastructure that is required for this to happen includes the following:
  1. Computers to be made cheaper and computer awareness to be increased
  2. Telecommunication costs to be made cheaper
  3. STD booths to be upgraded into info kiosks that can deliver Internet-enabled IT services to citizens
- The Working Group under the National IT Task Force had also identified area-wise requirements of citizens to include public grievances, police, rural services, social services, judiciary, registration of licenses and certificates, public information, economically weak section (EWS) services, agriculture sector, utility payments /billing, commercial taxes and returns filing, government procurement and so on.
- The Citizen–IT Interface Working Group under the IT Task Force had identified the following major areas for launching pilot projects in one or more states:
  1. Government tendering /electronic procurement
  2. Education
  3. Judiciary
  4. Land records
  5. Health (LAN-MIS for hospitals)
  6. Utilities payment/billing
  7. Government regulatory information
  8. Railway/road/airline time tables/fare charts
  9. Employment opportunities
  10. Agriculture related

11. Pension

12. Public grievance filing/tracking

13. Ration cards issuance

14. Driving license issuance, motor vehicles registration

- While endorsing the National E-Governance Action Plan in 2004, the Citizen IT Interface Working Group made the following key observations:

1. Wherever, possible, services should be outsourced.

2. Adequate weightage must be given for quality and speed of implementation in procurement procedures for IT services.

3. Connectivity should be extended up to the block level through National Informatics Centre's Network (NICNET) or State Wide Area Networks (SWAN).

4. Suitable system of incentivisation of states should be incorporated to encourage adoption.

5. The full potential of the private sector investment should be exploited.

6. Delivery of services through common service centers should be encouraged and promoted.

7. R&D should be undertaken in government systems.

- The Plan includes the following components:

1. Core policies

2. Core projects

3. Awareness and assessment

4. R&D (Research and Development)

5. Integrated services projects

6. Technical assistance

7. Support infrastructure

8. Human resource development/ training

9. Organizational structures

10. Core infrastructure

- The criteria for selecting mission mode projects under above Plan included the impact in terms of the number of people likely to be affected, likely improvement of the quality of service, the economy or economic environment in the country, the likely cost benefit of investments in the project, readiness and willingness of the ministry/ department to position a National Mission Project, and feasibility of implementing the project from a financial, administrative and political perspective within a reasonable time frame.

- These projects includes national citizen database, income tax, passports and immigration, department of company affairs' DCA21, banking, land records, road transport, EDI (e-commerce), India portal, e-procurement and E-Biz among others.

- The term eGovernance has different connotations:

  o **E-administration:** The use of ICTs to modernize the state; the creation of data repositories for MIS, computerisation of records.

  o **E-services:** The emphasis here is to bring the state closer to the citizens. Examples include provision of online services. E-administration and e-services together constitute what is generally termed e-government.

  o **eGovernance:** The use of IT to improve the ability of government to address the needs of society. It includes the publishing of policy and programme related information to transact with citizens. It extends beyond provision of on-line services and covers the use of IT for strategic planning and reaching development goals of the government.

  o **E-democracy:** The use of IT to facilitate the ability of all sections of society to participate in the governance of the state. The remit is much broader here with a stated emphasis on transparency, accountability and participation. Examples could include online disclosure policies, online grievance redress forums and e-referendums. Conceptually, more potent.

- Global shifts towards increased deployment of IT by governments emerged in the nineties, with the advent of the World Wide Web. What this powerful means to publish multimedia, support hyperlinked information and interactive information meant was a clearer avenue for G to C interactions and the promise of the attainment of the goals of good governance. Governments weighed down by the rising expectations and demands of a highly aware citizenry suddenly began to believe that there can be a new definition of public governance characterized by enhanced efficiency, transparency, accountability and a citizen-orientation in the adoption of IT enabled governance.

4.7 Indian Customs EDI System

- Indian customs has been among one of the first government regulatory agencies, in various parts of the world, to have introduced EDI in its interface with importers, exporters, and other players involved in international trade. Indian customs EDI system has carried out a major BPR exercise to improve its efficiency, and change its image from control to facilitation. The transition from customs controls to facilitation represents an attitudinal change on the part of customs agencies, which have traditionally been viewed as regulatory in nature. IT in general and EDI in particular, have helped re-engineer the processes related to customs clearance.

- The Indian Customs EDI System (ICES), designed, developed and implemented jointly by the National Informatics Centre (NIC) and the Customs Department, heralded an era of paperless trade in the country. Indian Customs EDI System has transformed the custom house into a paperless office. The working of the office has been redesigned according to re-engineered procedures through appropriate application software in ICES with a view to link the same with EDI transactions from across the organizational boundaries of the custom house.

- The pilot EDI project implemented at Delhi Custom House in May 1995, facilitated online clearance of import documents filed electronically by importers, and/or their clearing agents over NICNET.

- Indian Customs EDI System was extended to white shipping bills in May 1996, and to duty drawback shipping bills with effect from November 1996. Importers, Customs House Agents (CHA), and exporters would transmit bills of entry, shipping bills, and other related documents such as invoice, license, etc. over dial-up links to the NICNET EDI server, which, in turn, would submit them to the customs computer system for clearance.

- A CHA does not have to chase his documents physically from table to table in the Custom House for clearance. The project has since been extended to cover all custom houses in the country.

- Indian Customs EDI System comprises two main sub-systems, one is ICES/I for processing of bills of entry; and another is ICES/E for processing of shipping bills. Service centre modules have been incorporated in both these sub-systems, which allow entry of documents from the service centre located in the Custom House. CHAs who do not have their own computer systems, can bring their documents to the service centre for data entry and submission to the Customs system.

- Indian Customs EC/EDI Gateway (ICEGATE) was implemented in 2001-02. It has also been licensed by the Controller of Certifying Authorities to operate as a Certifying Authority (CA) under the IT Act, 2000. The iCERT CA—the legal CA entity under which the Customs CA operates—serves the community of users in ICES including customs officials, Custom House agents and importers /exporters.

- CHAs can use the Remote EDI System (RES) which is a standalone software package for preparation of Bills of Entry (BEs), Shipping Bills (SBs) and other related documents. It has been developed by NIC as part of the ICES project. Documents transmitted electronically are submitted to ICEGATE for clearance.

4.8 Service Centre

- CHAs who do not have access to computer systems use terminals in the service centre for having their documents entered into the computer system for processing. CHAs are able to see the status of their documents from the enquiry counter terminals positioned at the service centre. CHAs do not interact with the customs staff until the stage of physical examination of goods. On the basis of pre-determined criteria, ICES suggests the specific packages which may be checked by the customs staff in the examination unit.

- In addition to CHAs, importers, and exporters, ICES provides for integration of other agencies involved in the customs clearance through EDI technology.
- The Customs EDI Community System includes the following:

1. Directorate General of Foreign Trade (DGFT)
2. Punjab National Bank (PNB), and other banks
3. Airports Authority of India (AAI)
4. Apparels Export Promotion Council (AEPC)
5. The Reserve Bank of India
6. Custom House Agents (CHAs)
7. Importers/ exporters
8. Airlines
9. Port authorities
10. Shipping lines
11. Shipping agents

Fig. 4.6 shows the Customs EDI community system.

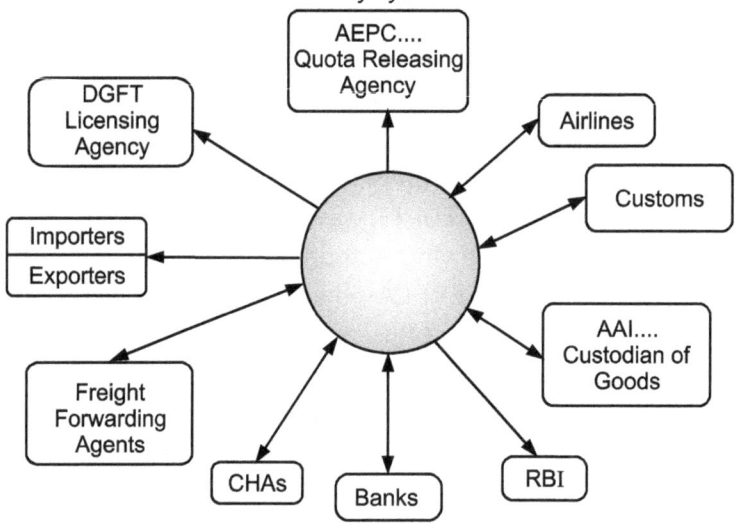

Fig. 4.6: Customs EDI community systems

- Import licenses issued by the Directorate General of Foreign Trade (DGFT), the quota release position of Apparels Export Promotion Council (AEPC), are directly available in the customs computer system through these EDI linkages. With this arrangement, there is no need for an exporter to get the allocation number endorsed on the body of the SB from

Apparels Export Promotion Council (AEPC). The Directorate General of Foreign Trade (DEEC) and EPCG certificates are no longer required from importers since they can be downloaded from DGFT computer systems. The GR-1 form required by the RBI can be directly transmitted from the customs computer system to the RBI computer system.

- During the very first stage of implementation, the computer system of Punjab National Bank (PNB), which is within the premises of New Custom House, was integrated with ICES. The advice for duty payment goes directly to Punjab National Bank (PNB) in addition to the printing of a TR-6 challan form in the service centre for the CHA, if he wishes to have a copy. The advice on the payment of duty is sent directly from Punjab National Bank (PNB) to ICES, and the information is available on the terminals in the examination unit at the import cargo shed.

- Airport Authority of India (AAI) is also a part of the customs EDI community system. Data about imports and exports are downloaded from ICES to its cargo management system. Similarly, Import General Manifests (IGMs) and Export General Manifests (EGMs), filed by the airlines with customs, are downloaded to AAI. The attempt in ICES is thus to capture the data only once from the agency that deals with that subject matter, and then make it available to others who need the same.

- ICES has eliminated a number of processes which were part of the erstwhile manual system. Some of the stages have been merged, while a few have been eliminated altogether. For example, at every stage, there were noting registers wherein entries would be made for the same document.

- ICES facilitates payment of duty drawback without the exporter having to submit a large number of documents for the purpose. In fact, he/she is no longer asked to submit any additional documents other than those submitted at the examination stage. No separate account numbers or ledger numbers are to be maintained by the exporter for the purpose of making drawback claims. The work related to the scrutiny of SBs for drawback claims has been integrated with appraising in ICES. Assessing officers verify the claims with respect to the drawback rates, quantity and value exported, and pass the bills for payment at the designated levels of Superintendent/Assistant Collector. All these documents are further examined by audit through an appropriate software module.

4.9 Import

- The BE (Bill of Entry), the import declaration, was assigned a unique number in the noting section, in a register. At all stages of processing, viz. appraising, comptist, Asst. Commissioner, audit, license, cash, bonds, bank, guarantee, examination, etc. entries would be made corresponding to the BE No. of the document being processed. The workflow software implemented in ICES keeps track of the movement of the BE. All registers stand eliminated. The noting section has been eliminated since ICES allocates a

BE number automatically. Comptist has been eliminated, since ICES computes the duty once assessment has been completed by the assessing officer and/or the Assistant Commissioner.

- The Import Policy should achieve national objectives, such as:

    1. **Import of Essential items:** Only essential items should be imported.

    2. **Promotion of Import Substitution:** The import substitutes should be promoted. The items which are manufactured in our county should not be imported. This will help to reduce import of goods in future.

    3. **Promotion of Export:** Only such goods should be imported which will help to promote export. Import Trade means trade that results in bringing goods from other countries to home country. The Importer is a person who imports goods. Import Trade may be carried on by the importer directly or through specialized agencies like Indent Houses or Firms. The procedure of Import Trade begins when the order is placed and comes to an end when goods are received and the importer makes the final payment. The procedure of import trade may differ slightly from county to country.

- The following are the important steps in import trade:

    o Import Licenses and Quota, 2. Obtaining Foreign Exchange, 3. Booking of Indent or placing of order, 4. Letter of Credit, 5. Sending orders or Dispatch of order by the Indent House/Importer, 6. Shipping of goods, 7. Preparation of Invoices and Bill for Payment, 8. Clearing of Goods.

    o ICES sends the assessed document to the bank connected with it on EDI. If the importer maintains an account there, and keeps a sufficient balance in it to enable automatic debit of the same, the duty payment becomes instantaneous. The BPR thus enables immediate transmittal of the BE to the examination sheds.

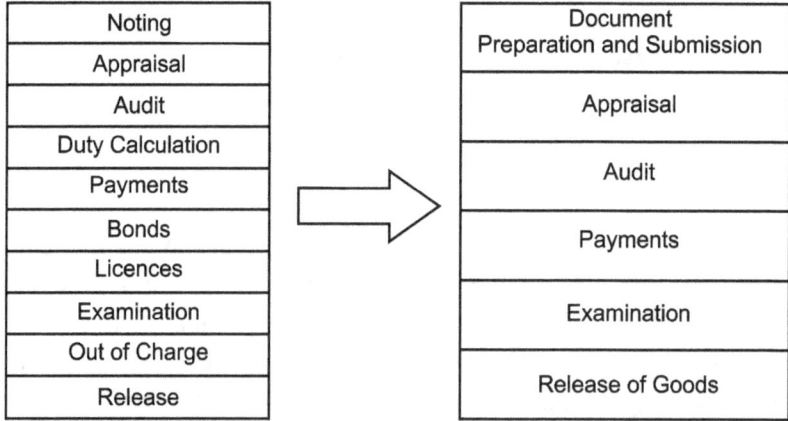

Fig. 4.7: Process reengineering for imports

- o ICES has facilitated green channel clearance for a number of importers with a good track record. On the basis of their reliability and reputation, importers are allowed to clear their consignments without any examination. But appraising is performed in a routine way. At Delhi, nearly 15 percent of the imports are allowed through this channel.
- o ICES has provision for system appraisal of the import declarations. The documents need not be appraised on the screen by assessing officers. System appraisal is carried out routinely in respect of imports of the following items:
  - ➢ Aircraft parts.
  - ➢ Defense supplies
  - ➢ Gold
  - ➢ Diplomatic goods
  - ➢ Books

  These account for nearly five percent of the imports at IGI Airport, New Delhi.

4.10 Export

- Every country desires to export goods to the possible maximum extent as it is an important source of earning foreign exchange. Hence, export assumes special significance in the economy of every country. Promotion of exports solves the problem of foreign exchange and also leads the country to economic and industrial development. The country is also able to maintain a prestigious position in the world market. "The backbone of every economy is exports, without it there is no other alternative but to perish". Export consciousness has to be created among the export manufacturers, export merchants and the Government. All concerned with this sector have to contribute to maximize exports.

- ICES has introduced more radical procedural changes in exports processing. In addition to eliminating the noting stage and all registers, appraising itself has been done away with for shipping bills related to non-drawback exports. In the case of drawback exports, an exporter is not required to file any separate application for release of duty drawback. No physical cheques are issued, instead the drawback payment is directly credited to the exporter's bank account.

Need for Export

- All countries in the world are dependent on each other. No country is completely self-sufficient. It is essential for every country to maintain trade relations. The need for exports arises due to following important reasons.
  1. **Balance of Payments:** Balance of Payment is an indicator of the international economic health of the country. Every country is serious about maintaining its

balance of payment. Our country, has to face a problem of unfavorable balance of payment position due to heavy imports. Export earning increases the reserves of foreign exchange and improves the position of balance of payment.

2. **To meet import needs:** In order to have industrial and economic development the developing countries have to import technical know-how, capital goods and components. Imports are necessary for strategic industries like petroleum, fertilizers etc. Exports only can meet these import needs.

3. **To increase production and employment:** An increase in exports may result in leading full use of production capacity, leading to increase in production which in turn result in increasing employment opportunities.

4. **To earn valuable foreign exchange:** The availability of valuable foreign exchange is essential for economic and industrial development. Foreign exchange earning enables countries to import basic raw materials, advanced technology and various components which accelerate process of industrialization and economic growth. The repayment of foreign debts becomes possible.

5. **To finance development plans and mobilization of domestic source:** Expansion and diversification of exports are necessary in order to finance development plans and mobilize domestic source.

6. **To make economic development:** Advanced countries are interested in export of technical know-how and capital goods to developing countries. Developed countries provide the necessary capital goods and technical know-how for development. They maintain trade relations with the developing countries. Thus, for making economic development of the country, exports are necessary.

7. **To increase purchasing power:** Increased exports leads to higher production and creation of more employment opportunities. Increase in employment results in increasing higher per capita income and national income. It also helps to increase purchasing power of people.

8. **To have optimum utilization of resources:** If a country is having excess production in the form of raw materials or finished goods it can be sold in the international market. Thus, effective use of surplus production becomes possible. The resources can be utilized in a proper way and waste can be avoided. Each country can receive the highest return from its resources.

9. **To help tertiary sector:** Export trade can help to build the economic life of the trade community. It can provide help to the tertiary sector activities such as banking, insurance, transport and other related activities.

10. **To facilitate debt servicing:** India has been borrowing on concessional terms from the World Bank and its associates over a longer period. This has resulted in a steady increase in the total external debt. Hence, there is urgent need to increase our exports substantially to meet our debts.

11. **To increase goodwill and reputation:** A country which is well-known in exports, enjoys more goodwill and reputation in the international market. High export earnings helps the country- to meet payments of import bills.

- Reduction in the number of processing stages, for a drawback Shipping Bill (SB), through BPR in ICES is shown in Fig. 4.8.

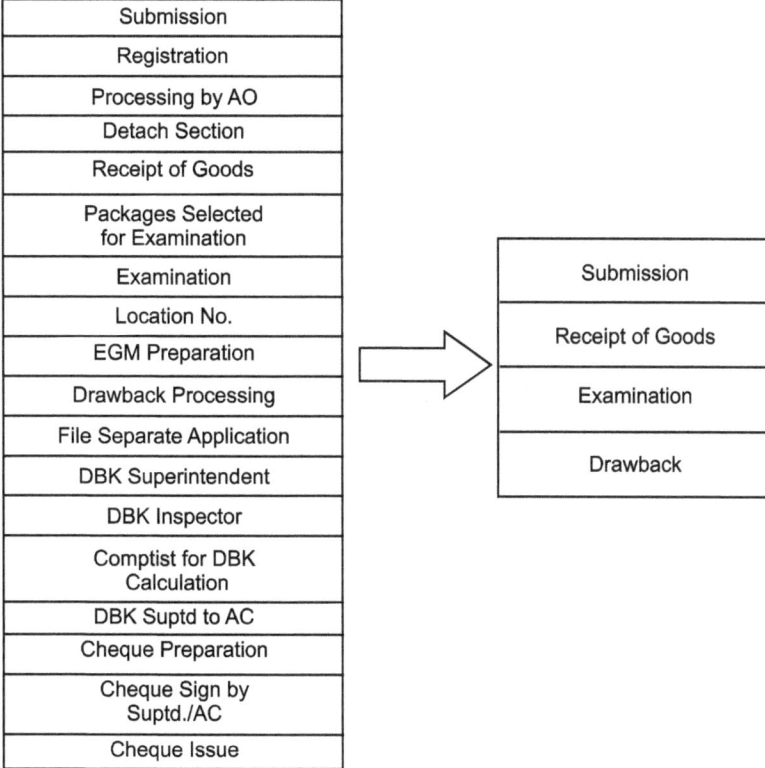

Fig. 4.8: Process reengineering for exports

- The most salutary gain of the ICES project at the Custom House is the achievement of the objective of 'customs facilitation' through an attitudinal change among customs officers. They accepted the system in a very positive manner. The trading community is happy about the transparency of procedures and new processes, and the accountability that goes along with it. The benefits of ICES can be summarized as follows:

1. Transparency of the system
2. Higher efficiency in customs operations
3. Nearly 50 percent of consignments being given green channel
4. No physical movement of document, thereby reducing processing time
5. Online enquiry
6. Minimum interaction with customs officers

7. Faster clearance of consignment

8. Customs EDI community system links all agencies

9. Electronic submission of documents over the network from anywhere

10. Truly a trade facilitator

11. Precedent search

12. Uniform assessment

Questions

1. What is meant by EDI?

2. Define the term EDI? State its advantages.

3. What are the components used by EDI?

4. Describe concept of EDI.

5. State various limitations of EDI.

6. Enlist various applications of EDI.

7. With suitable diagram describe EDI model.

8. Enlist various applications of EDI.

9. With suitable example describe operation of EDI.

10. List the disadvantages of EDI.

11. With a suitable diagram describe the Indian Customs EDI system.

12. Explain the term e-Governance of India.

13. What is meant by e-Governance?

14. What is meant by imports?

15. What is meant by exports?

16. With a suitable diagram describe service centre.

17. Compare exports and imports.

■■■

Chapter 5...

Electronic Payment System

Contents ...

5.1 Introduction

- E-payment or Electronic payment is any digital financial payment transaction involving currency transfer between two or more parties.
- Electronic payments are far cheaper than the traditional method of mailing out paper invoices and then processing payments received.

5.1.1 Electronic Payments

- The term 'electronic payment' is a collective phrase for the many different kinds of electronic payment methods available (also meaning online payment), and the processing of transactions and their application within online merchants and ecommerce websites.
- Electronic-payment is essential for all online businesses to be able to accept and process electronic payments in a fast and secure way. Businesses can gain a significant advantage over their competitors by providing an instant electronic payment service as it lets customers pay by their preferred way of credit or debit card.

- Electronic payments systems can also increase your cash flow, reduce administrative costs and labour and provide yet another way for your customers to pay.
- Care must be taken when choosing an electronic payment solution as it will need to fit within the constraints of your particular online business and integrate seamlessly within your website.

5.1.2 Electronic Payment System (EPS)

- EPS stands for Electronic Payment System.
- Electronic Payment is a financial exchange that takes place online between buyers and sellers.
- The content of this exchange is usually some form of digital financial instrument (such as encrypted credit card numbers, electronic cheques or digital cash) that is backed by a bank or an intermediary, or by a legal tender.
- An electronic payment system is needed for compensation for information, goods and services provided through the internet.
- The various factors that have lead the financial institutions to make use of electronic payments are:
  1. **Decreasing technology cost:** The technology used in the networks is decreasing day by day, which is evident from the fact that computers are now dirt-cheap and Internet is becoming free almost everywhere in the world.
  2. **Reduced operational and processing cost:** Due to reduced technology cost the processing cost of various commerce activities becomes very less. A very simple reason to prove this is the fact that in electronic transactions we save both paper and time.
  3. **Increasing online commerce:** The above two factors have lead many institutions to go online and many others are following them.

Definition

- Electronic Payment System (EPS) is a system which helps the user or customer to make online payments.

OR

- The term electronic payment can refer narrowly to e-commerce - a payment for buying and selling goods or services offered through the internet.

Advantages and Disadvantages

1. **Speed and convenience:** Using EPS Consumers can find what they want to buy and purchase it quickly. This immediate transfer of funds benefits businesses in several ways. Buyers are generally more willing to make purchases if the purchasing process is easy and immediate. Convenient and well-made e-payment systems also show consumers that the business cares about its customers and acts as a type of customer service.

2. **Flexible payment arrangements:** E-payments are also flexible. Many payment schedules allow for later billing or payment installments using a third-party vendor. Business websites typically give several options for customers to buy using a credit card, debit card or even a direct transfer from a bank account (Internet Banking). This also allows several types of transactions that are only available online, such as peer-to-peer electronic transfers.

3. **Security:** The flexibility that e-payments enjoy can also create security hazards. Malware and other hacking attempts can track keystrokes in order to copy account passwords and access payment information. Online databases can be hacked and important information can be stolen. Money can be stolen from online accounts like PayPal. It is difficult for businesses to guard against all possible security risks when creating online payment systems. A relatively modern invention is the electronic wallet, which contains customer's financial information in an offline database that is only accessed immediately when a purchase is made.

4. One of the most severe disadvantages of electronic payment systems is that of **identity theft**. The available security measures can prevent the sensitive information from being exposed. But it is important to use virus protection or firewalls for your computer. It is important to carry out money transactions over a secure server.

5. Mostly, **electronic cash is based on cryptographic systems**. The transactions are encoded by means of numeric keys while the transaction details travel across the net. Though electronic payments are resistant to forgery, the keys are vulnerable to attack.

6. **Payment system collision:** Because online payment systems are new and global in their perspective, problems can occur when it comes to applying them to all e-commerce businesses. Some types of payment that customers are used to depending on may not be available in other countries, even when purchasing online from those countries is an option. E-payments can also struggle to match up the values of different currencies or different types of bank accounts.

5.1.3 Process of Electronic Payment System

- Electronic payment systems have been in operations since 1960s and have been expanding rapidly as well as growing in complexity.
- After the development of conventional payment system, EFT (Electronic Fund Transfer) based payment system came into existence.
- It was first electronic based payment system, which does not depend on a central processing intermediary.
- An electronic fund transfer is a financial application of EDI (Electronic Data Interchange), which sends credit card numbers or electronic cheques via secured private networks between banks and major corporations.

- To use EFT to clear payments and settle accounts, an online payment service will need to add capabilities to process orders, accounts and receipts.
- But a landmark came in this direction with the development of digital currency.
- The nature of digital currency or electronic money mirrors that of paper money as a means of payment. As such, digital currency payment systems have the same advantages as paper currency payment, namely anonymity and convenience.
- As in other Electronic Payment Systems, (i.e. EFT based and intermediary based) here too security during the transaction and storage is a concern, although from the different perspective, for digital currency systems double spending, counterfeiting, and storage become critical issues whereas eavesdropping and the issue of liability (when charges are made without authorizations) is important for the notational funds transfer.
- Fig. 5.1 shows digital currency based payment system.

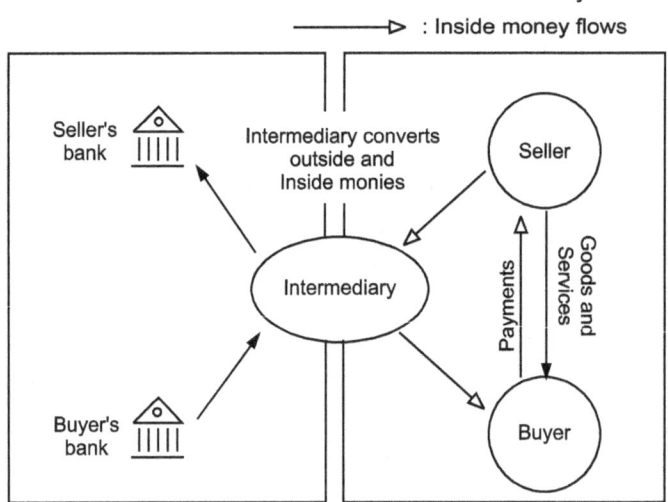

Fig. 5.1: Electronic payment system

- In Fig. 5.1, it is shown that intermediary acts as an electronic bank, which converts outside money (for example: Rupees or US $), into inside money (for example: tokens or e-cash), which is circulated within online markets.
- However, as a private monetary system, digital currency has wide ranging impact on money and monetary system with implications extending far beyond more transactional efficiency.

5.2 Types of Electronic Payment System

- At least dozens of electronic payment systems proposed in practice are found.
- The groupings of these can be made into three broad categories on the basis of what information is being transferred online.

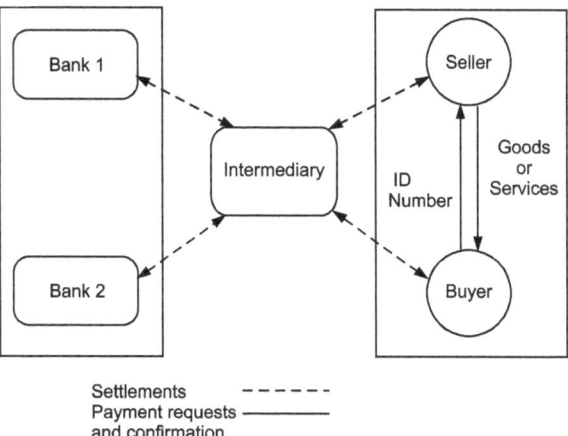

Fig. 5.2

1. **Electronic Funds Transfer (EFT):**

   EFT is the secure transfer of funds via an agreed protocol and system. In the recent years, banking and finance operations have long been dependent on EDI and EFT to ensure that money and securities are transferred to the company or individual that requested the action.

2. **Credit Card:**

   Now-a-days, people are afraid to operate through the internet using their credit card information. Your information can be used against you because of this, one wonders whether any business could be done at all. Customers are far more wary about providing credit information that ever before.

3. **Electronic Cheques:**

   Companies or organizations that pay the vendor through the Internet without sending your personal credit information or banks that use electronic cheques are examples of new services that are reducing the risk of providing credit information.

   - With the growing complexities in the e-commerce transactions, different electronic payment systems have appeared in the last few years.
   - At least dozens of electronic payment systems proposed or already in practice are found.
   - The grouping can be made on the basis of what information is being transferred online.
   - Basically six types of electronic payment systems:
     1. PC-Banking,
     2. Credit Cards,
     3. Electronic Cheques (i-cheques),
     4. Micro payment,
     5. Smart Cards, and
     6. E-Cash.
   - Kalakota and Whinston (1996) identified three types of electronic payment systems:
     1. Digital Token based electronic payment systems,
     2. Smart Card based electronic payment system, and
     3. Credit based electronic payment systems.

Dennis (2001) classified electronic payment system into two categories:

1. Electronic Cash, and
2. Electronic Debit-Credit Card Systems.

Thus, electronic payment system can be broadly divided into four general types (Anderson, 1998):

1. Online Credit Card Payment System,
2. Electronic Cheque System,
3. Electronic Cash System, and
4. Smart Card based Electronic Payment System.

- Following table shows Three broad categories of Electronic Payment Systems.

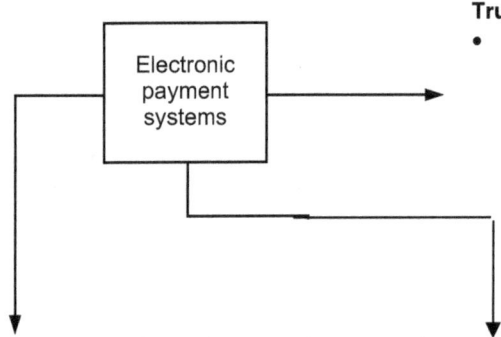

Trusted third party:

- It maintains all sensitive information such as bank account, credit card numbers and so on for its clients including buyers, sellers. When there is a transaction, order information is transmitted along with information about payment confirmation and clearing. This does not include sensitive information. No real financial transaction is done online.

Variations of digital cash, electrical money and coins:

- Difference of this from the other two categories are not due to simply the anonymity they afford, but the fact of what is being transferred in 'value' or 'money' itself.
- Digital money is just a convenient form of existing money, since digital money is created against existing money. In the long run, digital money may be created on its own if users accept it on its face value, which will be determined by how dependable its issuers are. All money are only as good as their users.
- Intercepting a message is an outright theft of your property, not just information. This differs from the second category wherein, some can commit fraud by lifting your message.
- Digital currency is very flexible since, it can be made to behave like electronic cheques situation warrants.
- Digital money currency are an encrypted serial number representing money, but money in all sense they are convertible to real money if desired. It took hundreds of years before people accepted paper money and cheques as payment.

Extension of the conventional notational fund transfer:

- In credit card transactions, sensitive information is being exchanged. Banks meanwhile, receive the information and adjust buyers and merchants accounts accordingly. The information being transmitted online in this case is encrypted for security. This type is now the mainstay of online payment methods, because consumers are familiar with this system and current players have vested interest in extending that system to the Internet. With proper caution and encryption, the internet may be more secure than phone lines for this same old payments methods.

5.3 Payment Types

- Payments are of two types which involves flow of funds inside corporations they are:
  1. Payments received from your customers, and
  2. Payments made to your suppliers.
- E-commerce helps in reducing these expenses by streamlining the cash collection and payment operations.
- While in other hand automating the supply chain, the receipt and payment processing functions could be automated along with the rest of the supply chain.
- The receipt of an actual product or conformation of delivery to the customer could automatically be deposited when they are received though the user of credit card software.

Receipt of Payments

- Receipt payments are from three sources:
  1. Retail customers,
  2. Wholesale customers, and
  3. Various miscellaneous payments.
- Before the advent of online electronic payment methodologies all the payment were received generally in cash or cheques and periodically the organisation would make a physical deposit at a bank.
- Modern electronic payment methods have made it simpler and transfer through the use of wire transfer making the funds transfer, possible without a physical deposit.

5.4 Traditional Payment System

- Traditional payment system uses currency, coins and cheques. Currency and coins in this payment system can be used to mediate transactions by physical exchange.
- Even though cash is legal tender for the payment of debts, it leaves no audit trails.
- Number of people ask for written receipts to show proof of payment when they pay a debt or purchase goods with cash.
- As an alternative to cash, number of people write cheques that tell their depository institution to transfer funds to the person/enterprise named on the cheque.
- The benefits and limitations are there in the cheque clearing process, cheque float and cheque information.
- The other systems which are recently in use are given below:
  1. Value exchange systems,
  2. Electronic Funds Transfer (EFT) system,
  3. Automatic deposit of payrolls and Social security payments,
  4. Bill payments by telephone,

5. Credit card systems,
6. National networks,
7. Shared terminal systems,
8. GIRO transfers,
9. Non-bank networks, and
10. Point of sale payment systems.
- Home banking has developed in many countries because of the reduced cost of computer and communication technology.
- In this banking, computers use connections over telephone lines or cable TV networks to access a depository institution's account records.
- Most allow people to check their account balances, pay their bills and transfer funds among accounts.
- Number of this banking also allow people to keep home budget, accounting and tax records in an organised fashion.
- People who use a home banking network can select an item to buy from an electronic catalogue, order the goods, transfer funds from savings to a checking account to replenish its balance.
- These people may also be able to record the item in the proper home budget category and note whether, it is a deductible item for tax planning.

Conventional Vs. Electronic Payment System

- To get into the depth of electronic payment process, it is better to understand the processing of conventional or traditional payment system.
- A conventional or traditional process of payment and settlement involves a buyer-to-seller transfer of cash or payment information (i.e., cheque and credit cards).
- The actual settlement of payment takes place in the financial processing network.
- A cash payment requires a buyer's withdrawals form his/her bank account, a transfer of cash to the seller, and the seller's deposit of payment to his/her account.
- Non-cash payment mechanisms are settled by adjusting i.e. crediting and debiting the appropriate accounts between banks based on payment information conveyed via cheque or credit cards.

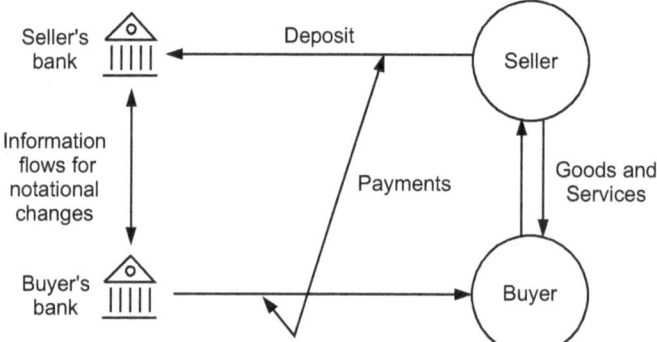

Fig. 5.3: Conventional/Traditional Payment System
- Fig. 5.3 is simplified diagram for both cash and non-cash transactions.

- Cash moves from the buyers bank to sellers bank through face-to-face exchange in the market.
- If a buyer uses a non-cash method of payment, payment information instead of cash flows from the buyer to the seller, and ultimate payments are settled between affected banks, who notationally adjust accounts based on payment information.

5.5 Value Exchange Systems

- Value Exchange Systems can work much like cheque clearing systems, although they transfer assets other than claims on demand deposits.
- The first and important widespread development of value exchange involved the use of credit cards.
- In Value Exchange System, credit card holders IOUs were exchanged for cash balances and subsequently these have been used to transfer debits to both demand deposits and other accounts.
- Accounts used for value exchange, in addition to demand deposits and credit card lines, include balances in individual's margin accounts held with stock brokers, balances in accounts held with money market, mutual funds and accounts held with other financial institutions.
- The key element necessary for a value exchange is that of the value of the item exchanged can be readily determined and agreed upon.
- IOUs of credit card customers and margin account customers have a fixed monetary value, as do shares in Money Market Mutual Funds (MMMF).
- Shares in other funds can also be exchanged if fractional share withdrawals are allowed when the net asset value per share in not equal to an even rupee.

5.6 Credit Card System

- A credit card is a plastic card having a magnetic number and code on it.
- It has some fixed amount to spend and customer has to repay the spend amount after sometime.
- It seeks to extend the functionality of existing credit cards for use as online shopping payment tools.
- This payment system has been widely accepted by consumers and merchants throughout the world, and by far the most popular methods of payments especially in the retail markets.
- Credit card is an instrument issued by bankers to enable credit purchases and cash withdrawals.
- The name itself makes it clear that it is a pre-approved loan which the customer uses.
- Credit Card is an instrument carrying a pre sanctioned credit limit by an issuing banker to its holder. It is an instrument facilitating current purchases to be paid in future.
- This form of payment system has several advantages, which were never available through the traditional modes of payment.
- Some of the most important are: privacy, integrity, compatibility, good transaction efficiency, acceptability, convenience, mobility, low financial risk and anonymity.

- Added to all these, to avoid the complexity associated with the digital cash or electronic-cheques, consumers and vendors are also looking at credit card payments on the internet as one of possible time-tested alternative.
- But, this payment system has raised several problems before the consumers and merchants.
- Online credit card payment seeks to address several limitations of online credit card payments for merchant including lack of authentication, repudiation of charges and credit card frauds.
- It also seeks to address consumer fears about using credit card such as having to reveal credit information at multiple sites and repeatedly having to communicate sensitive information over the Internet.

Fig. 5.4: Master card/Credit card

- Basic process of Online Credit Card Payment System is very simple.
- If consumers want to purchase a product or service, they simply send their credit card details to the service provider involved and the credit card organization will handle this payment like any other.
- This can be understood very easily with the format, (See Fig. 5.5) of Credit Card Payment Form.

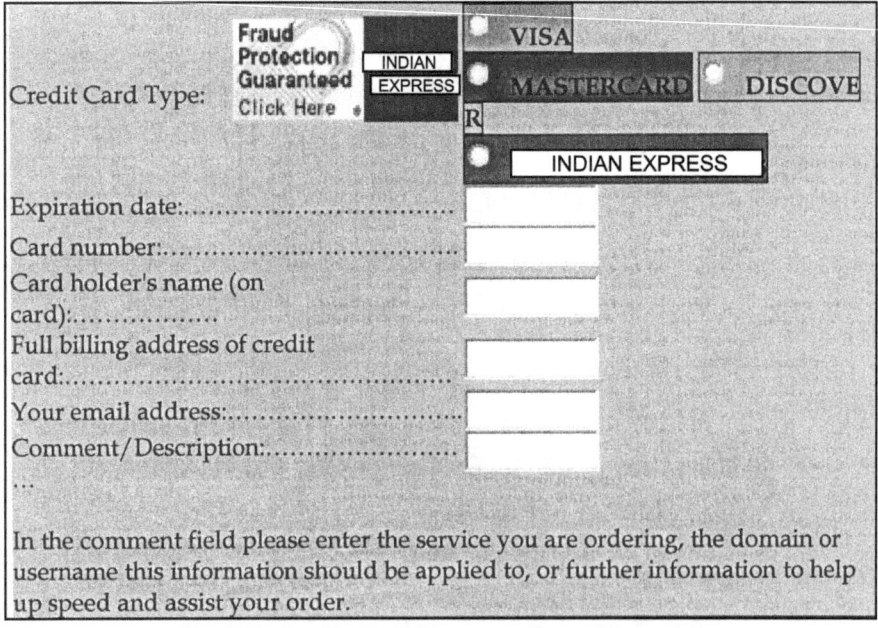

Fig. 5.5: Credit Card Payment Form (Sample)

Charge Authorization

* Do you authorize us to charge your credit card? By clicking "Yes" or signing below, (type in your name if submitting online) you hereby authorize, (any particular company) to use the above credit card to bill you for products ordered or services rendered, (which includes setup fees, normal monthly fees and any future services you request), until such time as you cancel such services, and you hereby state that you have the legal authority to use this credit card:

```
 ○ Yes   ○ No   | SIGNATURE:  [              ]
```

* Kalakota Whinston (1996), break credit card payment on online networks into three basic categories:
  1. Payment using clean credit card details,
  2. Payment using encrypted credit card details, and
  3. Payment using third party verification.

Credit Limit

* Each credit card holder shall be extended a credit limit.
* By Credit limit we mean the amount of credit sanctioned by the issuing bank to the card user.
* The amount sanctioned depends on the ability of a card user to repay which eventually depends on the card users salary.
* The card-issuing bank would ascertain the credit limit of its customer on the basis of his/her monthly/annual take home salary.
* For self employed i.e. business persons the credit limit is determined by the income generated by the business they carry.

Use of Credit Card

* A credit card would carry a definite credit limit upto which the card user would be allowed to spend.
* This credit limit is classified into:
  1. Cash withdrawal limit, and
  2. Credit Purchase limit.
* Cash withdrawal limit is a certain percentage of the total credit limit.
* For example A card user has a credit limit of Rs. 40,000/- of which say 20% is the cash withdrawal limit. In this case the card user can withdraw an amount equal to Rs. 8,000/- from the ATMs of the card issuing bank or any other ATM with which the card-issuing bank has ATM sharing agreement. The cardholder can have credit purchases worth Rs.32, 000/- thereby exhausting the entire credit limit.

- Credit card is not a generally accepted instrument. Hence, before making credit purchases one should ensure that the merchant establishment (i.e. the seller) does accept the card.

Advantages of using a Credit Card

1. Instantaneous purchase without cash.
2. No need to carry huge cash for completing transactions.
3. Reasonable acceptability.
4. Since, it is pre-approved loan, it can be used at any time especially in times of crisis.
5. Repayment over a period, that too in small installments, is possible.

Disadvantages of using a Credit Card

1. If the etiquettes of repayments are not followed could put its user in debt trap.
2. It could instigate unwanted purchases, which would not have been done if the person did not have the card at all.

5.7 Electronic Fund Transfer (EFT)

- EFT stands for Electronic Funds Transfer.
- EFT is a system of transferring money from one bank account directly to another without any paper money changing hands.
- One of the most widely-used EFT programs is Direct Deposit, in which payroll is deposited straight into an employee's bank account, although EFT refers to any transfer of funds initiated through an electronic terminal, including credit card, ATM, Fedwire and Point-Of-Sale (POS) transactions.
- It is used for both credit transfers, such as payroll payments, and for debit transfers, such as mortgage payments.

1. **Definition:**

- Electronic Funds Transfer is the paperless act of transmitting money through a computer network.

OR

- Electronic funds transfer (EFT) is the electronic exchange, transfer of money from one account to another, either within a single financial institution or across multiple institutions, through computer-based systems.

OR

- Electronic funds transfer means the online and computer transfer of money from one bank account to other bank account.

OR

- EFT (Electronic funds transfer) is the electronic exchange, transfer of money from one account to another, either within a single financial institution or across multiple institutions, through computer-based systems.

2. Basic Concept:

- Use of technology in the field of banking could be registered with the advent of MICR cheques. By MICR, we mean Magnetic Ink Character Recognition.

- These cheques were introduced with the objective of ensuring faster clearing. The MICR technology is based on the system of coded language. Each individual instrument (cheque) carries an MICR code line. This MICR code line contains numbers.

- These numbers indicate:

  1. First 6 digits conveying the cheque number.

  2. The next 9 digits are broken into 3 parts of 3 digits each. The first three digits stand for city code, next three for the bank code and the last three signify the branch code.

  3. To the right of these 9 digits are two digits with a reasonable gap between the two. These two digits stand for the type of account i.e. whether savings, current or cash credit etc.

- Coding of such comprehensive information in a single line enables quick sorting of cheques as per their drawee branch and city. This helps the bankers to claim their money quickly from the concerned bankers.

- Banks used reader sorters to ensure that the instruments are sorted on the basis of the information (data) captured in the MICR code line.

- The bankers use the same MICR code line to encode the information mentioned in the cheque.

- The collecting banker is required to sort these cheques as per the claims and these duly sorted and processed instruments are exchanged through the clearing house to reach the drawee bank.

- The process of clearing becomes quick due to the ability of the bankers to present their claims fast on account of MICR technology.

- Technological development led to the introduction of the following:

  1. EFT (Electronic Funds Transfer).

  2. ECS (Electronic Clearing System).

  3. RTGS (Real Time Gross Settlement).

- Electronic funds transfer is a system in which funds are electronically transferred from one bank account to another within 48 hours.

- The customer gives authority to a banker to debit his account.

- There is a wide variety of users of EFT techniques.

- Other uses often required Automated Clearing Houses (ACHs).

- One of the first uses was for the transfer of computerised credit card clearing information.

- The most sophisticated EFT operations are geared to ACH's and it can provide either:

   Credit transfers : The initiating institution sends funds through the system to be deposited in the recipient's account, or

   Debit transfers : The initiating institution withdraws funds from the depositor's account.

- It is similar to standing instructions given by the customer to his bank. The customer has to sign a form that authorises his bank to deduct payment on a certain date.

- He/She is required to give details such as beneficiaries account number, the amount to be deducted and other details of payment.

- This information is programmed into his/her account.

- As per this instruction on a specified date customer's account is debited and beneficiaries account is credited.

- By electronic funds transfer, we mean an arrangement wherein funds get transferred from one place to another without manual efforts.

- An electronic fund transfer involves transfer of funds taking the help of computers, and telecommunication.

- The concept of electronic funds transfer is very comprehensive.

- Any transaction in bank that involves a transfer that too via an electronic mode should be treated as Electronic Funds Transfers. This transfer could be a debit entry or a credit entry.

- The variants of electronic funds transfer are:

   1. Electronic Clearing System (ECS), and
   2. Real Time Gross Settlement (RTGS).

1. Electronic Clearing System (ECS)

- Electronic clearing system is an improved version of advanced paper based payment system.

- Now ECS is very commonly resorted to, where payments are in bulk and are to be made to large number of people.

- The frequency of such payment is another factor that led to introduction of a system like electronic clearing system.

- One can take examples of payment of interest and dividend by companies, payment of income tax refund, salaries etc.,

- The paying agencies prefer the electronic route over the manual route. The reason behind their preferences for electronic route is the drawbacks associated with the paper based payment system.

- They are as follows:
  1. Paper based payment system involves drawing/printing of an instrument, signing of the same, despatching them to the respective beneficiaries and ensuring that all claims/liabilities are cleared through the drawer's bank. The efforts involved in this process are too much and it is not as cost effective as the existing electronic clearing system.
  2. Paper based system also requires preservation of these documents which is difficult.
  3. The instruments dispatched by the drawer could be lost in transit and are also prone to material alterations. Therefore, an option to the paper based payment system came in the form of electronic clearing system.
- Electronic Clearing System involves transfer of data, which enables transfer of funds from the user of this service to the beneficiaries.
- It is very clear from the preceding discussion that ECS has been introduced because of the time and formalities involved in paper based clearing system.
- With growth of trade and business, the paper based clearing system was turning slow. Hence, quick transfer of funds was essential which came in the form of the Electronic Clearing System.
- Let us understand the parties involved in Electronic Clearing System.
- Let us understand that since clearing is a function of the Central Bank, the role of Central Bank in an electronic fund transfer is necessary. In fact, the Central Bank facilitates such transfer of funds.
- The other parties to ECS are the user of the service and the beneficiary.
- The user of the service is the person, institution, organisation that would want to transfer, or credit money and beneficiary would be one who would receive the money from the user.
- The user of this service could also be termed as the subscriber. The subscriber would obviously involve his bank called the sponsor bank in it.
- So we have:
  1. The clearing bank (RBI).
  2. The user of the service (the subscriber).
  3. The user's bank (sponsor bank).
  4. The beneficiary(who receives the payment).
- **The working of the Electronic Clearing System:** We must understand that there are two types of clearing under the Electronic Clearing System.

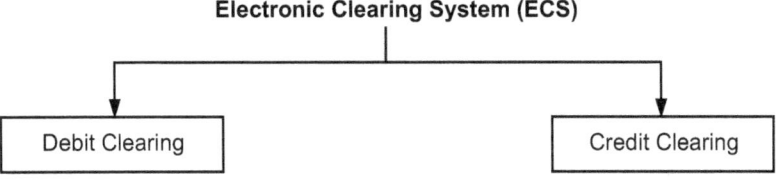

Fig. 5.6: Types of ECS

(i) Electronic Clearing System (Credit clearing):

- ECS (Electronic Clearing System) credit clearing would have a single user who would wish to transfer money to multiple accounts. For example an employer institution may want to credit salaries of its large number of employees. So this process involves multiple credits and a single debit.

- In this case, the user of the facility would very carefully prepare data about payment. This would be prepared using computer and later copied on the CD/floppy or any other removable electronic disk to hand over to his bank. i.e. the sponsor bank.

- This information given by the user would be accompanied with a mandate given to the clearing house to debit his account which he holds with the sponsor bank and credit the multiple accounts specified by him.

- The sponsor bank would hand over this data to that clearing house where the beneficiaries' bank is located.

- The clearing house would be authorised to debit the sponsor bank's accounts and credit the bank accounts of the beneficiaries.

(ii) Electronic Clearing System (Debit clearing):

- It is exactly opposite to credit clearing arrangement.

- Under the Electronic debit Clearing System there involves a single credit and multiple debits.

- This is useful from the viewpoint of the customers as large number of payments are collected through this system. For example, Telephone bills, electricity bills, payment of LIC premia etc.

- In this case, the user of the service is the institution/organisation that collects the payments, while the customer whose bills are being paid is the beneficiary.

- The clearing house, beneficiary's bank and the user's bank are the intermediaries. Before subscribing to this service the beneficiary is required to apply for this service by filling in a prescribed form.

- This form contains the information about the beneficiary's bank accounts. This form is infact a mandate given by a customer in favour of the collecting banker (i.e. the user's bank) to collect money from the beneficiary's bank.

- This mandate is an instruction given by the beneficiary to his bank to make payments whenever claims (for which the mandate has been given) on his account accrue.

- So the preceding discussion makes it very clear that making payments of bills is facilitated through Electronic Clearing System.

- The user institution for example telephone exchange, gives the details of beneficiary's (customer's) account and amount to be debited.

- Compiling this data on a computer does this and copying the same on either a floppy or a C.D., this is accompanied by a mandate given by the beneficiary.

- The clearing institution on the basis of the information available, debits the bank accounts of the beneficiaries and credits the account of the sponsor bank who in turn credits the account of its customer i.e. the user.

Advantages of Electronic Clearing System (ECS):

1. It saves time, money and energy involved in printing paper instruments.

2. The risk associated with loss of instruments in transit is done away with. The other formalities to be completed post loss of such instruments are also done away with.

3. Timely service to its clients is provided.

4. The customers do not have to go to their branches to deposit these paper instruments.

5. In case of electronic debit clearing, customers do not have to wait in long queues. They infact are not required to go to the bill payment centres at all.

6. In case of electronic debit clearing system, the data about the amount of debit is known and accordingly cash arrangement can be made.

2. Real Time Gross Settlement (RTGS)

- RTGS stands for Real Time Gross Settlement.

- The RTGS system was introduced in India on March 26, 2004.

- It is a comprehensive and secured on line payment and settlement solution.

- It is set up, operated and managed by the Reserve Bank of India.

- Prior to the introduction of the RTGS we had what was known as the Net Settlement System, wherein the settlement of transactions was netted usually at the end of the day.

- But under the RTGS system the inter bank payment instructions are processed throughout the day.

- These instructions are settled on individual basis, transaction by transaction, throughout the day.

- Since, the settlement is continuous it is called real time and since the same is not at the end of the day, (where debits and credits are netted and the balance if any settled) but on individual basis, it is also termed as gross. This is how we derive the RTGS system.

- To be a part of the RTGS system banks need to maintain the RTGS settlement account with the RBI. This account is linked to the current account of the bank with the RBI.

- The current account of the bank would cross fund the RTGS settlement account of that bank. This funding would be for a day.

- The balances in the RTGS settlement account would be transferred back to the bank's current account that very day. This makes the transaction an intra day transaction and the RTGS settlement account an intra day account.

- Hence, it is expected of banks to maintain reasonable balances in the RTGS settlement account that they hold with the RBI.
- There are two types of funds transfer under the RTGS. They are:

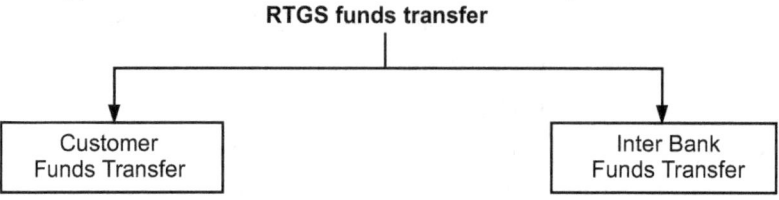

Fig. 5.7: RTGS types

(A) Customer Funds transfer:

- Under the customer fund transfer facility an individual can use this facility to transfer money from his account to the account of the beneficiary.
- The customer funds transfer takes two forms viz. Outgoing, and Incoming.

(i) Outgoing Funds Transfer:

- For seeking the outgoing facility, a customer of a bank would have to submit an application form duly filled.
- He/She needs to fill in an application form which is meant for RTGS. Usually banks provide a common application form for various remittances such as DD/MT/TT and now RTGS.
- In case of an RTGS system the parties involved are:
    1. The originating bank, from where RTGS is sought.
    2. The customer, who wishes to send money through RTGS.
    3. The beneficiary, to whom the money is sent.
    4. The clearing institution, the RBI.
    5. The Receiving bank, who receives money on behalf of the beneficiary or where beneficiary holds an account. It is also known as the destination branch.
- The customer would fill in an application form and submit it to the originating bank.
- The application would mention the account number and name of the person along with the name and place of the bank where money is to be remitted.
- The customer (remitter) has to ensure that the bank on which he is drawing the RTGS should be an RTGS enabled bank.
- Unless banks get linked under the RTGS system, they can not access this facility. So the customer and the originating bank should confirm that the destination bank (branch) is a member of the RTGS.
- The originating branch would receive the payment from the customer in cash or debit his account as the case may be and then inform the destination branch online.

(ii) Incoming Funds Transfer:

- The destination branch would receive a message pertaining to crediting the account of the beneficiary.
- On receipt of such a message, the authenticity of the same would be assessed and funds would be credited to the account of the beneficiary.
- The name and account number would be confirmed and the funds would be credited.

(B) Inter bank funds transfer:

- The inter bank funds transfer would also work the same way except for the fact that in place of an individual customer, there would be a bank.
- It is a bank to bank funds transfer.
- The system confers upon both its user and provider a number of benefits. Some of these benefits are as follows:
    1. It minimises cost involved in transfer of funds.
    2. It maximises benefits by transferring funds quickly.
    3. Increases the velocity of circulation of money by transferring money in no time.
    4. Reduces risks associated with other paper based modes of transfer.
    5. Provides liquidity, (cash) to the beneficiary on the date of transaction itself.

Advantages of EFT:

1. No more lost or stolen checks.
2. Quicker access to your funds.
3. Increased security of information.
4. Less time spent on claims tracking.
5. Expedited patient account reconciliation.
6. Easier retrieval of archived data.

- There are many benefits of using EFT through ecommerce website for financial transactions; some of them are as follows:
    1. Payments through EFT are much safer as compared to that of the cheques. There are no issues like lost or stolen cheques.
    2. Payments through EFT are quicker as compared to that of the cheques.
    3. Payments through EFT are quite convenient and easy.
    4. This is capable of eliminating the need to deposit and obtain the pay cheque or cash your pay cheque.
    5. Payments of EFT facilitate online baking though ecommerce website.
    6. Other benefits include lessen down of administration cost, greater security and increased efficiency.

5.8 Paperless Bills

- You may soon be able to pay all bills at a single website or internet.

- Indian consumers also now-a-days are flooded with bills almost everyday; bills for utilities, on internet, bills for medical expenses, bills for electricity, bills for income tax, bills for house taxes, bills for hotels, bills from post offices, bills for housing rent, bills for rental of various items and so on.

- The paper trail of cheques, bills and receipts is confusing at best, but the internet is offering a solution, electronic bill presentment and payment.

- Fig. 5.8 shows procedure for paperless bills.

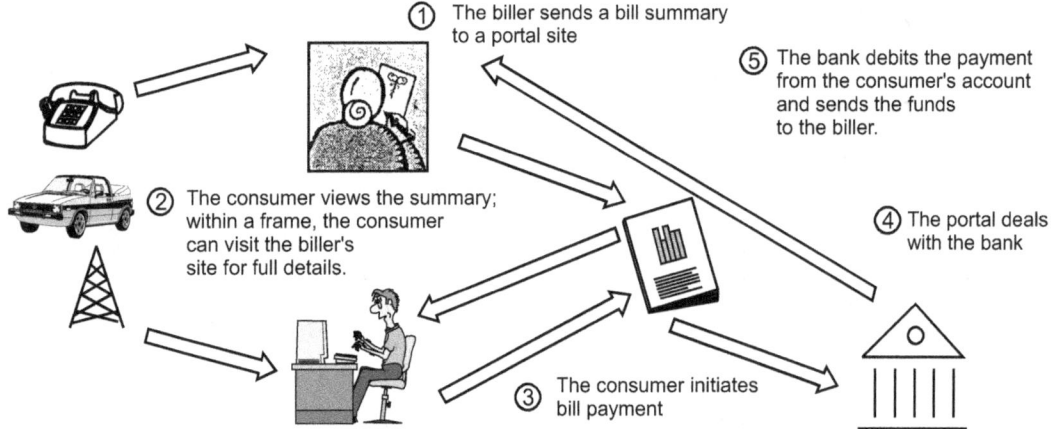

Fig. 5.8: Paperless Bills

What is Paperless Billing?

- Paperless billing is a service that allows T-Mobile subscribers to receive their billing information online rather than in a printed, paper format.

- Paperless billing subscribers will not to receive a paper bill in the mail and will instead receive an e-mail notification each month directing them to view and pay their bill online at the My T-Mobile Web site.

- Paperless billing is not available to certain types of accounts such as government, business.

- T-Mobile must receive full payment on at least one bill before you are eligible. A valid e-mail address and My T-Mobile account are required.

Note: T-Mobile example is given because no company in India is offering a very good paperless billing service yet.

1. **Automatic Deposits of Payrolls and Social Security Payments:**

   Regular payments to the same individuals can be made efficiently and effectively through automatic clearing homes.

As illustrated in electronic credit [See Fig. 5.9 (a)], the bank of the paying organisation gives the ACH a computer tape that provides information on the banks and account number of the organisation employee who are to be paid. The clearing house then credits the accounts of the receiving banks with the total due and provides data indicating which depositor's accounts should be credited. The bank that submits the tape provides funds to the clearing house if its payments exceeds its receipts at the clearing house from other sources.

For ACH operations to succeed, all organisations that submit tapes must use the same format and method of identifying the account numbers and amounts of funds transferred.

2. Bill Payment by Telephones:

This technique can be made efficiently and effectively through ACHs, and uses telephones or cable television lines. For making payments, the depositor dials the bank, enters his/her account number, the amount he/she wishes to pay and the bank and accounts numbers of the recipient of the payment. When the depositor provides data electronically the payment information can be verified and entered directly on a magnetic tape for submission to ACH, which will make the appropriate credit transfers.

3. Credit and Debit Transfers through an ACH:

An electronic credit transfer funds and information simultaneously from the payer to the payee. The debit transfer funds from the payer's bank to the payee's bank, but only after the payer gives the payee valid authorization to do so. Fig. 5.9 shows credit and debit transfer through ACH.

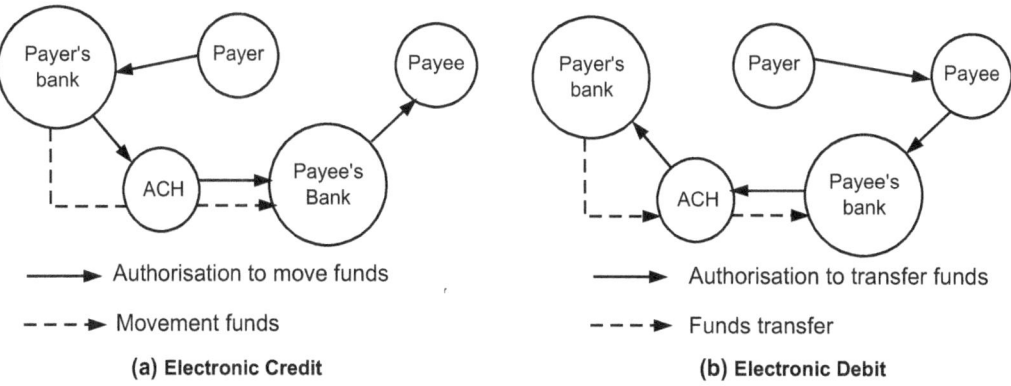

(a) Electronic Credit   (b) Electronic Debit

Fig. 5.9: Credit and Debit transfer through ACH

4. GIRO Funds Transfer Systems:

GIRO Funds Transfer System are widely used in Europe and it occurs when an individual instructs a financial institution to make a payment to another individual or firm who banks with another institution. The originating institution then transfers both funds and payment information telling which account should be credited to the receiving institution for this reason only one transfer is required for both funds and transmitted information. EFT system can make similar transfers if appropriate payment information is entered on magnetic tape and sent to an ACH.

5. **Point of Sale Payments System:**

Point of sale payment systems are more complicated and critical than payroll, pre-authorised transfer, or bill cheque payment systems. These systems require a two-stage transfer of information and funds, one transfer requires that information on the status of the customer's account be transferred to the point of sale so that the expenditure can be authorized.

These systems transfer requires that funds be transferred from the account to the retailer's account. This system has been slower to develop than other EFT functions. Fig. 5.10 shows typical point of sale EFT transfer system.

These transfers are more complicated and complex than pre-authorised transfers. In this system a customer first must prove that he/she is authorized to transfer funds from the named account. Usually, this is provided with a personal identification number or as secret code at the point of sale and second, the merchant must verify that sufficient funds are available to be transferred. This procedure is done by contacting a credit card or debit card authorization centre that has a record of the customer account.

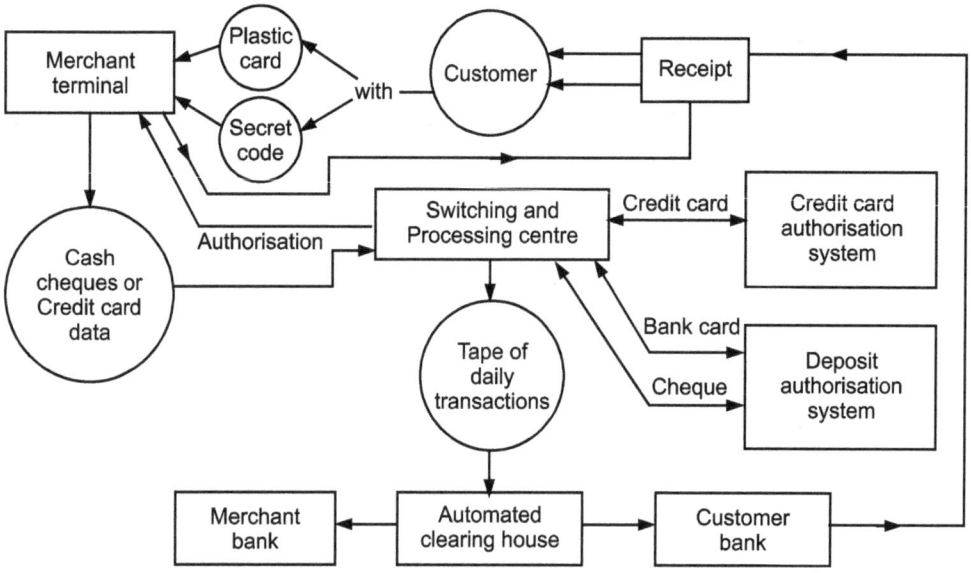

Fig. 5.10: Point of sale EFT transfers

5.9 Modern Payment System

* Modern Payment System are done through:
    1. PC Banking,
    2. Credit cards,
    3. Micropayments,

4. E-cash,

5. Smart cards, and

6. Electronic cheques or i-cheques.

1. PC Banking:

*   PC banking has been developed after the introduction of PCs and modems.

*   This banking involves externally accessible bank systems.

*   Earlier, payments were made to companies by retail customers through direct debit i.e. automatic withdrawals from the customers bank account or ATMs i.e. Automatic Teller Machine.

*   Fig. 5.11 shows PC banking network.

*   Today, there are numerous payment options.

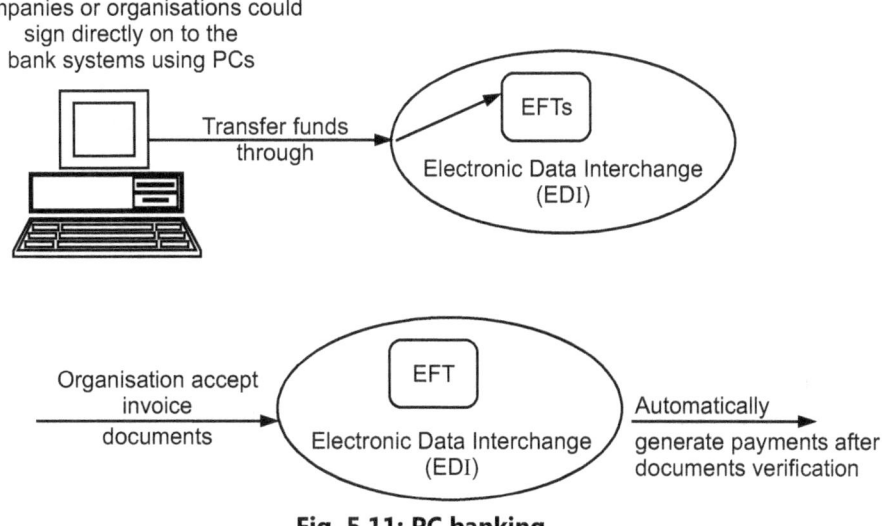

Fig. 5.11: PC banking

2. Credit Cards:

*   History of credit cards starts in using credit cards in 1958-1960, when the Bank of America issued certain cards in California to select group of users to pay for products by participating merchants, without cash.

*   The advantage of using credit cards is that users no longer have to carry cash to pay for a product.

*   Earlier, a credit card was provided imprinting a number. This was sufficient and efficient to complete the transaction.

*   Electronic processing was found necessary for online authorization and depositing functions. In the late 1990-1995, the Internet provided and unlimited opportunity if businesses could get paid for products or services sold electronically.

*   The credit card processing is simple and easy.

- After receiving from a customer details like his credit card number, name, expiration date, two more things should occur to complete the transaction.
  1. The electronic credit card information must be turned into an actual deposit at your financial institution.
  2. The credit card must be authenticated with the credit card firm or organisations so that you can receive an authorization number. This provides guarantee that the funds will be made available to you when you complete your deposits by ensuring the user of the card is not over his credit limited and that the card is not stolen.
- Fig. 5.12 shows processing of credit cards payment.

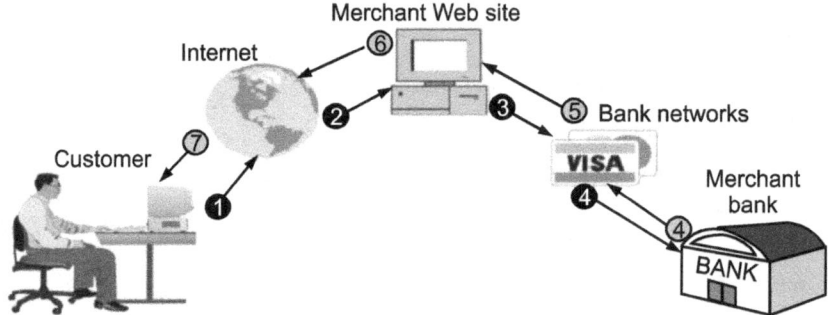

Fig. 5.12: Credit card payment process

3. Micro payments (Electronic wallet or Microtransactions):

- This payments is a very small fee paid when a visitor is sent from another website to your site.
- The payment is usually tracked by a third party and when a specific amount has been accumulated, say rupees thousand, the fee is paid to the website that sent the traffic.
- Micro payment mechanism helps a way for you to encourage other companies to add to your links to their website.
- This payments work based on the registration made within an organisation that verifies and reports on traffic levels between sites and next a very small payment per link or per click is calculated and when the total owing reaches a specified threshold, the payment is released from the customer's actual or virtual bank account to the vendor's account.
- Fig. 5.13 shows micropayment model.

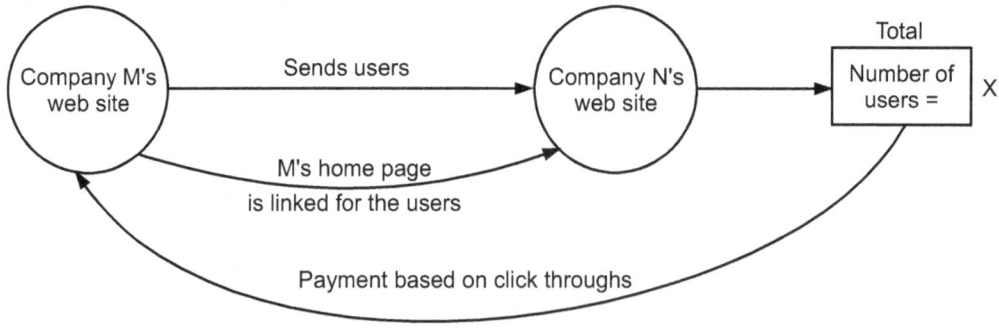

Fig. 5.13: Micro payments

5. Electronic Cheques:

- Electronic cheques also known as Internet cheques or i- cheques.

- They are used to make electronic payments between two parties through an intermediary and not very much different from the current cheque processing system.

- Electronic cheques address the electronic needs of millions of businesses, which today exchange traditional paper cheques with the other vendors, consumers and government.

- The e-cheque method was deliberately created to work in much the same way as conventional paper cheque.

- An account holder will issue an electronic document that contains the name of the financial institution, the payer's account number, the name of payee and amount of cheque.

- Most of the information is in uncoded form. Like a paper cheques e-cheques also bear the digital equivalent of signature: a computed number that authenticates the cheque from the owner of the account.

- Digital chequing payment system seeks to extend the functionality of existing chequing accounts for use as online shopping payment tools.

- **Electronic cheque system has following advantages:**

  1. They do not require consumers to reveal account information to other individuals when setting an auction.

  2. They do not require consumers to continually send sensitive financial information over the web.

  3. They are less expensive than credit cards, and

  4. They are much faster than paper based traditional cheque.

- But, this system of payment also has several disadvantages. The disadvantage of electronic cheque system includes their relatively high fixed costs, their limited use only in virtual world and the fact that they can protect the users anonymity. Therefore, it is not very suitable for the retail transactions by consumers, although useful for the government and B2B operations because the latter transactions do not require anonymity, and the amount of transactions is generally large enough to cover fixed processing cost. The process of electronic chequing system can be described using (Fig. 5.14) and follow the following steps.

Step 1: A purchaser fills a purchase order form, attaches a payment advice (electronic cheque), signs it with his private key, (using his signature hardware), attaches his public key certificate, encrypts it using his private key and sends it to the vendor.

Step 2: The vendor decrypts the information using his private key, checks the purchaser's certificates, signature and cheque, attaches his deposit slip, and endorses the deposit attaching his public key certificates. This is encrypted and sent to his bank.

Step 3: The vendor's bank checks the signatures and certificates and sends the cheque for clearance. The banks and clearing houses normally have a private secure data network.

Step 4: When the cheque is cleared, the amount is credited to the vendor's account and a credit advice is sent to him.

Step 5: The purchaser gets a consolidated debit advice periodically.

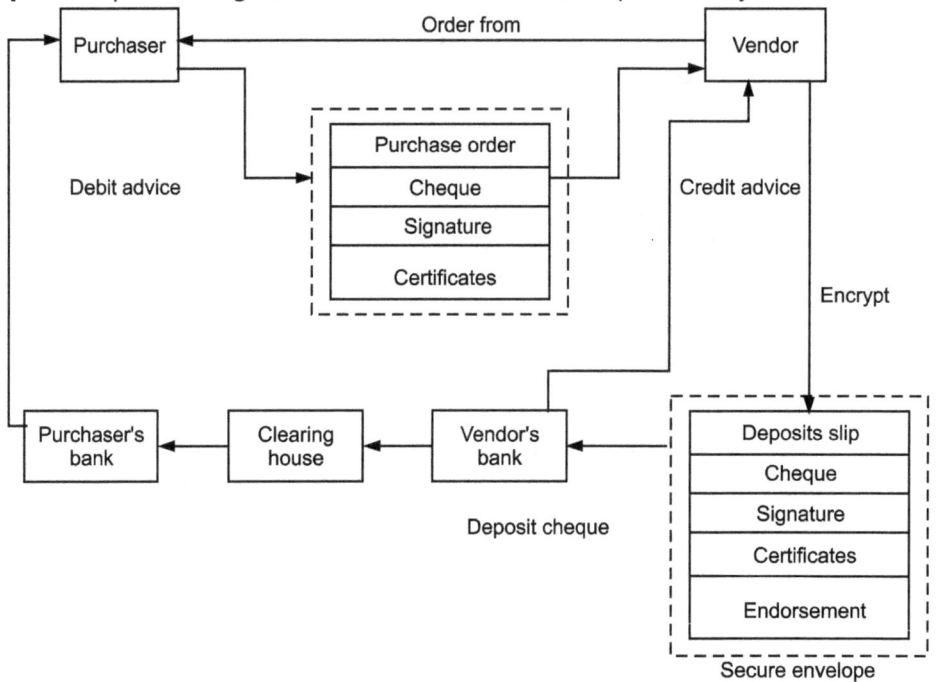

Fig. 5.14: Clearing cheque payment electronically

- E-cheque provide a security rich Internet payment option for businesses and offer an easy entry into electronic commerce without a significant investment in new technologies or legal systems.

5. **Smart Cards:**

- A smart card can be considered as a portable device that contains some non-volatile memory and a microprocessor.

- Smart card contains some kind of an encrypted key that is compared to a secret key contained on the user's processor.

- Some smart cards have provision to allow users to enter a Personal Identification Number (PIN) code and these are being relatively common with billions of cards expected to use worldwide.

- These smart cards will emerge as the ultimate interface device for the mobile digital economy.

- These smart cards will hold your cash, ID information, house and office keys, subway tokens, all types of preference files and other information.

- A smart card, unlike a credit and debit card, is a card that is embedded with either a microprocessor with a memory chip or only a memory chip with non-programmable logic.

- While the microprocessor can add, delete and otherwise manipulate information on the card, a memory-chip card can undertake only predefined operations.

- Smart cards' are receiving renewed attention as a mode of online payment. They are essentially credit card sized plastic cards with the memory chips and in some cases, with microprocessors embedded in them so as to serve as storage devices for much greater information than credit cards with inbuilt transaction processing capability.

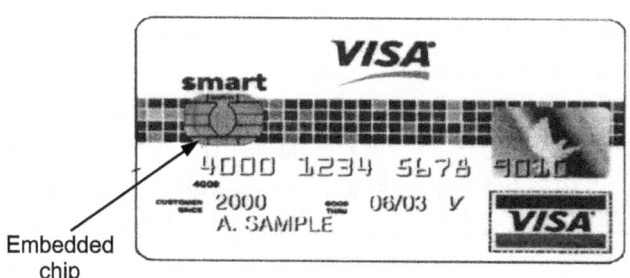

Fig. 5.15: A smart card

- This card also contains some kinds of an encrypted key that is compared to a secret key contained on the user's processor.

- Some smart cards have provision to allow users to enter a Personal Identification Number (PIN) code.

- Smart cards have been in use for well over the two decades now and have been widespread mostly in Europe and Asian Countries.

- Owing to their considerable flexibility, they have been used for a wide range of functions like highway toll payment, as prepaid telephone cards and as stored value debit cards.

- However, with the recent emergence of e-commerce, these devices are increasingly being viewed as a particularly appropriate method to execute online payment system with considerably greater level of security than credit cards.

- Compared with traditional electronic cash system, smart cards based electronic payment systems do not need to maintain a large real time database.

- They also have advantages, such as anonymity, transfer payment between individual parties, and low transactional handling cost of files.

- Smart cards are also better protected from misuse than, say conventional credit cards, because the smart card information is encrypted.

- Currently, the two smart cards based electronic payment system Mondex and Visa Cash are incompatible in the smart cards and card reader specification.

- Not knowing which smart card system will become market leader; banks around the world are unwilling to adopt either system, let alone other smart card system.

- Therefore, establishing a standard smart card system, or making different system interoperable with one another is critical success factors for smart card based payment system.

- Kalakota and Whinston, classified smart cards based electronic payment system as relationship based smart cards and electronic purses. Electronic purses, which may replace money, are also known as debit card.

- Further Diwan and Singh and Sharma and Diwan, classified smart cards into following categories:

  1. **Memory cards:** This card can be used to store password or pin number. Many telephone cards use these memory cards

  2. **Shared key cards:** It can store a private key such as those used in the public key cryptosystems. In this way, the user can plug in the card to a workstation and workstation can read the private key for encryption or decryption

  3. **Signature carrying card:** This card contains a set of pregenerated random numbers. These numbers can be used to generate electronic cash

  5. **Processor cards:** These cards carry a co-processor that can be used to generate large random numbers. These random numbers can then be used for the assignment as serial numbers for the electronic cash.

- The origin of smart cards can be traced to a frenchman named Ronald Moreno, way back in 1970.

Smart Card Standards		
o Open card Frame work	o Supported by Sun Microsystems, IBM, Oracle and Netscape	o It is a standard for NCs, emphasizes portability and personalization and adopts Java.
o Personal Computer Smart Card (PCSC)	o Proposed by Micro-soft and supported by Schlumberger Electronic Technologies	—
o Sun's Java Card API	o Endorsed by Citibank, Visa, First Union National Bank, Verifone	—
o Motorola Smartcard Systems Business Unit	o Contactless cards using radio	—

- The smart card technology is widely used in countries such as France, Japan, Germany and Singapore to pay for public phone calls, transportation and shopper loyalty programs.
- The basic idea has taken more time to catch on in the US, since highly reliable and fairly inexpensive telecommunication system has favoured the use of credit and debit card.

Smart Card Processing

- Fig. 4.16 shows smart card processing steps are listed below:
    1. User opens account and receives smart card.
    2. User downloads tokens onto card.
    3. User inserts card in reader.
    4. Tokens are transferred from user card to vendor.
    5. Goods delivered.
    6. Vendor redeems tokens.

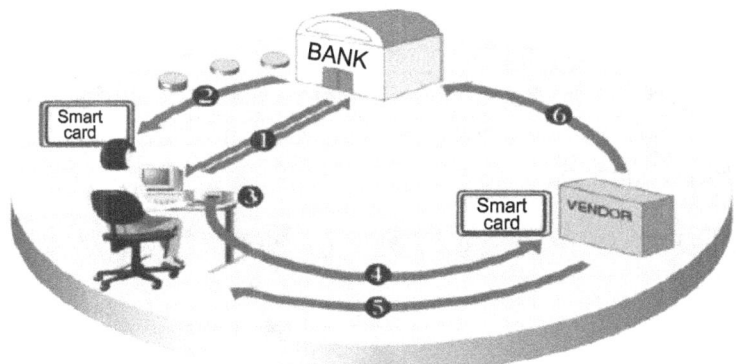

Fig. 5.16: Smart card processing

Types of Smart Cards:

- **Smart cards are of two types:**
    1. Relationship based smart credit cards, and
    2. Electronic purses.

1. **Relationship based smart credit cards**

    (i) **Traditional credit cards:** They are fast evolving into smart cards as consumers demand payment and financial service product, that are user friendly, convenient and reliable.

    (ii) **Relationship based smart card:** This card are an enhancement of existing card services and/or the addition of new services that a financial institution delivers to its customers via a chip-based card or other device.

2. Electronic purses:

This cards are wallet sized smart cards and embedded with programmable microchips that store sums of money for people to use method of cash for every thing from buying food, photocopies etc.

- There are three categories of smart cards are:

  1. **An intelligent memory card:** It contains beside data, some built in logic, usually used to control access to the memory of the card. These cards have certain data processing capabilities.

  2. **A processor card:** It contains own microprocessor and an operating system. These cards can process and store data on their own.

  3. **A memory card:** It stores data. It will need an outside processor to access and work with this data.

- Two other types of cards are:

  1. **Contact-less cards:** They are passed near an antenna to connect via a radio signal. They have both a microchip and an antenna embedded. This allows the smart card to communicate without physical contact.

  2. **Contact smart cards:** They are inserted into a reader or validator for the data to be read. When the card is inserted into the reader, it transfers data to and from the chip via electrical connectors.

5.10 Other Types of Modern Payment System

1. Electronic Cash

- (e-cash) is a new concept in online payment system because it combines computerized convenience with security and privacy that improve on paper cash. Its versatility opens up a host of new markets and applications.

- E-cash presents some characteristics like monetary value, storability and irretrievability, interoperability and security.

- All these characteristics make it more attractive payment system over the Internet.

- The predominance of cash indicates an opportunity for innovative business practice that revamps the purchasing process where consumers are heavy users as cash.

- E-cash is based on cryptographic systems called digital signatures. A pair of numeric keys work in tandem, one for locking (encoding) and other for unlocking (decoding).

- Messages encoded with one numeric key can only be decoded with the other numeric key, not otherwise, the encoding key is kept private and the decoding key is made public.

- E-cash is an electronic or digital form of value storage and value exchange that have limited convertibility into other forms of value and require intermediaries to convert.

- This payment system offers numerous advantages like authority, privacy, good acceptability, low transactions cost, convenience and good anonymity.

- But, this system of payment also has many limitations like poor mobility, poor transaction efficiency and high financial risk, as people are solely responsible for the lost or stolen.

- Gary and Perry, just like real world currency counterpart, electronic cash is susceptible to forgery. It is possible, though increasingly difficult, to create and spend forged e-cash.

E-cash Structure:

- e-cash structure could be identified as a string of bits that represents certain values such as reference number and digital signature, which could be used for the security purpose to prevent forgery and criminal use. But, the structure proposed by Wright needs some extension to make e-cash more secure.

- Therefore, the present model (Fig. 5.17) adds a digital watermark to e-cash structure to protect it from the illegal copy and forgery activities further, the model modified the structure of the reference number to support tractability as shown in the Fig. 5.17.

Currency	Value	Reference	Digital Signature	Digital Watermark

Fig. 5.17: E-cash structure

- The proposed e-cash structure is comparatively better than suggested by Wright, because security issue is given importance of top most priority in the present model.

- But, still there are certain concerns to be addressed for an electronic cash system. For example, who has the right to issue electronic cash? Can every bank issue its own money? If so how do you prevent fraud? And who will monitor the banking operations to protect consumers?

- Many of these concepts relate to the legal and banking regulatory aspects. However all these issues are beyond the scope of the study and therefore, cannot be included here. But, these issues must be addressed before establishing a complete e-cash based payment system.

- **E-Cash Processing (Fig. 5.18 shows processing of e-cash):**
  1. Consumer buys e-cash from Bank.
  2. Bank sends e-cash bits to consumer (after charging that amount plus fee).
  3. Consumer sends e-cash to merchant.
  4. Merchant checks with Bank that e-cash is valid (check for forgery or fraud).
  5. Bank verifies that e-cash is valid.
  6. Parties complete transaction.

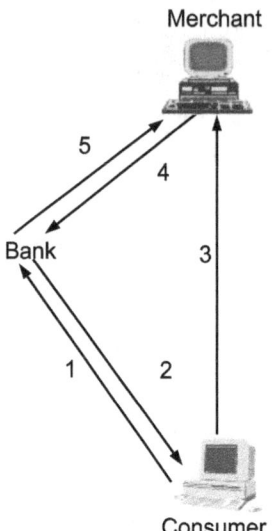

Fig. 5.18: E-cash processing

Advantages:

1. E-cash can be carried around.

2. E-cash is guaranteed by the government and does not normally lose its value in the short range.

3. E-cash is anonymous. Traders cannot normally say who gave a particular currency note.

4. E-cash is universally recognized as having value and accepted as legal tender.

5. Any person having cash can exchange it for goods or services without the help of a third party such as a bank.

6. Privacy of transactions is ensured because of anonymity.

Disadvantages:

1. E-cash is bulky.

2. E-cash is not safe. If you loses your purse you will be lucky to get your cash back.

Comparison of Electronic Payment Systems

- The electronic payment system- the ability to pay electronically for goods and services purchased online- are an integral part of e-commerce and an essential infrastructure for e-commerce models.

- One of the major reasons for the widespread of e-commerce transactions is perhaps the rapid development and growth of various electronic payment systems.

- In the developed countries, credit cards have been used even before the advent of Internet.

- The present part of the study revealed many electronic payment systems and broadly these electronic payment system can be grouped or classified into four categories: Online Credit Card Payment System, Online Electronic Cash System, Electronic Cheque System and Smart Cards based Electronic Payment System.

- These payment systems have numbers of requirements: e.g. security, acceptability, convenience, cost, anonymity, control, and traceability.

- Therefore, instead of focusing on the technological specifications of various electronic payment systems, the researcher have distinguished electronic payment systems based on what is being transmitted over the network; and analyze the difference of each electronic payment system by evaluating their requirements, characteristics and assess the applicability of each system.

- Following table presents the comparison of various electronic payment systems.

Features	Online Credit Card Payment	Electronic Cash	Electronic Cheque	Smart Cards
Actual Payment Time	Paid later	Prepaid	Paid later	Prepaid
Transaction information transfer	The store and bank checks the status of the credit card	Free transfer. No need to leave the name of parties involved	Electronic checks or payment indication must be endorsed	The smart card of both parties make the transfer
Online and offline transactions	Online transactions	Online transactions	Offline transfers are allowed	Offline transfers are allowed.
Bank account involvement	Credit card account makes the payment	No involvement	The bank account makes the payment	The smart card account makes the payment
Users	Any legitimate credit card users	Anyone	Anyone with a bank account	Anyone with a bank or credit card account
Party to which payment is made out	Distributing Bank	Store	Store	Store

contd. ...

Consumer's transaction risk	Most of the risk is borne by the distributing bank, consumers only have to bear part of the risk	Consumer is at risk of the electronic cash getting stolen, lost, or misused	Consumer bears most of the risk, but the consumer can stop check payments at any time	Consumer is at risk of the smart card getting stolen, lost or misused
Current degree of popularity	Credit card organizations check for certification then total the purchases. Therefore, it can be used internationally, and is the most popular payment type	Unable to meet financial internet standards in the areas of expansion potential and inter-nationalism.	Can not meet international standards, therefore its not very popular	Credit card organizations check for certification then total the purchases. Therefore, it can be used internationally and is becoming more widely used.
Anonymity	Partially or entirely anonymous	Entirely anonymous	No anonymity	Entirely anonymous, but if needed, the central processing agency can ask stores to provide information about a consumer
Small payments	Transaction costs are high. Not suitable for small payments	Transaction costs are low, suitable for small payments	Allows stores to accumulate debts until it reaches a limit before paying for it. Suitable for small payments	Transaction costs are low. Allows stores to accumulate debts until it reaches a limit before paying for it. Therefore, it is suitable for small payments

contd. ...

Database safeguarding	Safeguards regular credit card account information	Needs to safeguard a large database, and maintain records of the serial numbers of used electronic cash.	Safeguards regular account information	Safeguards regular account information
Transaction information face value	Can be signed and issued freely in compliance with the limit	Face value is often set, and cannot be changed	Can be signed and issued freely in compliance with the limit	Can be deducted freely in compliance with the limit
Real/Virtual world	Can be partially used in real world	Can only be used in the virtual world	Limited to virtual world, but can share a checking account in the real world.	Can be used in real or virtual worlds.
Limit on transfer	Depends on the limit of the credit card	Depends on how much is prepaid	No limit	Depends on how much money is saved.
Mobility	Yes	No	No	Yes

- After analysis and comparison of various modes of electronic payment systems, it is revealed that it is quite difficult, if not impossible, to suggest that which payment system is best.
- Some systems are quite similar, and differ only in some minor details. Further, all these systems have ability or potential to displace cash. Added to this, widely different technical specifications make it difficult to choose an appropriate payment system.
- On the basis of above analysis it is concluded that, smart cards based electronic payment system is best. It has numerous advantages over the other electronic payment systems.
- Therefore, establishing a standard smart card based system, or making different system interoperable with one another is critical success factor for the smart cards based payment system.
- Smart card organizations around the world must establish a smart card interface standard and a conformance testing organization to make all smart card system compatible; otherwise smart card related products will not develop fully.

2. ATM:

- ATM Stands for Automated Teller Machines. It is one of the modes of Electronic banking. ATMs have changed the banker customer relationship substantially.

- ATM is a self-operated machine. ATMs are basically used for dispensing of cash from out of customers account. The basic idea with which ATMs were introduced was only cash withdrawals.

- ATMs initially were introduced to facilitate the transactions of the Credit Card holders. But with further improvements in technology the same facility was even extended to all other demand deposit accounts of banks.

- The ATMs today can be used for various purposes such as:
  1. Depositing money,
  2. Withdrawal of money,
  3. Balance enquiry, and
  4. Lodging requests for cheque book etc.

Advantages of ATMs:

1. Transactions through ATM becomes impersonal. If there is personal contact there is a possibility of conflict or disagreement over some issues, which is completely done away with.
2. The facility is available 24 hours a day and 365 days in a year.
3. If the ATMs of banks are spread throughout the city, then the customer may not need to go to his branch for withdrawing cash. This offers bank customers a lot of convenience in transaction.
4. If the user of an ATM uses the same with due care and diligence then the possibility of any fraudulent practice associated with ATM is remote.
5. Since, ATMs run through the implicit software, the accounts of the bankers and also the customers are immediately updated.

Limitations of ATM:

1. Undisturbed power supply is needed for ATMs to work.
2. Literacy in general and computer literacy in specific, among ATM users, is essential for functioning of ATMs.
3. Psychology of the people may limit working of ATMs. People in underdeveloped nations may have fear of using ATMs. The very fear about the ability to use the card, keeps many away from ATMs.
4. ATMs are a target during unrest of any kind in society. A mere pelting of stones at the ATM centre may cause a heavy damage.
5. Lack of orientation of bank employees.

3. Debit Card:

- This is one more form of Plastic Card.

- This is somewhat similar to that of a Credit Card. The only difference is that there is no credit facility available to the debit cardholder on his debit card.

- With the help of debit card the cardholder can withdraw and can pay for purchase of goods and services.

- On purchase of goods or services the cardholder's account is instantaneously debited.

- This card can be used only if credit balance exists in the account of the debit cardholder. This card is more suitable to those who wish to manage within their monthly income and who usually do not want to borrow.

- Hence, debit card is a card without any borrowing facility. Many banks issue ATM cum debit cards.

  1. Debit card gives twin benefits of cash withdrawal and cashless purchases.

  2. The facility of cash withdrawal is available 24 hours a day and 365 days in a year.

  3. It offers its users the facility of convenient banking as withdrawals are possible from anywhere through the ATMs of the bank or any other bank.

Limitations:

1. Undisturbed power supply is needed for cash withdrawals through ATMs.

2. Literacy in general and computer literacy in specific, among debit card users, is essential for general use of debit cards.

3. Psychology of the people may limit working of debit cards. People on account of illiteracy may carry fear of using debit cards. The very fear about the ability to use the card, keeps many away from the use of debit cards.

4. Debit cards do not have general acceptability. They are not widely accepted in all shops and hence cannot be taken as substitutes to money.

5. Debit cardholders do not have any credit facility and are accepted only to the extent of balances in the account of the debit card holder.

3. Internet Banking:

- Online banking or Internet banking allows customers to conduct financial transactions on a secure website operated by their retail or virtual bank, credit union or building society.

- Internet banking is changing the banking industry and is having the major effects on banking relationships.

- Banking is now no longer confined to the branches were one has to approach the branch in person, to withdraw cash or deposit a cheque or request a statement of accounts.

- In true Internet banking, any inquiry or transaction is processed online without any reference to the branch (anywhere banking) at any time. Providing Internet banking is increasingly becoming a "need to have" than a "nice to have" service.

- The net banking, thus, now is more of a norm rather than an exception in many developed countries due to the fact that it is the cheapest way of providing banking services.

- e-banking first offered in 1995, online banking is the latest twist in the ever-growing world of technology. Now that over 68% of U.S. households have access to the Internet, bank customers are discovering it's easier and more expedient to do the following online:

  o Check account balances
  o Balance a checkbook
  o Transfer money between accounts
  o Track recent account activity
  o Authorize electronic bill payments
  o Request copies of past statements and processed checks
  o Order traveler's, cashier's, and regular checks
  o Issue stop payment requests
  o Apply for auto, mortgage, home equity, student, or personal loans
  o Receive investment product and service information

- To get started, all you need is a computer with a modem or other dial-up device, a checking account with a bank that offers online service, and the patience to complete about a one-page application--which can usually be done online.

Advantages of Internet Banking:

1. An internet banking account is simple to open and use.

2. Internet banking costs less.

3. Comparing internet banks to get the best deal is easy.

4. Bouncing a check (accidentally) should be a thing of the past because you can monitor your account online any time, day or night.

5. You can keep your account balanced using your computer and your monthly statement.

6. With the ability to view your account at anytime, it is easier to catch fraudulent activity in your account before much damage is done.

7. Internet banking offers a great deal more convenience than you could get from a conventional bank.

Disadvantages of Internet Banking:

1. Need an account with an Internet Service Provider (ISP)
2. Security concerns, like "hackers" accessing your bank accounts
3. Original setup for bill paying time is time-consuming but will ultimately be a time-saver
4. Switching banks can be more cumbersome online than in person
5. Must have basic computer skills and Internet knowledge
6. Must be comfortable using a computer

4. E-Cheques

- A system that transfers money electronically from the buyer's current account to the seller's bank account

Benefits of E-Cheques

1. Well suited for clearing micro payments. Conventional cryptography of e-cheques makes them easier to process than systems based on public key cryptography (like digital cash).
2. They can serve corporate markets. Firms can use them in more cost-effective manner.

Advantages of E-Cheques

1. Similar to traditional cheques. This eliminates the need for customer education
2. Since Electronic cheques use conventional encryption than Public and private keys as in e Cash, Electronic cheques are much faster than traditional cheque.

5. RTGS

- RTGS-The full form of 'RTGS' stands for Real Time Gross Settlement, which can be defined as the continuous (real-time) settlement of funds individually on an order by order basis (without netting).
- 'Real Time' means the process of instructions that are executed at the time they are received rather than at some later time.
- 'Gross Settlement' means the settlement of funds transfer instructions occurs individually (on an instruction by instruction basis). Considering that the funds settlement takes place in the books of the Reserve Bank of India, the payments are final and unalterable.]

5.11 Security Measures of Online Transactions

1. Ensure that your computer is defended against Internet threats

- o Help protect your online transactions by using firewall, antivirus, and antispyware software. Encrypt your wireless connection at home. Keep all software (including your web browser) current with automatic updates.

2. **Create strong passwords that are used effectively and changed regularly**

   o Strong passwords are easy for you to remember but difficult for others to guess. They should be kept secret and should be changed regularly.

   o Use unique passwords for bank accounts and other important financial transactions. And avoid using the same password everywhere. If someone steals that password, all the information that the password protects is at risk.

3. **Look for signs that your information will be safe online**

   o Before you enter sensitive data on a webpage, ensure that the site uses encryption – a security measure that helps protect your data as it traverses the Internet. Signs of encryption include a web address with "https" (the "s" stands for "secure") and a closed padlock beside it (the lock might also be in the lower right corner of the window). And always double-check that you are at the correct website (for example, at your bank's site, not a fake one that has a similar URL).

4. **Perform confidential transactions on a private and personal computer over a secure wireless network**

   o Never perform any confidential transactions (especially any financial ones, such as paying bills, banking or shopping) on a public or shared computer, or on devices such as laptops or mobile phones that are on public wireless networks. The security is unreliable.

5. **Find the web address yourself**

   o Links in email messages, text messages, instant messages, and pop-up ads can take you to websites that look legitimate but are not. To visit websites, type the address yourself or use your own bookmark or favorite.

6. **Use common sense**

   o To help protect yourself against fraud, watch out for scams. For example, be wary of deals that sound too good to be true, alerts from your "bank" that your account will be closed unless you take some immediate action, notices that you have won a lottery, or a refusal to meet in person for a local transaction.

   o Typically this kind of message, whether sent by computer or phone, is designed to entice you to visit a phony website where criminals collect your financial data. (If you doubt the message's authenticity, call the company.)

   o Threats of payments system

5.12 Threats of Payment System

1. **Threats:**
   o Anyone with the capability, technology, opportunity, and intent to do harm.
   o Potential threats can be foreign or domestic, internal or external, state-sponsored or a single rogue element.

   Example: Loss of Privacy/confidentiality, data misuse

   o Intellectual property threats - use existing materials found on the Internet without the owner's permission, e.g., music downloading, domain name (cybersquatting), software pirating

2. **Client computer threats**
   o Trojan horse
   o Active contents
   o Viruses

3. **Communication channel threats**
   o Sniffer program
   o Backdoor
   o Spoofing
   o Denial-of-service

4. **Server threats**
   o Privilege setting
   o Server Side Include (SSI), Common Gateway Interface (CGI)
   o File transfer
   o Spamming

Questions

1. What is meant by electronic payment system?
2. Define electronic payment system.
3. With suitable diagram describe process of electronic payment system.
4. Enlist various types of electronic payment system.
5. Describe the following terms:
   (i) Credit card, and
   (ii) Smart card
6. State various types of payments in short.
7. Explain the term value exchange systems in brief.
8. What is meant by paperless bills? How they work?

9. With suitable diagram describe micropayment system.

10. Describe the term modern payment system in detail.

11. What is meant by credit card? How it works?

12. What is electronic cash? State its advantages and disadvantages.

13. With suitable diagram describe traditional payment system.

14. Compare electronic cheque and e-cash.

15. Differentiate between smart and credit cards.

16. Compare traditional and electronic payment systems.

■■■

www.ingramcontent.com/pod-product-compliance
Lightning Source LLC
Chambersburg PA
CBHW080731020726
47503CB00010B/2868